Hunted

by

Sharon C. Cooper

DEDICATION

To my friend Cheris—a fellow Mustang girl.
Keep doing you, Diva!

Prologue

Whitney hated this part of her job. The photos she had taken over the past four weeks would no doubt change the dynamics of her client's family.

Watching Margaret in silence as she sifted through the pictures, Whitney brought her steaming mug of coffee to her lips. At seven in the morning, she needed all the caffeine she could get.

Taking a careful sip of the strong brew, she glanced around the cozy cafe. They were just north of Macon, Georgia, in an out-of-the-way area that Whitney had never heard of before, much less visited. Like her client, she preferred meeting someplace where there was a slim chance of running into anyone she knew. Spying for the CIA for so many years had made her paranoid on almost every level, but she now enjoyed working for herself. As a private investigator, she chose her assignments, decided how much she wanted to work, and what level of danger she would allow.

A couple of months ago, Margaret had hired her to find out if her husband was cheating. Unfortunately, Whitney had just handed over proof that not only was he cheating, but he also had a drug problem.

"I can't believe he would do this to me." The woman's hazel eyes brimmed with tears, and red splotches covered her fair skin that had gone pale. "I didn't want to believe it, but the signs were there. Late hours. Money disappearing. Lying about where he'd been. The smell of perfume on his clothes. Each time I questioned him, he had an excuse."

"Well, it's probably good you know now," Whitney said, unsure of what else to say. Seemed lately this was the type of work she'd been getting, and it wasn't always the men who were caught cheating. She'd had her share of male clients wanting her to spy on their cheating wives or girlfriends.

"After twenty years and three kids, he steps out on me. I thought we had a good marriage. I don't know what I'm going to do."

"Can I get you ladies anything other than coffee? Maybe pancakes? Waffles?" the server asked.

Margaret stared at the photos as if still trying to wrap her brain around that she'd been right about her loser husband.

"That'll be it," Whitney answered for the both of them. "You can just bring me the check."

As Whitney went back to drinking her coffee, a strange sensation crept down her back. The feeling of being watched was stronger than it had been the day before. Yesterday, while she was running errands, she thought it might've been her imagination, but two days in a row? No. Something wasn't right.

She set her coffee mug on the table while casually glancing around. Sitting toward the back of the cafe, she had a good view of most of the tables, except those few on the side. Her gaze bounced from person to person as they dined and chatted. Considering the early hour, the place was somewhat full. Nothing seemed out of place or looked unusual.

Yet, that eerie feeling consumed her.

"I appreciate your help with this," Margaret said, cutting into Whitney's thoughts. She stuffed the pictures into her large handbag. "You're as good and efficient as I heard you were. I just wish I had been wrong about my husband."

Margaret slid a white envelope across the table to Whitney. She had requested to pay in cash up front, thinking it would be easier to hide the investigation from her husband.

Whitney stuffed the payment into the back pocket of her blue jeans while dividing her attention between Margaret and their surroundings. Her client rambled on about how she planned to handle her cheating spouse, and Whitney's pulse pounded in her ears. She hated the anxiousness swirling inside of her.

"All right, ladies. You can take care of this whenever you're ready." The server set the check face down on the small table. "Oh, and the cute guy at the counter…" she glanced back, pointing to where several people sat at the bar. "Well, he was there a minute ago. Anyway, he told me to give you this."

Whitney accepted the folded piece of paper while taking another glance at the counter. Five people were sitting there, some talking to the person next to them, while others hunched over their plates eating. She didn't recognize any of them and wondered where the person who sent her the note had disappeared to.

"Thanks." She accepted the slip of paper. "Can you describe him?"

The server's brows drew together and her sienna-toned face scrunched as if trying to remember. "A little shorter than my husband. He had to be around six feet or so with broad shoulders and olive skin. He was wearing a heavy black jacket with a baseball cap pulled low above his eyes," she said to Whitney. "He was just there a minute ago."

"I guess you have an admirer," Margaret said after the server walked away.

Whitney gave a half-hearted shrug. She hoped that's all it was, but her gut was still churning with trepidation. She'd wait to read the note in the car.

Margaret took care of the bill, and once they were outside, Whitney shook her hand.

"If there's anything else I can do, you know where to find me."

"I do, and thanks again."

They said their goodbyes, and Whitney hurried to her car. Repeated glances over her shoulder revealed others were leaving, but no one was following her. Maybe her imagination was working overtime, and she was being paranoid. Either way, she wouldn't feel comfortable until she was back at home.

After starting the vehicle, she unfolded the now crumpled slip of paper and skimmed the words written in block lettering.

I know who you are, Samantha Cooley. You will pay for destroying my family.

Whitney's heart slammed against her chest, and her blood turned to ice in her veins as she balled up the paper.

Samantha.

Heart racing. Pulse pounding. She glanced over her shoulder and out the back window, searching for anybody who might be watching her. Seeing no one, she hurried and started the car, then peeled out of the parking lot.

Going through her mental rolodex, she tried to remember the last time she had used the name *Samantha Cooley*. It had been her final alias before leaving the CIA.

Whitney searched her mind to recall the details of that last case. She'd been in Colombia for months on assignment. An assignment that had been chaotic and mishandled on so many levels. She had almost been killed, which was why she had decided it was time to leave the CIA.

You will pay for destroying my family.

Whose family? Whose family had she destroyed? And why now? Why come at her after so many years? She had always feared that one day her work with the CIA would come back to haunt her. Gathering intel from all over the world had been dangerous, but she had always been careful. Not once had her real identity been compromised.

At least that's what she thought.

How the heck had someone connected her to Samantha? That just anyone could get ahold of that information. Unless somehow her target at the time had managed to make the connection. Whitney had moved around for years, never staying in one city for long until she settled in Atlanta.

With a death grip on the steering wheel, she checked her mirrors for the hundredth time. Thankfully there wasn't much traffic, and she wasn't far from the highway that would take her back to Atlanta.

"Okay, just stay calm," she mumbled to herself as she entered the on-ramp for I-75. Her mind raced as she weighed her options. The last thing she should do was head home. Chances were, they probably knew where she lived. Maybe if she changed cars and laid low for a while, she could delay whatever this person had planned.

Whitney's thoughts raced as her fear increased while debating on what to do first. Maybe it would be best to head back to Atlanta. If this person knew her, they might also know about Collin and Myles.

Myles. I have to call Myles. He'll know what to do.

"Damn," she mumbled, seeing traffic backed up ahead. Just once, it would be nice to travel around Georgia and not worry about traffic.

She pressed the brake, but the car didn't slow down.

"What the…"

Panic roared through her body as she kept pumping the brake.

Nothing happened.

"Oh, dear God."

At sixty miles an hour, her car raced toward the crawling vehicles ahead.

Tension seized her shoulders.

Icy fear twisted inside her chest.

She had to do something.

At the last second, Whitney jerked the steering wheel to the right so hard, pain shot through her arms. Terror clouded her vision. The car hurtled across the shoulder of the road. An ear-piercing scream ripped from her throat as the vehicle flew through the air toward trees.

"Oh, God!"

She crossed her arms in front of her face just before impact.

Everything went black.

Chapter One

Three days earlier...

"Any day now, Gen. I need to get out of here," her sister Journey said as she strolled from the office in the back of the salon and sat in Geneva's styling chair.

"Don't be trying to rush me now. You're the one who's been on the phone for the last thirty minutes," Geneva said, grateful the phone call had given her just enough time to finish up another client before getting back to Journey's hair.

"Yeah, sorry about that. I was waiting to hear from one of our investigators regarding a case," her sister explained.

"I don't know how you juggle a demanding job, a husband, and a one-year-old."

"Girl, sometimes I don't know either. It never slows down in our office." As a Georgia assistant district attorney, Journey worked crazy hours but seemed to take it all in stride.

Geneva couldn't do it. She couldn't see herself married, much less a mother raising a child. Neither had ever been on her radar. At least not until lately. She had caught herself over the last few weeks entertaining the thought of settling down. All because of one virile, irritating, sexy hunk.

Myles Carrington.

The one man she couldn't have.

7

"So, what's up with you and Myles?" Journey asked as if reading Geneva's mind. "You heard from him lately?"

Geneva sighed loudly as she flat-ironed her sister's hair. Just once, she wished they could share the same space and not discuss Myles.

"How many times do I have to say it? Nothin's up with us."

At least that's what Geneva kept telling herself. She didn't do serious, long-term relationships. Yet, here she was, thinking about him every few minutes. Months ago, he had dared her to kiss him during their friends Kenton and Egypt's wedding reception held at Journey's house. Geneva never walked away from a dare, and that evening was no different.

The intense lip-lock with Myles led to a quickie with him inside Journey's guest bathroom, and Geneva hadn't been able to think straight since. They'd had an agreement. One and done. Instead, they had run into each other six weeks ago at a mutual friend's birthday party, and that intense connection from months ago was still there. After the party, they met for a drink. One thing led to another, and they ended up back at her place. Since then, Geneva hooked up with him again, and again, and yet again.

Their chemistry was like nothing she had experienced with any other man. Before long, they were hanging out like a couple. Meeting for coffee. Camping out in front of the television and watching sports or movies late into the night at her place. The week before he headed to California, Geneva had even cooked for him.

"Laz made it sound as if you and Myles were an item," her sister said of her husband, Lazarus Dimas, a former detective with the Atlanta Police Department. He was now a personal security specialist who worked with Myles. "You might as well admit—" Journey winced when Geneva pulled her hair. "Ouch, Gen! What's wrong with you?"

"Pick something else to talk about. Myles is off-limits."

"Fine, I won't mention him again, but don't take your frustrations out on me or my hair."

Geneva heated up a curling iron, planning to bump the ends of Journey's hair after she finished flat-ironing it.

"Come on, Gen. When are you going to face the fact that you're feeling him?" Journey asked as if they hadn't just agreed to change the subject.

"Don't talk to me about Myles while I have a hot flat iron in my hand. I might *accidentally* let it slip."

Journey *tsk*ed. "And if you do, I'll have you arrested for assaulting a government official."

Geneva gasped and held the flat iron up and away from her sister as she glared at her through the mirror. "That's cold. I cannot believe your ass went there," Geneva ground out.

Journey, who was two years older, knew that Geneva was only afraid of one thing in this whole world—going back to jail. That experience was one thing she never joked about and a subject that was entirely off-limits.

"Okay, I'll admit that was a low blow, but you started it," Journey shot back, remorse in her tone. "I shouldn't have said that, but you're the one who's tripping. Don't get mad at me if you're not willing to admit that you have feelings for Myles."

Geneva released a long, frustrated sigh. Her sister was right. Myles was a sensitive subject, and it irritated the hell out of Geneva. He was just a man. Like every other, it should've been easy for her to move on and not look back.

But something inside of her shifted. She wanted more. She wanted *him*.

It didn't matter now, though. Myles had shut down their little fling and moved on. He'd even had the nerve to give her the *it's me, not you* speech.

No man had *ever* kicked her to the curb. Instead of being pissed, Geneva had been shocked, and if she was honest with herself, she was a little disappointed. She actually liked the asshole. A lot.

"Why'd I have to fall for him," she mumbled under her breath but realized too late that she'd said it out loud.

"I knew it!" Journey said, practically leaping out of her seat.

Geneva yanked on her hair.

"Ow. Dang, Gen! I'm getting a little sick of you tonight. So what if you like Myles? You can do a lot worse. Heck, you have, more times than not."

"Would you just shut up and leave it alone? I'm done talking about him."

"Fine. I won't say anything else about him."

"Good."

"By the way, I'm loving the hot pink styling chairs. They go perfect with the black and white color scheme."

Geneva smiled. "Thanks, they arrived a few days ago. Business has been booming, and I had to add two more stylists and another nail tech. I figured since I had to get more chairs, I might as well get what I've been wanting."

The spa-like space was fun, yet elegant, and was turning into everything Geneva had dreamed. It had taken years to finally find her true passion. She had always been into makeup, fashion, and anything involving her appearance, but she hadn't considered doing hair until Journey suggested she enroll in cosmetology school.

Geneva owed her success to her sister and their parents. After being released from jail, she had still toed the line of that reckless stage of life. Now, she was a business owner trying to keep her head on straight and her butt out of trouble. She owed the change in her to her family. They not only supported her emotionally during those troubled years; they had also invested in the salon. For them to trust her enough to put money behind her dream meant everything, and it was something she wouldn't soon forget.

"Hold your head down some," Geneva said, trying to curl the back of Journey's hair. "Almost done."

The loud chime on the door sounded.

"Sorry, we're closed," she called out just as she was finishing the last lock of hair.

"Then why isn't the door locked?"

Geneva's hand stilled. She'd recognize the deep rumble of that voice anywhere.

She placed the curling iron back into its holder, then glanced over the half wall that separated the styling area from the waiting room. Heat soared through her body at the sight of the man she couldn't get out of her system.

Goodness.

After the watered-down *it's me, not you* speech he spouted before leaving town, she hadn't expected to see him. At least not until the next time one of their mutual friends had a cookout or some type of party. Yet, here he was…in her shop…looking sexy as sin.

Dressed in a leather jacket with a gray T-shirt underneath and black jeans and Timberland boots, he looked good enough to eat. Everything about the man screamed badass. That laid-back, devil-may-care vibe that was such a part of him was in full force.

"Hey, Myles," Journey said as Geneva removed the black salon cape from around her.

"What's up, Journey? It's good seeing you." Myles hugged her and placed a kiss on her cheek, but his gaze was on Geneva.

Very little made her nervous, but she had to keep herself from fidgeting under his perusal. She broke eye contact and glanced at her salon station, where she noticed Journey had left money. Geneva never charged her, but the woman insisted on paying.

"Well, I'm gonna get out of here and let you two catch up. Gen, walk me to the door," Journey said, humor radiating from her eyes.

When they reached the door, Geneva returned Journey's cash and lifted her hand when her sister opened her mouth to speak. "Don't say a word about him. I don't want to hear it. Just take your money and go."

"Talk to him…" Journey managed to say before Geneva pushed her out the door.

11

When she turned, Myles was standing in the middle of the styling area, his arms folded across his chest. Maybe it was his rugged badass swagger that attracted her. A former underground MMA fighter, something he did during college to make extra money, he still kept in shape. He wasn't a big, bulky man like some of the security specialists he worked with, but at six feet tall with a lean, muscular build, he was still intimidating.

Right now, his dark gaze bore into her. He didn't speak, didn't smile, just stood there with an all-too-familiar unreadable expression. It was sexy and irritating at the same time. The indecipherable mask probably served him well while he was with the CIA. Though he had never confirmed or denied it, she'd heard that he'd been a spy. Whatever training he'd gone through probably enhanced his ability to always appear cool, calm, and confident.

Like now. The look was suddenly grating on her nerves and pissing her off.

She yanked the door back open. "You're not welcome here. Get the hell out."

Chapter Two

Unfazed by Geneva's order to leave, Myles let his gaze travel the length of her. Though sometimes he hated how seductively she dressed, he couldn't deny that she was one gorgeous woman.

Her hair was piled on top of her head in a messy bun just the way he liked. Knowing she had a sexy body with curves in all the right places, Geneva never hesitated to show off her hourglass figure. She seemed to revel in the attention she attracted. The fitted, black long-sleeved shirt with a plunging neckline accentuated her more-than-a-handful breasts that he was very familiar with. His gaze slid over her narrow waist and moved down to the holey, bleached washed jeans that revealed more skin than they covered.

Geneva sighed loudly, and his attention shot back up to her lovely face. Her golden-brown skin glowed beneath the overhead lights, only bringing more attention to her scowl.

She released the handle and let the door close, then crossed her arms. "What do you want, Myles?"

That was a loaded question. He could give her a list of everything he wanted from her, but that would defeat the whole purpose of putting distance between them.

"Laz sent me to lock up with you, but first, I need a haircut." He also needed a shave, but he'd take care of that once he got home.

When he received the work assignment to go to Los Angeles, Myles thought it couldn't have come at a better time. Not only did he get to spend a little time with his brother Ray, a doctor in the Hollywood Hills, but he needed time away from Geneva. A two-week break from the stunning beauty in front of him was supposed to help him forget her.

Instead, Myles found himself thinking of her day and night.

That never happened.

He didn't get attached.

While with the CIA, he traveled constantly. There had been no time to build deep connections that weren't work-related. That hadn't changed since he left the agency a few years ago and started working for Supreme Security. At least not until he and Geneva hooked up.

His first mistake.

Falling for her was the second.

Breaking things off hadn't gone as planned. Ordinarily, he could move on from a woman without thinking twice, but Geneva wasn't easy to walk away from. There was a charged energy that surrounded him whenever they were near. Like now. She might've been shooting daggers at him with her eyes, but all that did was turn him on more.

Which meant he clearly needed to have his head examined.

"I don't need your help in locking up," Geneva snapped.

Now he was the one sighing. He'd only been back in Atlanta for a couple of hours and hadn't even had time to go home yet. Laz had called a short while ago, telling him that the strip mall where Geneva's shop was located had been having problems with thugs hanging around. It was after nine o'clock at night, and neither of them thought it was a good idea for her to lock up the place alone.

Stopping by seemed like a good idea at the time. He'd get to see her for a minute, as well as make sure she was safe. But seeing Geneva again only intensified his desire to be near her.

He had it bad for the woman. The worse part was that he was treading into new territory and wasn't sure what to do with his feelings.

"Oh, and our barber won't be in until tomorrow morning at nine. Do you want me to add you to his schedule?" She turned and walked away.

"No. I want you."

She stopped short, whipped around, and glared at him. His words came out wrong, but that's what he was feeling. He wanted her. Plain and simple.

His attraction to Geneva was more than about sex, which he'd admit was amazing. Everything about the woman turned him on. Her wit, her fierceness, and there was a sweetness about her that not too many people got a chance to see.

Yeah, Myles wanted her in his life, which was such a bad idea. His world wasn't conducive to long-term connections. It wasn't that he couldn't commit to a monogamous relationship, because he could. He just didn't want to for more reasons than he cared to explain to her.

"I want *you* to cut my hair," Myles finally said and walked past her to hang his jacket on the hook next to her smock. Then he sat in her chair. The way she was glowering at him didn't go unnoticed. Letting a pissed-off woman cut his hair might not be one of his smartest moves.

"Myles, I'm not doing this with you. I—"

"Gen, just cut my hair."

"What makes you think I have time to cut your hair?"

"Because you're just standing around. Besides, no one was in your chair."

Facing the mirror, Myles didn't miss the various emotions flashing across her face. She might not be happy that he was there, but he hadn't missed the longing in her eyes when he first arrived. Geneva wasn't good at hiding her feelings. As a matter of fact, she usually said whatever was on her mind. Except now...she seemed conflicted.

He glanced over his shoulder at her. "The sooner you get started, the sooner we can get out of here."

"Sometimes I can't stand you," she grumbled.

He chuckled and turned back around to face the mirror.

Geneva rolled her eyes and shook out a cape before draping it around him and fastening it at the back of his neck.

"So, how would you like it done?"

"You already know how I like it."

"You know what? You're pushing it. How the hell do you want your hair cut? And just answer my fucking questions without making everything sound so damn suggestive!" she snapped.

"That mouth of yours..." Myles shook his head and spun the chair around to face her. Unable to stop himself, he tugged on the front of her shirt and drew her to him. He held her chin, keeping her from moving away. God, he wanted to kiss her, but he wouldn't. "What'd I tell you about the vulgar words that you let slip between those gorgeous lips?"

She swallowed hard, and her gaze jockeyed from his mouth to his eyes and back to his mouth again.

His heart thudded against his chest. If either of them acted on what they both clearly wanted, there would be no turning back. They both had agreed that a committed relationship wasn't what they wanted. One of them had to be strong, and at the moment, Myles wasn't sure it could be him.

Geneva braced her hand on the arm of his chair. The fresh, seductive scent of her fragrance danced around him, adding to the struggle to keep his distance. His barely controlled willpower teetered.

"If you quit pissing me off, then you won't be subjected to my *vulgar* words, as you call them," she ground out between gritted teeth.

Myles's lips twitched. He couldn't fight the grin that broke through. She had a quick temper, but he loved her fire.

"Just tighten my hair up around the ears and line up the back," he said.

Geneva stepped out of his hold and turned his chair back around to face the mirror where she stared at him. Seconds ticked by before she huffed out a breath and grabbed her clippers.

Twenty minutes later, she was done. Just as she removed the cape from around him, the door chimed. Myles assumed she had locked it. Apparently not.

Unease clawed through him. It was too late for anyone to be stopping by, and the way the chair was positioned, he couldn't see the visitor.

He started to reach into his back pocket where he'd stored his switchblade, but Geneva squeezed his shoulder, stopping him. The person came into view.

Reuben Jackson.

He smiled at Geneva, and Myles stiffened. His protective instincts went on high alert. He wasn't a confrontational person, but the way the man was leering at her, Myles wanted to snatch him up and toss him through the nearest window.

"Hey, beautiful. Can I holler at you for a minute?" Reuben asked, his toothy grin spreading wider.

Myles hated the guy. Not because he knew him personally—he didn't—but the man's reputation preceded him. A friend of Myles had an encounter with Reuben and some of his friends years ago that landed him in the hospital. At over six feet tall, Reuben was powerfully built, and looked like he should've been on a professional football team. Instead, he'd spent much of his life with the Minauros Devils, one of Atlanta's most dangerous gangs. Reuben had ended up doing a stint in jail for a different crime. After his release, he somehow managed to leave the gang life and the city. A year ago, he returned to Atlanta.

"Now's not a good time," Geneva said to Reuben as she used a neck duster to brush hair off of Myles's collar. "Give me a call later."

"Come on, baby."

Myles's blood heated as it rushed through his veins. He didn't want her with any man, but he sure as hell didn't want her to be anywhere near Reuben Jackson. Some claim he had cleaned up his act. Myles doubted it. The man still associated with his old crew, which told Myles all he needed to know.

Reuben moved a little closer, made eye contact with Myles, but returned his attention to Geneva. "You don't have a minute?"

"No, I don't," she bit out.

Now both of her hands were gripping Myles's shoulders. Could she sense the tension building inside of him?

"Right now is not a good time," she repeated with authority.

Myles couldn't see her face, but the way Reuben's shoulders sagged, it was safe to say she was giving him that death stare that she had mastered.

He threw up his arms. "Fine. I'll call you later."

The moment Reuben walked out of the shop, Myles bolted from the chair. Geneva startled when he got in her face, their noses almost touching.

"Stay the hell away from him," he said in a low growl.

Momentarily stunned, she stared at him with wide eyes. But that shocked expression quickly turned into rebellion.

"What you ain't gon' do is come up in my shop and tell me who I can and can't see. Besides, what do you care who I hang out with? You're no longer interested. Remember?"

She moved away from him, but he gently grabbed her arm. "I mean it, Geneva. Stay the hell away from—"

She shook out of his hold and went to lock the door. "You telling me not to do something is like telling me to go for it. Is that what you're saying?"

Myles said nothing, and if he clenched his teeth any tighter, they were going to crack. What could he say? He had no claims on this woman, even if there was a part of him that felt like she was his.

"I'm sorry." The words felt like sandpaper on his tongue. He couldn't remember the last time he had apologized to someone. "You're right. What you do is none of my business, but just because you and I aren't...we're not..."

The rest of the words stuck in his throat. They might not be a couple, but the possessiveness he felt when it came to her made it hard not to claim her as his own.

"You know what? Do what you want." He slipped into his jacket. "I just don't want to see you hurt."

"You're right. It's none of your business, but for the record, I'm not involved with Reuben. He and I used to hook up years ago. Despite what you think of him or what you've heard, he's actually a nice guy. He's cleaned up his act."

"Yeah, if you say so. From what I've heard..."

The faint sound of a car alarm at the back of the building could be heard where they stood.

Geneva growled under her breath. "That sounds like my car." She stomped past him, but Myles stopped her before she opened the back door.

"Give me your keys and wait here."

"Dang, you have a bad habit of telling me what to do." She mumbled something Myles couldn't decipher, but then she pulled keys from the back pocket of her jeans and handed them to him.

He was glad when the phone in her office rang. Otherwise, she would've followed him out.

Myles unlocked the wood door that led to the alley behind the building and slowly inched it open. A gust of chilly air kissed his warm cheek as he started to step out into the night, but he stopped.

His skin prickled, igniting all of his senses and putting him on high alert. Not because the car alarm was blaring like crazy. No, it had everything to do with instinct. Someone was on the other side of the door.

Illumination came from a single light bulb overhead and a couple of light poles down the alley. Still, it wasn't enough light to see through the small opening.

As a former spy, listening to his gut kept him alive on many dangerous assignments. He still relied on that and the sixth sense, an extrasensory awareness, that he'd been born with.

Instead of opening the door further, Myles kept it propped open with his foot. He couldn't see anyone, but he felt their presence. He let the alarm continue squawking and hoped Geneva would stay in her office a little longer. Pocketing her keys, he wasn't sure what to expect in the alley. But instead of pulling the gun from his ankle holster, he dug into his pocket and pulled out his switchblade, his preferred weapon.

Without another thought, Myles shoved the door open, slamming it against the person behind it.

"Owww," someone shrieked in pain, and Myles eased into the alley. He barely had time to dodge a fist aimed for his face.

Pulse pounding loudly in his ears, he blocked the half-assed punch with his forearm. With his free hand, he landed a left hook against the man's jaw. The blow was hard enough to stun the person but not hard enough to break anything.

The guy howled in pain and stumbled back, holding his jaw. Myles ignored the blood streaming from the man's nose. Anger crackled inside of him and drove him forward. The bastard had been out there waiting for Geneva. He deserved an ass-kicking.

Myles swept his leg out, catching the man at the ankle and knocking him off his feet. He didn't care that the man was howling. He started to kick him while he was down but stopped when realizing he was just some punk kid. The pimply-faced teen couldn't have been more than sixteen.

"Get your ass up," Myles demanded. He shoved the knife back into his pocket and shut off the car alarm.

The kid staggered to his feet while bleeding all over himself. Myles didn't want to kill the worthless piece of crap, but he definitely wanted to teach him a lesson.

"Get off of him!" Shouts came from behind Myles.

He whipped around in time to see two teens charging toward him. On reflex, he lifted his right knee, pivoted slightly, and quickly extended his leg in a spinning roundhouse kick. His booted foot caught the taller one in the left ear. It threw the kid off balance, sending him crashing into the shorter guy before falling face-first to the ground. The short, stocky kid scrambled to his feet. Before he could take a step toward Myles, the back door swung open. Myles spotted a black aluminum bat before Geneva made an appearance.

"Are you shitting me?" she screamed at the top of her lungs and turned her attention to the kid standing a foot away from her. "Y'all punk-asses busted out windows of a vintage Mustang?" Within a heartbeat, she swung the bat like a major league baseball player, catching the guy in the back and knocking him into the building.

Myles quickly turned to the first kid, expecting him to attack. Instead, the bloody-faced teenager stood frozen. His wide-eyed gaze bounced frantically from Myles to his friends on the ground and back to Myles. Without a word, he turned and hightailed it down the alley before disappearing around the corner of the building.

"Your ass is mine!" Geneva lifted the bat, and Myles ran over and caught hold of the weapon in mid-swing.

"Give me that before you kill him."

"He deserves to die," she shrieked and rushed to her vehicle. "Look at my car!"

Myles huffed out a breath and winced when he saw the gash on the side of the kid's head where he'd run into the side of the building. The boy was dazed and groaning in pain.

Myles left him and went to check on the thug he had knocked out with a kick, the one lying facedown on the concrete. Placing two fingers against the guy's neck, he confirmed he was still alive.

"Stupid jerk," Myles mumbled under his breath and stood. A former MMA fighter, Myles had knocked out plenty of opponents during his matches. He always fought to win, even though he hated the sport. He only participated because it was a means to an end, earning him enough money to pay for college. But going at someone outside of a boxing ring? Always a last resort. His hands and feet were considered deadly weapons.

This was not how he saw his evening going. After the long flight from California, he'd planned to head home and camp out in front of the television for the rest of the evening. Helping Geneva lock up her shop was supposed to be a quick pit stop.

He pulled out his phone to call 911 and watched Geneva as she angrily stomped around her restored 1966 Ford Mustang, checking out the damage. The sleek, light silver-blue pony with chrome bumpers and trim was normally in pristine condition. Not anymore. Not with two slashed tires and a shattered driver's-side window. And that was just what he could see from where he was standing. Why she chose to park at the back of the building was a mystery to him, but telling her it wasn't safe would be a waste of time.

After explaining everything to the 911 operator, Myles disconnected and roamed around to the other side of the vehicle and cursed under his breath. Three teens, two slashed tires, and two smashed windows? And the guys stuck around... This wasn't a robbery. This was a message.

"I cannot believe this!"

"Geneva," Myles said.

Normally, her bark was worse than her bite. Yet, when she whirled around, the murderous glare in her eyes could've killed someone on the spot.

"Don't you dare tell me to calm down! They are going to pay." She charged toward the boys, but Myles stopped her.

"I already called the cops. They'll be here shortly."

"I don't need the cops," she snarled, panting, her chest rising and falling as fury marred her beautiful face. "I'm going to make them regret the day they ever touched my car!"

"I think they got the message." Neither kid moved, but one moaned in pain. "Do you know these kids?" Myles asked.

"The one I hit with the bat I've seen around. I just can't believe they...oh, no!" She gasped, fear glittering in her eyes before she jerked away from Myles.

"What? What is it?"

Geneva ran back to the car and yanked the driver's side door open. She almost dived into the front seat before Myles grabbed her around the waist.

"Hold up." She wiggled in his arms, and he forced himself to ignore the way her lush backside brushed against him.

"Geneva! Would you just slow down a minute?"

"I can't, Myles. I had something in the car I shouldn't have. If it got into the wrong hands, I could get in—"

"What? And where'd you leave it?" Myles edged her away from the car, then used the sleeve of his jacket to wipe tiny pieces of glass from the driver's seat. If she had drugs hidden in the vehicle, that was a deal-breaker for him. The excuse he needed to move on.

"It's in the back, under the passenger seat," she said, then ran around to the other side of the car. By the time she got the door open, Myles had found what she was hiding.

"Really, Geneva?" He held up the 9mm, shocked and a little relieved it wasn't drugs she'd been trying to stash. Then something else dawned on him and he lowered his voice. "Why are you rolling with a gun?"

She waved her arms around. "Look at where we are, Myles. I'd be a fool not to carry—"

"You shouldn't be carrying, no matter where you are. Are you trying to go back to jail?"

Chapter Three

Geneva's heart thudded against her chest, surprised that Myles would know something so personal about her. Something she rarely shared with anyone. But her initial surprise quickly spiraled into anger. If there was one thing she hated, it was people reminding her of the biggest mistake she ever made.

"I'm not going to even bother asking where you got that information," Geneva growled under her breath, her pulse still racing, thinking that someone had stolen her gun.

For a moment, she wasn't concerned about the bastards who had vandalized her car. All she could think about was that Myles knew about her past. Laz, her brother-in-law, probably told him. Or as resourceful as Myles was, he could've easily found out on his own. That was one of many problems in falling for someone with his background.

God, what he must think of me.

She usually couldn't care less what people thought of her, but him? This was Myles. A man she cared about more than she dared to admit.

What was it about this night? First, her sister threatened to send her back to jail. Then she learned that Myles knew about her stint behind bars. Both pissed her off.

"What were you thinking?" he asked in that cool, calm way that grated on her nerves.

As a convicted felon, it was against the law for her to purchase or possess a firearm. If caught, she'd be tossed back in jail, and her parents would kill her. The last thing she wanted to do was disappoint them again.

"Carrying this around is asking for trouble, but what I want to know is why you have it in the first place," Myles said in a low voice. The teens were nearby but not close enough to hear the conversation.

Silence fell between them as they stared each other down. He was still in the driver's seat while she stood inside the opened passenger door.

Geneva didn't bother telling him that she'd been having trouble with some punk kids who had been terrorizing the area. She only recognized one of them on the ground from a couple of weeks ago.

"Listen," Myles continued, but Geneva lifted her hand to silence him.

"No. You listen. Hand over my gun and get the hell out of my car. Better yet, leave. I'll deal with the cops myself. I don't need your judgment right now or your help in locking up."

Without a word, Myles ejected the magazine, made sure there wasn't a bullet in the chamber, then handed her the empty gun. He climbed out of the car and slammed the door, causing more glass to skitter to the ground.

Anger propelled Geneva around to the driver's side of the vehicle. Before she could get to Myles, he had his cell phone to his ear and stared her down. It was as if he was daring her to try and take the ammunition from him.

"Myles, you're crazy in your head if you think I'm letting you leave here with my—"

"Yeah, this is Myles. I need a favor," he said to whoever was on the other end of the call. He didn't take his eyes off of Geneva, and his voice remained calm as if she weren't glaring at him. She half-listened as he told the person on the other end of the line about her car and how she needed the vehicle towed.

Geneva heard sirens in the distance, and they were getting closer. She glanced down at the gun in her hand. He was right. Bullets or no bullets, she couldn't be caught holding a pistol.

She stomped back into the building and hurried to her office, where she shoved the weapon into her Coach bag in the bottom desk drawer. Had she stayed outside any longer, she probably would've shot Myles.

"That's if I had bullets," she grumbled. She knew he was right...about everything, but she would never admit that to him.

"Geneva, the cops are here," he said from the back door, and she reluctantly left her office.

For the next forty-five minutes, they spoke with the responding police officers. Both kids, suspected to have concussions, had been placed under arrest and carted off in ambulances, a police officer with each of them. Myles was concerned that one of the boys got away, but the cops seemed confident that one of the others would give up his identity.

Right after the officers left, Myles's friend showed up with a tow truck. Geneva wanted to cry at the sight of her Mustang. Her father had given her the car years ago, and over time, she had dumped a fortune into it to have it fully restored. He had suggested that she not drive it on a daily basis. But what was the point of having a gorgeous vehicle if she wasn't going to drive it?

She left Myles and his friend outside talking while she went back to her office. Not only was she still pissed about the car, exhaustion consumed her. Dropping down in her office chair, she propped her elbows on the desk and covered her face with her hands.

What a day. It had already been long, but dealing with thugs, the police, and Myles had taken its toll. Not to mention that she had to watch her beautiful car get hooked up to a tow truck. All she wanted to do now was head home, pour herself a big glass of wine, and take a long, hot bubble bath.

"You ready to go?"

Geneva screamed and bolted out of her chair and snatched up the crystal paperweight from her desk. She was prepared to use it as a weapon when she turned to find Myles standing a couple of feet behind her.

"What the fu..." With her chest heaving, she caught herself before dropping the f-bomb. "What is wrong with you? You shouldn't sneak up on people like that," she yelled. Her grip on the rectangular paperweight was so tight that it was cutting into her palm.

Myles glanced from her face to her hand with one brow arched. He didn't miss anything, and the way he moved around like a damn ghost was a bit unnerving. His stealthiness was so creepy at times, she wouldn't be surprised if he could walk through the damn walls.

Geneva blew out a tired breath and set her makeshift weapon on the desk.

"My guy can take care of your tires in the morning. Unfortunately, he doesn't have windows for your car on hand, but he can get a hold of them in the next day or two."

Geneva released a long sigh. "Thanks," she finally said. She never liked asking for help. Never wanted to owe anyone. Yet, at that time of night, had Myles not been there, she didn't even want to think about what could've happened to her.

A shiver rocked her body just thinking about how things could've played out had she stepped into that alley alone. Her bat might not have been enough.

"I appreciate you being here and handling those delinquents tonight." Closing her eyes and pinching the bridge of her nose, she also knew she needed to apologize to Myles. "And sorry about being a...a jerk and giving you a hard time tonight about...about everything," she murmured.

Myles stepped forward and gently brushed a loose strand of hair away from her eyes, and Geneva swallowed hard. This man was such a temptation. The woodsy scent of his enticing cologne surrounded her like a cozy blanket and sent her body temperature rising. His nearness and his fragrance made her want to bury her nose into the crook of his neck for a better whiff. He smelled just that good.

How could she stay annoyed at him when her body craved every inch of the man?

"I'm glad I was here," he said. "Laz and I will coordinate something to make sure you don't have to lock up alone while we get to the bottom of whoever's terrorizing the area."

Geneva recognized that statement as his way of saying *we won't be sitting around waiting for the cops to get a handle on the situation.*

"Come on. Let's get out of here," Myles said. With no other option available, Geneva reluctantly grabbed her stuff and followed him out.

When they were finally on their way to her house, Myles said, "Let's talk."

Geneva held up her hand. "Let's not. Unless you're planning to give me my ammunition back."

Without taking his eyes off the road, he dug into the pocket of his jacket and pulled out the magazine for her 9mm.

"Here. Now, tell me how you ended up in jail."

Geneva didn't bother slipping the magazine back into the gun. She just dropped it into her handbag. "So, you know I did time, but you don't know why?"

"Just tell me. I want to hear your version."

Geneva sighed and stared out the passenger side window of his BMW as her mind took her back to that dark time. "I was twenty-one and dating this guy who my parents hated. You know how it is. The more they forbid me to see him, the more I wanted to. I'll admit he was bad news, but back then, so was I."

Myles didn't comment, not that she expected him to. One thing she had learned during their time together was that he was a good listener.

"My parents were out of town, and he and I were hanging out at their house. Anyway, we started arguing about something. I can't remember what the disagreement was about, but I told him to get out. When I opened the door for him, he backhanded me. He hit me so hard I thought he had broken my jaw."

Geneva didn't miss the way Myles's hands tightened around the steering wheel or the way his jaw clenched.

"And then what?"

"I got one of my dad's handguns and went after him. He was getting in his car, and I went off on him. Telling him that he was crazy in his head if he thought he could hit me and get away with it. I didn't take shit from nobody back then."

"Back then?" Myles's lips twitched as if to keep from smiling.

"Okay, that hasn't changed. I'm just a little smarter now. Anyway, he didn't know I had the gun. He got in my face and was calling me names and talking trash. Then he wrapped his hand around my neck and shoved me against his car. That's when I pulled the gun from the back of my waistband. Needless to say, he backed the hell up."

"You shot him?"

"Only a warning shot near his feet to keep him away from me. Heck, I could've killed the bastard if I wanted to, *but I didn't*. I told him the next time wouldn't be a warning."

"Why'd you end up in jail?"

"At the time, I didn't notice the neighbor or any kids outside. Someone called the cops, and I was arrested and charged with aggravated assault with a deadly weapon."

"And your mother couldn't get you off," he said as a statement instead of a question.

Having a mother as one of the best defense attorneys in the state and a retired cop for a father might've been a good combination for getting her out of some jams, but not that one.

"She tried. Since it was considered a public altercation, and I had endangered others, they sentenced me to three years in jail. Thanks to my mom, I only ended up serving eight months in jail and two years of probation."

Geneva stared back out the window, watching the landscape pass in a blur. It was a wonder her parents hadn't disowned her for all the crap she had pulled over the years.

"I know you don't have a permit. How'd you get the gun?"

Geneva hesitated but knew she could trust Myles. "Laz hooked me up."

Myles mumbled something under his breath and shook his head. "Why? Why would he get you a gun when he knows you could end back up in jail if caught with it?"

"That's none of your business. The only reason I told you that much about me is because I figured you already knew most of it."

For the rest of the drive, Myles remained quiet.

Her big mouth and her past had probably ruined any chance of them hooking up again. It was probably for the best. It didn't matter that they were attracted to each other and that their chemistry between the sheets was off the charts. Myles was no good for her. He would never harm her physically, but he had the power to hurt her emotionally. Geneva wasn't about to let that happen.

He pulled up in front of her house, and she glanced at the adorable two-bedroom, two-bathroom bungalow that she had called home for the past couple of years.

Myles put the car in park. "I still can't get over you living in something that looks like a gingerbread house."

Still gazing at her home, Geneva smiled. He was right. The house did look like a life-sized gingerbread house with the dark brick and a light gray roof. It even had a white picket fence around it.

To her family and friends, the place didn't match her personality, but Geneva loved her little slice of paradise. Her retreat. She had purchased the house at a state auction. Then she and her father had spent the last couple of years renovating it. She even had a garden in the backyard.

She turned to Myles. "Wanna come in?"

That hadn't been what she'd planned to say to him, but that's what came out. "You know what? Never mind," Geneva said, thinking better of the invite.

It wasn't a good idea, and they both knew it. They might not want anything serious, but it was evident that their attraction to each other was stronger than ever.

"It's late. I have to get up early, and I'm sure you do, too." She opened the car door. "Thanks for your help tonight."

"Anytime. Do you need me to drop you off at work tomorrow?"

He made it so hard to despise him. "Nah, but thanks. I'll find a way there."

Myles looked at her in that unsettling way that felt as if he was able to see deep into her soul. "I'll let you know when the car is ready."

She nodded and climbed out of his vehicle.

He's not the settling-down type. He's not the settling-down type. Geneva told herself that over and over as she strolled up her walkway. Heck, she wasn't either, but her heart and body said otherwise. She wanted him. She wanted him badly.

Now what to do about it…

*

The next day, Geneva leaned on the back of her salon chair and glanced around the shop while waiting for her client to return from the bathroom. It was late afternoon, and to say the salon had been busy would be an understatement. Even with five hairstylists, they'd barely been able to keep up. If they kept bringing in that amount of business, she'd finally be able to relocate to a larger space.

"What time is your last appointment?" Christy whispered next to her. She was one of the stylists, as well as one of Geneva's best friends. They had attended cosmetology school together and hit it off immediately.

"I have one more after Mrs. Norris." Geneva glanced at her watch, thinking that her client, Wendy, should be there soon. "Why do you ask?"

"Tonight, Kim and I are planning to hit up that new restaurant near Ponce City Market. I hear the food is amazing. You in?"

"Umm, maybe."

Honestly, she wasn't in the mood to hang out, but if she went home, all she'd do was think about Myles. Seeing him the night before had already caused her a sleepless night of tossing and turning. Maybe it would be good to hang with the girls.

"Yeah, I'm in, but you guys don't have to wait around for me. I'll meet you there around eight."

"Cool, but aren't you gon' need a ride since your car is in the shop?"

"Nah, I'll get there." Laz was planning to stop by and help lock up, and she could always get him to drop her off.

They were just tying up the details for their evening when Geneva's client returned.

"Whew! Thanks for the break. Those two cups of coffee this afternoon might not have been a good idea. Got me running to the bathroom every thirty minutes."

Geneva smiled at Mrs. Norris. "No problem. I'm almost done with your hair. I'll have you out of here in about ten minutes."

"Sounds good."

The rest of the day flew by, especially since Geneva's five-o'clock appointment had canceled. The timing couldn't have been more perfect. It gave her a chance to wash a load of towels and take care of some paperwork.

A soft knock sounded on the office door, and she looked up. Vanessa, one of their most recently hired stylists, was standing in the doorway. "Hey, there."

"Hey, Gen. My last client just left. So, it's just us. Do you still have time to give me a quick updo?"

"Oh, yeah, that's right. I'm glad you reminded me." Geneva hopped up from her desk, stuck her cell phone in her back pocket, and grabbed the shop keys. "Can't have you going on this blind date looking any kind of way."

Laughing, they went back out to the salon, and Vanessa settled into Geneva's chair.

"All right, girl. With all of this thick hair, how do you wa…"

The sound of a car screeching to a halt in front of the building captured their attention seconds before the shop's front window shattered. Shards of glass flew everywhere, pelting them like torrential rain. Geneva's heart slammed against her chest, and she dropped to the floor, pulling Vanessa down with her. Screams filled the air, and she wasn't sure if they were hers or Vanessa's.

"What the hell is—"

The loud crash against a nearby wall halted Geneva's words. Her arms flew up, covering her head as glass exploded, echoing through the space like large hail ping-ponging off the walls. A burst of white powdery substance detonated into a massive cloud of smoke.

Geneva coughed and blinked several times, unable to see through the sudden fog. Panic rioted within her as her mind raced, trying to figure out what was happening. Body pulsing with adrenaline, she stood but banged the side of her head against the corner of a cabinet.

Pain blasted through her skull.

Nausea clawed at her throat.

Heart racing and head pounding, fear seized Geneva. She couldn't see through the thick swirl of powder. Vanessa? Where was she?

"Vanessa!" The word flew from her mouth in a hoarse panic. "Vanessa!"

"I'm here. I'm here," she cried.

Geneva heard her moving around nearby, crying and mumbling something Geneva couldn't understand. She reached out, patting her hands aimlessly around on the floor as her anxiety grew with each piece of glass she touched.

"Gen? Where are…" Vanessa made contact with Geneva, pulling on her pants leg. "Oh, thank God. We… *Ohmigod, ohmigod!*"

Geneva startled at Vanessa's sudden scream.

"Fire! Gen, we gotta get out of here."

"Gas…I smell gasoline," Geneva rasped on a cough.

Fear propelled her into action. She and Vanessa blindly grabbed onto each other. Pulling. Tugging. They stumbled. Collided. Banged into furniture.

Geneva didn't stop moving. "Run! Run! This place is going to blow!"

Chapter Four

Myles had a problem. He either needed to figure out how to move on from Geneva or admit that he wanted a relationship with her. Otherwise, he was going to mess around and lose his job. He couldn't keep zoning out at work with thoughts of her like he'd been doing for much of the day.

For years he'd been able to keep a wall around his heart and not get attached. One stupid dare to get a kiss out of her, and he'd ended up screwing himself. Geneva was an addiction. An obsession of sorts. One that Myles might not be able to break.

"Like I said, you guys did a great job in Los Angeles. The feedback has been outstanding," Mason Bennett said, cutting into Myles's thoughts.

The owner of Supreme Security-Atlanta glanced around at the small group of people in the office. He rarely called impromptu meetings, but since those who had been on the trip were in the building, he pulled everyone together for a quick debriefing.

Myles straightened in his seat and forced himself to pay better attention. They were in Hamilton Crosby's office. He was Myles's supervisor and a managing partner of the company. Also present were three others from their security team, sitting at the small round conference table. While Hamilton sat behind his desk, and Mason stood near it.

"In the future, though, Atlanta's Finest won't be traveling around the country to train security specialists," Hamilton added.

Years ago, management affectionately referred to their security personnel as Atlanta's Finest. Some were former military, but the majority had law enforcement backgrounds. Everything from beat cops to FBI agents was represented at Supreme, and their skill sets were second to none.

"We decided that we'll start offering training here on-site," Hamilton continued. He explained that with the number of requests they were getting from around the country, it made better financial sense to do training at their headquarters.

Myles admired Hamilton and Mason. They were well connected, and with their business acumen, there was no telling how far they could take Supreme Security. The company initially started in Chicago and had expanded to Atlanta. Now there was talk that they might branch out to other cities in the near future.

Myles glanced at his watch, realizing he'd been away from his post for over twenty minutes. Unlike the others in the meeting, he had to get back to the front desk.

He stood and buttoned his suit jacket. "I need to get downstairs before Parker thinks I've abandoned him."

Like most of the team, Myles hated when he was assigned front desk duty. Too much sitting around. He understood the need for making sure the building was secure, but they all preferred to be out in the field.

"All right, Myles. Thanks again for your help these past couple of weeks," Mason said, then snapped his fingers. "Oh, and don't you guys forget London's birthday party next week. We want to see all of you. There will be plenty of food, drinks, and music. It's going to be a good time, so don't miss out."

Myles assured him that he'd be there and then headed to the stairs that would take him to the main level. The ten-thousand-square-foot renovated warehouse had everything they could possibly need, with room to expand. Mason and a design team had outdone themselves. The state-of-the-art building included a huge fitness center, crash rooms, a well-stocked kitchen, an indoor shooting range, and it even had a helipad on the roof.

When Myles reached the ground floor, Parker stood at the other end of the long hallway. The former SWAT officer had moved to Atlanta from Chicago well over a year ago and fit right in at Supreme.

"Laz is on the main phone line. He said he's been trying to reach you."

"Really?"

Myles pulled his cell from his pocket as he walked behind the long counter that overlooked the reception area. Glancing at his cell phone screen, he realized he had two missed calls. He picked up the receiver and pressed the red button that was blinking.

"Laz, what's up, man?" Myles sat in one of the high back leather chairs located behind the desk counter.

"Someone tossed a Molotov cocktail into the front window of Geneva's salon."

Myles sprung forward. "*What?* Is she okay?"

"I'm not sure. I'm on my way there now, but I wanted to find out if you heard anything else about last night's incident with her car. There might be a connection."

"Nah, and I haven't talked to Gen. I might see if I can reach Ashton," Myles said of Laz's old partner, a detective with Atlanta's police department. "Maybe he can shed some light on where that case stands. Who called you about the Molotov?"

"Journey. She's in Alpharetta with Dakota and the kids," Laz said, referring to Hamilton's wife. "She's worried because Geneva called her pretty upset. It scared her, man, and you know there's not much that shakes my sister-in-law. I'll let you know what I fi—"

"I'm on my way." Myles hung up, then realized he needed someone to cover the desk for him. "How long are you here for?" he asked Parker.

"For a couple of hours. Go ahead and leave. I'll get someone to cover for you while you go check on your girl."

"She's not my girl," Myles said in a rush. He snatched his phone from the desk, then searched the area to make sure he wasn't leaving anything behind.

"If she's not your girl, what is she?"

"She's my…"

"Your what?" Parker pressed.

Myles glared at him. He didn't have time for this. All he could think about at the moment was getting to Geneva and making sure she was okay. "Hell, I don't know what she is, but don't call her that."

Parker shook his head. "Man, you guys are dropping like flies."

"Yeah, whatever. I'll be in touch."

You guys are dropping like flies. The words played around in Myles's head as he drove to the salon. Three of Atlanta's Finest had gotten married in the past year and a half. The same ones who had vowed to never marry.

Was there something in the air?

Myles hoped not. He had no intention of ever settling down, and it was crazy even to imagine him and Geneva as a couple. Hell, it was crazy to imagine himself with anyone. A bachelor for life. Myles did what he wanted, when he wanted, and with whom he wanted, with little care about those outside of his immediate circle of family and friends.

Then why was his heart practically pounding out of his chest with worry? Why was he driving like a madman through the city?

He knew the answer. To get to Geneva.

He turned the radio up in the car, hoping the contemporary jazz flowing through the speakers would drown out his thoughts. He was just going to check on Geneva and make sure she was all right. That's it. Nothing else. It didn't mean anything.

At least that's what he kept telling himself.

*

Anger and helplessness warred inside of Geneva as she sat on the bumper of the ambulance with a blanket wrapped around her shoulders. An EMT was tending to the cut on the side of her forehead and had also removed a few slivers of glass from her hand. Geneva couldn't take her eyes off of the front of the salon. The large plateglass window had been obliterated, and black smoke clung to the exterior brick around the opening.

It all seemed like a bad dream. One minute she was about to do Vanessa's hair, and the next, they were running for their lives. Firefighters were still on-site, but the sprinkler system—which hadn't come on immediately—had contained the flames at the front part of the salon. But it hadn't come on soon enough for Geneva. The building managers were going to get an earful by the time she was done with them. It wasn't until she and Vanessa were almost out of the building did the sprinklers activate.

Thank God they'd been the only two in the salon at the time. Had it been an hour earlier, some clients would have definitely gotten hurt.

A Molotov cocktail.

Geneva couldn't believe someone had thrown one into her beauty shop. The cops' initial assessment was that the perps threw two bricks through the window first, followed by two large bottles. The first bottle had been filled with gasoline and motor oil. The other was filled with baking soda, of all things. Geneva couldn't figure out the purpose of that one.

It didn't matter, though, because once she got her hands on those responsible, she'd risk going back to jail to make them pay. Deep down, she knew the guys from the night before had something to do with it. Last she heard, one was locked up because of warrants, but the other had paid the fine and was out. They still didn't have the name of the one who got away. His boys hadn't rolled on him.

Either way, there was no way she was letting someone get away with this. She had worked too damn hard to make a success of her business, and she sure as hell wasn't going to let some cowards ruin everything.

"This is a pretty nasty gash you have here, but it doesn't look like you'll need stitches," the EMT said. The woman was so petite, she could've easily been mistaken for a fifteen-year-old. "Besides the headache, are you experiencing any dizziness or nausea?"

"Just a headache," Geneva said, but it was more like a jackhammer had been set loose inside her skull. It was probably a combination of bumping into the cabinet and the stress of having her salon destroyed.

Laz's voice snagged her attention. He had arrived a few minutes ago, and after making sure she was all right, he went to talk to the police officers. Some of them he had worked with in the Atlanta PD.

Geneva winced when the EMT put a large bandage over the cut.

"Sorry about that. It's probably going to be tender for a little while."

Once the EMT was done asking her questions and bandaging her up, Vanessa walked over.

"Are you all right?" she asked and hugged Geneva. They clung to each other, both sighing loudly as if it was the first time they'd been able to take a breath.

"I will be. What about you?"

Vanessa hadn't sustained any injuries, but she had broken down into tears when they finally made it out of the building. Crying hysterically, it took Geneva several minutes to calm her down.

"I'm okay. I guess my blind date is off." She gave a humorless laugh and wrapped her arms around herself. Tears filled her eyes again, but none fell. "I'm just glad we made it out."

"Yeah, me too." Geneva squeezed the young woman's arm, hoping to offer some type of comfort. "I'm so sorry you had to go through this."

"I'll be fine. The initial shock is wearing off, and my dad just got here. I'll stay with him and my mom a couple of days until I get my nerves under control." Her voice shook, and she gave a little laugh. "I can't stop shaking."

"I know the feeling. Call me if you need anything. I mean it, anything. I'll be working with the insurance company and figuring out the next steps. I should be in touch with you in a couple of days to let you know where we go from here."

"Thanks, Gen. Take care of yourself."

"Yeah, you too."

Dread lodged into Geneva's chest as she watched Vanessa walk toward an older gentleman.

What am I going to do?

Anxiety swirled around inside of her. From employees to clients, people were counting on her to get the next steps right. She had to figure out how to get her business back up and running soon, but how? She wasn't even sure where to start.

"Gen!"

Geneva turned at the sound of the deep male voice. She huffed out a breath when she saw Reuben rushing toward her. As promised, he had called and left a message on her voicemail the night before, but she hadn't returned his call.

"Are you all right?"

She nodded and tightened the blanket around herself. She wasn't surprised to see him. A friend of his had recently opened a coffee shop that Reuben frequented at the opposite end of the strip mall.

"What the heck happened? Was anyone else hurt?" he asked, the concern in his eyes warming Geneva's heart. Some in the community thought he was still the same old gangbanger from years ago, but she had seen the change in him.

Geneva told him about the Molotov, the fire, and how she and Vanessa had barely escaped. Her voice cracked on the last words. She wasn't a crier but glancing at the front of the shop, where the huge window used to be, was almost her undoing.

"Come here. Everything is going to be okay. I'll check my contacts to see if anyone has any information. We'll find whoever did this."

Geneva allowed Reuben to pull her into a hug, but she kept her hands securely in front of her, where she held onto the blanket. Numbness enveloped her. She might not ever be okay. Her dream had literally gone up in flames.

Reuben tightened his hold, and she immediately felt uncomfortable when he nuzzled her neck. Maybe in the past, she would have welcomed his attentiveness, but those days were gone. She had no intentions of picking up where they left off years ago.

Geneva pulled back, easing out of Reuben's hold. She appreciated his concern but couldn't deal with him right now. Standing in front of the storefront, her gaze swept the interior of the salon. Charred furniture. Black, soot-covered walls. Water damage. Moments ago, she'd been angry enough to put a serious beating on someone. Now, misery consumed her. She swallowed the despair in her throat, only for it to return seconds later.

What a mess.

She had worked so hard to build her business. Everything she had went into making it a success. Time. Money. Determination. What did she have to show for it? A shell of a space that still smelled a little like gasoline.

Her heart ached.

What am I going to do?

The words were like a roar in her head. Geneva was building her savings and planning to relocate to a larger facility, but that wasn't for another year. Financially, she couldn't make that move yet, and she sure as hell wasn't asking her family for money. They had already done more than enough to help her realize her dream of being a business owner.

Dread settled around her and the tension in her chest intensified.

"I'll get someone to board up the place," Reuben said and turned her to face him. "Then I'll take you home."

"She's not going anywhere with you."

Geneva's head jerked up and her gaze collided with Myles. Standing slightly behind Reuben, he was looking tall, fierce, and in complete charge. Supreme required their security team to dress in all black when on duty, and the black suit and shirt molded over his lean, muscular body like it had been tailored just for him. His team was also required to wear black ties, but Myles wasn't the buttoned-up shirt and tie kind of guy. He had discarded his.

Geneva didn't know what it was about seeing him, but tears filled her eyes.

She didn't cry.

She never cried.

Yet, that's exactly what she felt like doing.

She didn't know if she moved toward him. Or if he moved toward her. All she knew was that one minute she was standing in front of Reuben, and the next, she was clinging to Myles.

I will not cry. She told herself that as she buried her face in the crook of his scented neck.

I will not cry.

Myles secured the blanket around her. His arms, like steel bands circling her back and waist, tightened as he held her against his hard body. No words were spoken, which wasn't a surprise. His quiet strength was more than Geneva could ask for at the moment.

All the emotions she'd been feeling the last few minutes collided, and her tears flowed freely. She had put everything into her salon, and with one evil act, it was ruined. Everything she had worked so hard for was destroyed.

Myles placed a gentle kiss on her cheek that made her tears come harder. "Besides your head, are you okay?"

She nodded, unable to quiet the sobs that were wracking her body and stealing her voice.

"Shhh... Sweetheart, this can all be fixed," Myles cooed close to her ear. "I'm just glad you're okay."

Keeping one arm around his waist, Geneva swiped at her tears that wouldn't seem to stop. His kind words were like a salve to her defeated spirit. Of all the people to soothe her, she never expected it to be Myles. Heck, she wasn't even sure how he found out about the fire.

He placed another kiss near the bandage on the side of her forehead. "Don't cry. This could've been a lot worse. As for you getting banged up, it's a good thing you have a big, hard head."

Geneva sputtered a laugh and elbowed him playfully in the ribs. "You're such an asshole."

"Yes, I've been told," Myles said, the deep rumble in his voice bringing her even more comfort. She was glad he was there. He might've been a stubborn, bossy jerk at times, but deep down, Myles was a good guy who had shown her his true character on more than one occasion.

He was also right. The incident could've been so much worse. She and Vanessa could've been seriously hurt, and the place could've burned to ashes. And though the shop was a wreck, structurally, it was fine. So, it wasn't a total loss. She had to dig deep and look on the bright side and not lose hope.

Geneva lifted her head and, with the heel of her palm, dabbed at the tears. She must've looked a mess. But the kindness in Myles's intense dark eyes helped ease some of the anxiety that had been sparring inside of her.

Cupping her face, he brushed the pads of his thumbs across her cheeks. Geneva's heart melted at his tenderness. Who knew this tall, strong, unyielding man had a sensitive side?

"Thank you," she said. "I can't tell you how glad I am that you're here with me."

He placed a lingering kiss on Geneva's lips that sent fireworks shooting off inside her body, then lifted his head and gazed into her eyes.

"There's no other place I'd rather be."

Chapter Five

Myles would be the first to admit that he liked driving with quietness surrounding him. But having a silent Geneva in the passenger seat was unsettling. In the time that he'd gotten to know her, she always had something to say. She could keep a running monologue about nothing and everything, not caring if he interjected or not.

He liked that about her. Well, most of the time. He had never been a big talker, preferring to listen, knowing he could learn more about a person if he let them do most of the talking. As long as Geneva's one-sided conversations weren't about fashion, hair, or gossip, he could tolerate them.

Right now, though, her silence bothered him. She wasn't her animated self. She had barely spoken two words since leaving her shop. Myles couldn't imagine what she must've been feeling seeing her place of business destroyed within minutes, but she was a fighter. She'd bounce back, especially since he and Laz planned to help her. They had already discussed some ideas regarding the salon. Now all he had to do was figure out what to do about Reuben. Myles didn't like the way the guy hung around. And he definitely hated the way the man looked at Geneva.

Arriving at the strip mall and finding her hugged up to the piece of slime had caught him off guard. If it hadn't been for Laz telling him to slow his roll, Myles probably would've done something stupid, like punch the former gangbanger. He wasn't usually a violent man, unless he had to be, but he didn't trust Reuben. For all Myles knew, the guy could've been responsible for the fire, as well as sending those guys to the shop to destroy her car. No doubt, the two incidences were connected. Reuben could claim to be reformed all he wanted, but Myles wouldn't believe it until he saw proof. In the meantime, he didn't want Geneva anywhere near the man.

Glancing at Geneva, who stared out the passenger window, Myles reached for her hand. He wasn't the most compassionate person and had no clue on how to console her. Maybe it hadn't been the best decision to insist she go home with him, but there was no way he was letting her out of his sight. At least not until the police determined if the two incidents were retaliation for something.

"Are you hungry?" he asked.

"No."

She might not be hungry, but he was. After he shooed Reuben away from the shop, Myles and a couple of guys from Supreme boarded up the salon. He then drove Geneva home so she could shower and pack an overnight bag for her and her dog, Coco.

Myles glanced in the back seat. The two-year-old black-and-white border collie-boxer mix lifted her head and looked at him as if he had called her name. The intuitive beauty had stuck close to Geneva at the house as if sensing her distress.

Myles squeezed Geneva's hand, and she glanced at him. She gave a slight smile but still didn't say anything before turning back to the window.

Releasing her hand, he activated the car's Bluetooth and called his neighborhood pizza joint. He ordered a large veggie pizza and a medium Hawaiian chicken pizza that he knew Geneva liked.

"Can you add a side of wings and cinnamon sticks to the order?" Geneva asked. With the phone on speaker, the woman on the line heard her.

"I sure can." The woman's chipper voice rang out. "Will there be anything else with the order?"

Geneva shook her head.

"No. That'll be it," Myles said.

After the woman gave him the total for the order, he disconnected the call and went back to holding her hand. He didn't hold hands. Yet, the need to touch her was stronger than he could resist.

"I thought you weren't hungry."

"I wasn't until you mentioned Hawaiian chicken pizza. Now I'm starving."

Myles chuckled. Some of her humor was peeking through. Unfortunately, her smile didn't quite reach her eyes.

After picking up their meal, he pulled into the underground parking of his loft. The old warehouse had been converted years ago and now housed several loft-style units. He had purchased the three-bedroom, two-and-a-half-bathroom place from Mason a couple of years ago. His boss and Mason's wife London had lived in the loft until they finished building a massive home out in Kennesaw, Georgia. Even though Myles didn't entertain much, it was the perfect bachelor's pad. The exposed brick and ductwork gave the place an industrial feel while still feeling homey.

When he let Geneva and Coco into the house, Geneva made a beeline to the wall of windows. Myles set her bag near the stairs and stood back, watching as she stared out into the night. Four stories high, his unit had a good view of the manicured park across the street that hosted blooming trees and flowers for much of the year. Geneva had once commented that the scene had a calming effect.

"I'll take Coco outside. Make yourself comfortable."

The dog trotted over to him as if she understood everything he had just said. Sitting at his feet, her tail thumped loudly against the hardwood floor, patiently waiting for him to grab her leash.

Considering Geneva could be loud and quick-tempered, her dog was calm and well trained. Myles had taken a liking to Coco immediately, especially since she had a similar demeanor as his dog, Pepper, a black Labrador retriever he and his siblings had growing up. Pepper had a sixth sense, able to detect their moods, especially Myles's. When he was happy, she was playful. If he had a bad day, it seemed she stayed close to him, wanting to offer comfort. Similar to what Coco had done with Geneva.

Instead of heading out the door as planned, he strolled across the dark hardwood floor toward her. She didn't turn to him, but he was sure she saw him approach through the window. Wrapping his arms around her, he pulled her back against him and placed a kiss just below her left ear.

Myles held her without speaking. He normally wasn't the cuddling, comforting type, but with Geneva, it was different. He was different. He didn't recognize himself whenever they were sharing the same space. She brought out a side in him that Myles didn't know existed. And right now, all he wanted to do was hold her. She felt so perfect in his arms, and he never wanted to let her go.

"I got you," he said quietly. "Whatever you need. I'm here, and you're going to get through this. All right?"

Geneva turned her head slightly as if to say something to him, but instead, she pulled her bottom lip between her teeth and nodded.

Coco whined near the door, but Myles wasn't ready to release Geneva. He held her a few minutes longer before placing a kiss on the side of her head and slowly stepping back. "I'm gonna take her out and be right back."

"Okay," she said.

He hooked on Coco's leash and opened the door.

"Myles," Geneva said, glancing over her shoulder at him. "Thank you for everything."

His heart squeezed at the sadness in her eyes and the defeat in her tone. "No problem. We'll be back in a minute."

Once outside, a strong, cool breeze whipped around him, and he shivered, wishing he had thought to slip into a heavier coat than just his suit jacket. As Coco sniffed around the yard, Myles stood with his shoulders hunched and a billow of vapor coming from his mouth with each exhale.

He glanced around his surroundings, taking in the quiet block and tree-lined street as he waited for the dog to handle her business. His mind immediately went to Geneva and the situation with her salon. Furniture, equipment, drywall, and a host of other items would need replacing. Also, a good cleaning would have to happen before she could operate again. It would be weeks—or maybe even a month—before she'd be able to get back to work.

Myles wanted her business up and running again, but in a better neighborhood. Which was why he planned to talk to Geneva about finding another location. She might balk at the idea, but it couldn't hurt to put the suggestion out there.

The wind picked up, and an uneasy sensation crept across the back of Myles's neck and down his spine. His CIA experiences had sharpened his senses and had saved his life on more than one occasion.

Now he stood frozen in place, his ears straining to hear anything outside of Coco's movements. The eerie feeling of being watched was strong, stronger than anything he'd felt in a while.

Coco lifted her head, then glanced up at Myles.

Okay, so he wasn't the only one who sensed something. Then again, it could be nothing, and he was on edge after having a long day. Still, Myles took in the neighboring building, a warehouse that had also been converted to lofts. His gaze swept over the few cars parked on the street. Empty. No one in sight. That didn't mean he wasn't being watched.

Hearing movement behind him, he slipped the switchblade out of his pocket quicker than most people could blink. Holding it close to his side, he remained perfectly still. Waiting. Listening.

Coco's low growl turned into barking, and she ran toward the street, but the leash held her back just as two kids on skateboards came rolling into view. They were laughing and talking but grew quiet when they saw the dog. Seeing that she wasn't going to chase them, they kept rolling until they were around the corner and out of sight.

"Quiet," Myles said when Coco continued barking. She stopped, but her attention stayed on the direction the kids had disappeared. After a few minutes, she went back to roaming around the grassy area.

Myles kept his blade out. The tension swirling inside of him eased, but not completely. He didn't relax until he and Coco were back inside the building.

When they walked into his unit, Geneva was nowhere to be seen. The two pizza boxes and wings were still on the counter and hadn't been touched. No sounds flowed through the loft.

Myles washed his hands in the half-bath, then dug around in the canvas bag that held some of Coco's items. He found two bowls and set them out near the door, filling one with dog food and the other with water.

Once Coco started eating, Myles headed upstairs and shrugged out of his suit jacket along the way. After barely getting any sleep the night before and having an early morning, the plan had been to get home at a decent time, eat a little something, then hit the sack.

So much for making plans. The day had been nothing like he expected.

Myles pulled up short at the bedroom door, surprised to see Geneva stretched out across the bed. Still fully clothed, she hadn't even bothered to kick off her black ankle boots.

He dropped his suit jacket on the bench at the foot of the bed. Staring down at the woman who had crashed into his life like a meteor slamming through the earth's atmosphere, a calmness swept through him. Even though Geneva drove him nuts with her smart mouth, quick temper, and her ability to invade his mind at the most inopportune time, Myles loved having her around.

He stood over her, brushing a few strands of hair away from her eyes. Originally it had been piled on top of her head but was now hanging loosely around her shoulders and face. The bandage on the side of her forehead stood out like a blinking neon sign, reminding him of her traumatic day.

Not wanting to wake her but wanting her to be a little more comfortable, Myles gently tugged off her boots and set them on the floor. No way was he removing her clothes. No sense in torturing himself with seeing her in the sexy underwear she usually wore. He lifted her slightly and moved her higher up on the king-sized bed. Geneva mumbled something, snuggled into the pillow, but didn't wake up.

She had only been to his place a couple of times, and Myles had never planned to have her in his bed again. Yet, here she was. He was playing with fire. His feelings for her were stronger than anything he had ever experienced with a woman, but if he wanted to ensure things between them didn't go any further, this setup was a bad idea.

Say what you mean. Mean what you say.

That was something his father constantly preached before dying a few years ago. Words that Myles lived by. Until now. He meant it when he told Geneva he wasn't looking for anything serious. She was only supposed to be a one-time hookup. Yet, there was something special about the complex woman that kept him from moving on.

If he were smart, he'd sleep in the guest room to eliminate any temptation. He wasn't feeling that smart at the moment. Curling up on the bed with her securely in his arms was an enticement he didn't know if he could walk away from. Then again, she'd just been through hell. The least he could do was act like he had some type of self-control. But when it came to Geneva, his self-control and common sense were nonexistent.

Myles shook his head and huffed out a breath. "It's going to be a long night."

Chapter Six

Cyrus slowly pulled over to the shoulder of the road. He had intentionally kept his distance several vehicles behind Samantha Cooley. Or as he now knew her, Whitney Spencer.

Finally, *finally*, he had gotten a little justice, though it had taken over four years. It took that long to learn the identity of the CIA agents responsible for destroying his family.

But they would all pay. Them and their families.

The CIA had buried their true identity under layers and layers of bureaucracy and lies, making it nearly impossible to track them down. But Cyrus wasn't a quitter. He never gave up. After serving in the army and doing three tours in Afghanistan, protecting his country, he had learned patience and had gained a never-say-quit attitude. He only left the military because of his father's plan to run for president. His dad would've been a great commander-in-chief, and Cyrus had intended to return home and work on his father's campaign.

He never got the chance.

His family had been ripped apart, shredded into tiny pieces, and practically left destitute because of lies. Just thinking about that time in his life had him squeezing the

54

steering wheel tighter. His father had given his life to politics, with Cyrus's mother right by his side. But devastating lies dug up by the CIA and the FBI had ruined them. They had ruined everything, and his parents hadn't been able to withstand the shame that came along with them. The smear campaign had resulted in his father's suicide and his mother dying from alcoholism.

Cyrus vowed to destroy those responsible. It might've taken him going around and around in circles for over four years, but his determination had finally paid off.

Whitney was his first target.

Now he just had to make sure she was dead.

He pulled up behind an old orange pickup truck. The driver had stopped right after Whitney crashed and was now hurrying out of his vehicle. The man, tall with a beer belly, had red hair and a long scraggly beard the same color covering his alabaster skin. Wearing worn overalls and dusty work boots in the farming area, it was safe to assume he was a farmer. Besides Cyrus, the guy was the only person to stop. Every other motorist just peered at the scene through their car windows as they crept through traffic.

Cyrus couldn't have planned the accident better. Traffic was backed up, and Whitney hadn't had a chance to travel far before needing her brakes.

Putting his truck in park, he turned on his blinkers. He didn't think he'd need it, but he made sure the Atlanta PD badge was in his pocket. At a quick glance, not even a police officer would know it was a fake.

He climbed out of his truck and tugged the Atlanta Braves baseball cap lower on his head. To complete his disguise, his wraparound sunglasses were securely in place, covering his light brown eyes and some of the freckles on his light skin. He rushed toward Whitney's vehicle. Any observer would dismiss him as another Good Samaritan.

He had been traveling three cars behind and had seen the crash. There was no way the woman could've survived it, especially after slamming into the huge eighty-foot trees at the speed she'd been going. The only other thing that would have given him more pleasure was if the car would've exploded on impact. Now that would've been sweet justice.

There was still a little satisfaction, though. The way the front end of her Toyota Camry was mangled, she had to be dead. Cyrus needed to make sure.

"Hey, thanks for stopping," the farmer said. He had to be around six feet tall, an inch or two taller than Cyrus, and at least thirty pounds heavier. "The door is jammed. Let's see if we can get it open. The driver might still be alive."

"Let me grab my crowbar."

For her sake, she better not be, Cyrus thought as he rushed to the rear of his truck, grabbed the tire iron, and ran back. He peered through the driver's side window. The airbag had deployed, and the windshield was shattered. Whitney's face bled from its many cuts, and her head was arched at an odd angle. More importantly, she wasn't moving.

That's a good sign.

Cyrus stuck the crowbar between the door and the body of the vehicle. He wanted to make his effort to help look good. While he tugged, trying to pry the door open, the other guy kept yanking on the door handle.

"I'll go around to the other side and break the window," Cyrus offered, surprised it hadn't shattered on impact like the windshield.

Just when he lifted the crowbar to crash through the window, he heard sirens in the near distance. He needed to move quickly if he wanted to ensure his target was dead. If she wasn't, he planned to finish her off.

Once he busted through the window, Cyrus carefully reached in and opened the passenger door. He shook her gently, careful not to touch anything else, and then placed two fingers against her neck to feel for a pulse.

Nothing.

Relief spread through him. Considering how close the other man was behind him, it would've been hard to kill her under his watchful eyes. Now he didn't have to worry about that. She was dead.

"Is she…" the other man started, but his words trailed off when Cyrus climbed out. His phony expression of being distraught must've worked. The farmer shook his head and cursed.

Seconds later, a police car and a fire truck were on the scene. Emergency personnel flooded out of the vehicles. The farmer was talking a mile a minute to anyone who would listen. He explained how he and Cyrus had tried to help the woman.

"All right, all right, we'll get your statements," a large burly police officer said with his arms spread wide, blocking their view of the wreckage. "Right now, though, I need you two to move back. Step over there." He pointed to a spot at least twenty feet away where another officer waved them over.

The farmer was questioned by that cop, while Cyrus was stuck with the burly police officer, who, after a few minutes, he wanted to punch. The guy kept having him to repeat almost everything Cyrus said, as if not believing him. The only thing that made the situation bearable was when the black coroner's van showed up.

Sweet victory.

One CIA agent down.

One to go.

*

After taking Coco outside, Myles returned to his bedroom and climbed back into bed. He had slept soundly except for when he vaguely remembered Geneva getting up, bumping around downstairs in the middle of the night. At some point, she had even replaced the large bandage on the side of her forehead with a regular-size Band-Aid.

What he hadn't realized until this morning was that she had also stripped out of her clothes.

Laying on his side and propped on his elbow, he pulled the sheet up over Geneva's bare breasts, not wanting to be any more aroused by her naked body. Just the sight of her had him hard as granite. Add that to the fact that he hadn't had sex since the last time they were together, two weeks ago, and his penis was ready to punch a hole through his lounging pants.

Agony. Being this close and not touching her was pure agony.

Geneva stirred, moaning in her sleep. Eyes still closed, she yawned and slowly stretched her arms up and out. Each move she made caused the bed sheet to slide lower. Her voluptuous breasts and perky nipples that begged to be sucked peeked from under the covers again, stoking the growing fire within him.

Damn. Even in her sleep, she insisted on torturing him.

Laying on her back, she yawned again, and her eyes eased open. She glanced up at the ceiling, blinked several times, then turned her head toward him. Their gazes locked, and a slow, sensual smile spread across her gorgeous mouth.

"Good morning, handsome," she crooned.

Myles's shaft twitched at the huskiness of her melodious voice. She rolled onto her side, facing him, and his whole body yearned with need.

He wanted her.

Wanted to touch her, any part of her, but a touch would lead to a kiss. A kiss would lead to heavy petting. Heavy petting would lead to the point of no return.

Not a good idea. At least not until they had a chance to talk about their relationship...or whatever was happening between them.

"Morning," he finally said and kept his hands to himself. "How do you feel?"

She searched his face for the longest time before speaking. "Horny. I'm feeling horny as hell."

Okay, *that* wasn't what he expected her to say.

"Instead of just staring at me, why don't you help me out with that," she purred and moved even closer. Her fingers took a slow stroll down his chest, and his body heated from the inside out.

"Gen…" Myles started, unsure of what to say. Of course, he wanted to help with all of her sexual needs, but she was more than a quick lay—something he realized while in Los Angeles those couple of weeks.

Geneva was important to him. Important enough to where he wanted to change their initial agreement. At first, neither of them was looking for anything serious, but now…

Yeah, they needed to talk.

Myles needed to tell her that he didn't just want a sex partner. He wanted her in his life. He wanted her to be his woman. But the realization of that was too crazy to even form the sentences that would be needed to tell her. He didn't do relationships. He didn't let women get this close.

Not just because he loved his drama-free life. No, there were a number of reasons why: one being his past life. The life of a spy had been dangerous on so many levels. Though he no longer worked for the CIA, Myles never knew when something or someone from his past would creep into his present. He never wanted to put his loved ones in danger because of something he might've been a part of in the past.

"Don't overthink this, Myles. I'll respect your wishes and keep my distance…tomorrow. Right now, though, I want you as much as I think you want me."

She slid her hand lower over his stomach and kept moving south, sending sparks of desire shooting to every nerve in his body. He sucked in a breath when she cupped his shaft, rubbing him gently before squeezing.

"Let's just help each other out, for now; then I'll move on."

"I'm not sure I want you to move on," Myles groaned out as his shaft grew harder within her grasp to the point of being almost unbearable. He covered her hand with his. He didn't want her to stop stroking him, but they needed to clear the air. "About what I said a couple of weeks ago. I've—"

"Just be quiet and kiss me." Geneva didn't give him a chance to respond. She barely finished her sentence before releasing him, then straddling his thighs and covering his mouth with hers.

Pleasure pulsed through his body as she kissed him with an intensity that had him vibrating with need. Yeah, they could talk later. Much, much later. All Myles wanted to do at that moment was refamiliarize himself with every inch of her luscious body. But as she ground against his hardness, his brain short-circuited, and he could barely think straight.

His little vixen not only kissed with a hunger that matched his, but Myles had learned early on that her sexual appetite was just as ferocious as his. He'd been a fool thinking he could have just one taste of her and be satisfied.

It wasn't even just their sexual chemistry that turned him on and kept him coming back for more. It was everything about the woman. Her wittiness. Her intelligence. Her boldness. Myles had never met anyone quite like her. Whenever they were together, in and out of the bedroom, Geneva stoked something so exciting and uncontrollable inside of him, he couldn't ever see moving on from her.

She was now stretched out on top of him. Chest to chest, thigh to thigh, no part of them wasn't touching. The only thing that kept him from sliding into her sweet heat was his pants, but Myles could feel all of her.

He moaned when she circled her hips on top of him, making him even harder if that was possible. He cupped her bare butt, planning to slow her moves since he didn't want this to be over before they even began. But unable to help himself, he started kneading and squeezing her ass, crushing her more to him and loving how perfectly she fit into his hands.

"Myles," Geneva groaned against his lips as her body gyrated more.

"I know, baby." He knew her patience was wearing thin.

Myles flipped her onto her back and deepened the kiss, ravishing her mouth and unable to get enough of her sweetness. She was the sexiest woman he'd ever been with. Having her naked beneath him stirred every erotic desire he'd kept bottled up for the last couple of weeks. The lust-arousing sounds she was making only intensified his need to have her, but Myles didn't want to rush.

He moved his mouth from hers and nibbled her earlobe, eliciting a whimper from her as she wiggled against him. He nuzzled her neck.

"Man, you smell good." The vanilla fragrance was even more pronounced than it had been the night before. "And this body..."

With his hand, Myles traced a path down the center of her body and cupped her firm breasts, pushing them together before lowering his head to taste her. He swiped his tongue over a pert nipple. Teasing, Licking. Sucking.

"Baby, that feels good," she said, moaning and trembling under his touch.

Even her moans were sexy.

Myles kissed a path down her chest to her stomach and lingered near her bellybutton.

"My—Myles," Geneva breathed, her hands gripping his head as she moved beneath him. He knew what she wanted when she spread her legs, and he was just the man to satisfy her every desire.

He took his time, kissing his way lower, wanting to savor every minute with her. More than anything, Myles wanted to prolong their time in bed.

"I think we need some chocolate syrup."

Geneva giggled between panting. "Later...we'll get it later. Don't stop."

Myles smiled against her scented skin. She was always torturing him one way or another, especially in the bedroom. A little payback right about now wouldn't hurt.

He stopped abruptly and hopped off the bed.

"Nooo..." Geneva choked out a laugh that turned into a groan as she pounded her fist on the mattress. She squeezed her thighs together as if in pain. "You are not right. You can't leave me like this."

"Oh, but you're going to love every minute of what I have planned for you."

He wanted to torture her some, but in hindsight, maybe it wasn't one of his best ideas. The woman had him so damn hard, he could barely walk. Taking a few deep breaths, he took uncomfortable steps to the bedroom door.

"You're going to pay for this," Geneva grumbled.

Yeah, he was already paying, but it would be worth it.

When he opened the door, instead of Coco running into the bedroom as Myles expected, she headed to the stairs, glancing over her shoulder to see if he was following.

Myles closed the door and followed the dog downstairs.

"Instead of chocolate, maybe some whipped cream," he mumbled to himself, quickly grabbing the can out of the refrigerator and heading back to the stairs.

Bzzzz. Bzzzz. Bzzzz.

Whoever was pushing on his doorbell wasn't letting up. Coco started barking and prancing around, trying to figure out where the sound was coming from before running over to the intercom.

Myles rarely had visitors, and no one dared stop by without calling. But whoever was ringing the bell was intent on getting his attention.

He strolled to the door. Instead of using the intercom, he activated the built-in monitor connected to cameras at the front and rear of the building. Buying the loft from a person who owned a security firm had its advantages. Mason had outfitted the unit with a state-of-the-art security system.

When the person came into view, Myles's heart slammed against his chest. Tension gripped his shoulders. His mind raced with scenarios that would explain the visit, and not one of them was good.

Coco sat next to his legs, whining as if sensing his sudden anxiety. Myles placed his hand on her head, petting her with soothing strokes to quiet her. The gesture even helped him some, but there was still a slight churning in his gut as he braced himself for whatever was about to come.

He buzzed her in, knowing it would take a few minutes for her to ride the elevator to his unit. Hurrying over to the coat closet off of the kitchen, he grabbed a sweatshirt off of the top shelf and slipped it on. Then he stuck his bare feet into a pair of running shoes.

He was back at the door and opening it before his visitor had a chance to knock.

"She's gone, Myles," Yvette choked out. Her red-rimmed eyes and quivering lower lip had his pulse racing. "Whitney...she's gone."

Tears leaked from her eyes, and her shoulders shook while Myles stood in shock, attempting to process the news. Numbness seeped into his body. With Yvette showing up on his doorstep, he knew that something terrible had happened, but not that.

Dead.

Whitney was dead.

The news hit him like a back kick to the face. This didn't make sense. He had just talked to her the night before. Now she was gone? Dead?

Coco started whining again, and Myles glanced at the dog, who nudged his leg with her nose as if to *say snap out of it.*

"Where's Collin?" Myles asked.

Yvette reached for the stroller that was out of view and pulled it forward. "She dropped him off early this morning at my place, saying that she had to meet a client. She was only supposed to be gone a few hours, but..." Yvette covered her face with her hands and sobbed outright.

Myles's chest tightened, and he pulled her into his arms. She and Whitney had grown up in foster care and ended up in the same foster home at the age of twelve. Since then, they'd been closer than some biological siblings. Not only had Yvette lost her sister, but the sleeping child would grow up without his mother.

Seconds ticked by as they stood, holding each other while Myles grappled with the news.

Yvette eventually pulled out of his hold and wiped her face feverishly with the sleeve of the fleece jacket. "I saw her this morning, only a few hours ago. Now...I just can't believe she's gone."

"Yeah, I can't either. Come in." He helped maneuver the jogging stroller into the loft and locked the door behind them.

Yvette released a long sigh. "It doesn't seem real."

Collin stirred, and she pushed the stroller back and forth.

"Here, let me take him out of there."

Myles lifted the boy from the stroller and adjusted him so that the child's head rested on his shoulder.

"Tell me what happened."

When Yvette started crying again, Myles adjusted Collin in his arm, then wrapped his other arm around her. He hoped to offer some comfort, but it wasn't easy when emotion clogged his throat. Whitney was gone. He had spoken with her the day before, not knowing that it would be the last time.

"I'm sorry, Myles. I just can't seem to get myself together."

"I know, but you'll...we'll get through this."

Myles held Yvette close until her sobs stopped. Then he stepped into the half bath next to the stairs and grabbed her a few sheets of tissue.

"Thank you." She dabbed at her eyes. "The cops are still investigating, but they said according to witnesses, Whitney lost control of the car and drove off the road."

"Where?" Myles asked.

That didn't make sense. Whitney was an excellent driver. How had she lost control of the car? Had she fallen asleep at the wheel? Did she swerve to miss an animal in the street? Did someone run her off the road? Questions he knew Yvette didn't have answers to bombarded his mind.

"She was meeting the client just outside of Macon, but she didn't say exactly where."

"Did the cops say anything else?"

"No. They're still investigating. The accident happened hours ago. They sent someone to Whitney's house, but of course, no one was there. Eventually, they found my number in her cell phone. I was the last person she called. Thank God she had me listed as a sister."

"I'm not surprised," Myles said. "She always thought of everything."

Collin squirmed, and Myles rubbed the child's back as he rocked him, hoping they hadn't awakened him, but Collin lifted his head. His sleepy eyes blinked several times before zoning in on Myles, who couldn't help but smile.

"Hey, little man. You're awake."

"Hi...Daddy."

"Daddy? *What the hell*, Myles!" Geneva yelled from behind him.

Myles closed his eyes and braced himself for his human tornado.

"You have a kid and a baby mama and didn't think to tell me?" she screeched, the sound sending goosebumps over his skin the way it would if fingernails were clawing down a blackboard.

"Geneva," Myles said with impatience as he turned.

The rest of his words died on his tongue. She was wearing one of his white dress shirts and making it look way better on her than it did on him. It stopped mid-thigh and showed off her long shapely legs that he'd been between only moments ago.

She jammed her hands on her hips, causing the hem of the shirt to rise. Myles was pretty sure she was naked underneath and hoped the hem didn't rise any higher.

His gaze went back to her face. The way she was glaring, he'd be a pile of dust if her eyes were weapons.

"Your ass better start talking before I raise hell up in here."

Chapter Seven

"Geneva, meet Collin...my son."

Geneva shook with barely contained rage and balled her fists at her sides as she glared at Myles. Gritting her teeth, she fought against herself to keep from saying anything that she might regret, especially in front of the little boy.

A son. He has a son.

How the heck had she not known that?

"Go upstairs and get dressed, then I'll explain everything," Myles said in a casual tone as if they were planning to discuss the merits of Kwanza.

His tone only made her angrier, and instead of arguing, Geneva stomped to the stairs, her bare feet slapping against the hardwood floors. Stopping suddenly, she turned to call Coco, but the four-legged traitor was too caught up in the little boy who was now on the floor petting her.

Geneva hiked up the steps, mumbling angrily under her breath. As soon as she was dressed, she was getting out of there. Myles didn't have to explain a damn thing to her. It was too late. She didn't want to hear it. She might've loved children, but dating men with kids was a deal-breaker. And she definitely didn't tolerate baby mama drama.

Growling under her breath, her teeth were clenched so tight, it was a wonder they didn't crumble into small pieces.

She tore through her overnight bag, yanked out a sweater and yoga pants, and slammed them on the bed. Then she pulled out her pink lace underwear and hurried into them.

"What. An. Idiot! How could I have not known?"

Granted, Myles rarely talked about himself. Much of their time had been spent in her bedroom. Outside of that, for the weeks they hung out, she typically controlled the conversations while he listened and interjected periodically. Yet, he had plenty of opportunities to tell her he had a kid.

Had she missed any signs of a child being in his life?

She glanced around his bedroom. *No pictures.*

No surprise there.

There were no photos, paintings, or anything else hanging on the walls or sitting on any flat surfaces throughout the loft. As a minimalist, it was a wonder Myles even had furniture. He had the bare minimum on the main floor, and the king-sized bed, two nightstands, and a bench at the foot of the bed were the only pieces of furniture in the bedroom. A small chest shoved into a corner of the closet held folded clothes, and there wasn't much hanging on the rods except for a few shirts and suits.

Furniture or no furniture, it didn't matter. Nothing about Myles mattered anymore. Clearly, he was a man of secrets, and Geneva wanted no part of it.

She quickly dressed in the pink off-the-shoulder sweater and black leggings. And once her boots were on, she gave the bedroom one last glance and headed for the stairs, but pulled up short. Glancing down the hallway, there were two bedrooms and a bathroom. At least that's what Myles had told her. He hadn't actually given her a tour of the place, and she never bothered to look around either. That wasn't her style. She didn't snoop...normally.

Geneva marched down the hall and slowed when she reached the full bathroom, only giving it a cursory glance. The other two doors were closed, and she shoved the first one open. Except for a futon and a dresser that held a television, the rest of the room was bare. She turned on her heels to the door across the hall and shoved it open.

Her breath caught and a twinge of something sharp settled in the center of her chest. She wanted to scream. Geneva wanted to be angry. And she wanted to punch someone. But what good would any of that do? She'd been had, and the only person she could really be mad at was herself. She should have never fallen for Myles. The asshole.

Her shoulders sagged as she glanced around the brightly decorated space.

Collin's room.

As her gaze took in the beautifully decorated room, it was hard to stay mad at Myles. It was clear the love that had gone into every detail.

Geneva strolled inside, taking in every inch. A bluish-gray feature wall was covered with twinkling stars that gave the space a warm, inviting feel. The twin-sized blue, black, and red bed was shaped like a train and an overhead roof acted as the headboard. It even had wheels. The rest of the furnishings, including a hutch and a small dresser, matched the bed frame and headboard colors.

This is too frickin' cute. The rest of the house barely looked lived in, but no expense had been spared in decorating his son's space. Every possible toy and book were meticulously organized on the far side of the room, along with a small table with two chairs.

Geneva gave the space one last look before heading to the stairs. She wanted to be mad, but some of her anger dissipated as she went down the stairs.

"I'll update you once I learn more and figure out the next steps. I still can't believe she's gone, Myles."

"Yeah, me either."

Not intending to eavesdrop on their conversation, Geneva couldn't help wondering what and who they were talking about.

Myles glanced at her just as she made it to the second from the bottom step. He and the woman were still standing near the breakfast bar, their faces lined with worry. Leaving without giving him a chance to explain had been Geneva's plan, but the weariness in his intense dark eyes rooted her in place. Whatever was going on was serious.

Myles reached for her hand. "Come and let me introduce you."

Geneva stood in shock, staring at him, wondering what the heck was happening. She was angry at him. At least she wanted to be. But there was something about the way he looked at her that had her moving forward and reluctantly accepting his extended hand.

Myles blew her away even more when he pulled her to his side. He should've been pissed at the way she snapped earlier, embarrassing him in front of his guest. Instead, he held her close with an arm around her waist and his hand resting on her hip.

"Geneva, this is Yvette, Collin's aunt. His mother's sister. Yvette, this is my..." Myles started to speak but stopped and gave his head a slight shake. "This is Geneva."

Interesting. What had he been about to say?

Geneva didn't get a chance to play the question around in her mind. Collin giggled from across the room, snagging all of their attention. The open concept gave an unobstructed view into the living room where he was rubbing Coco's back.

The anger Geneva battled with while upstairs slowly dissipated, especially now seeing the boy with her dog. Clearly Collin wasn't afraid of Coco, and her fur baby was eating up the attention.

"He loves dogs," Yvette said quietly.

Short, with a reddish-black afro, light-brown complexion with blotchy skin, probably from crying, the woman appeared to be in her late twenties, possibly early thirties.

"Geneva, I'm sorry about barging in on you guys. I called Myles earlier. When I didn't get an answer and couldn't reach my husband right away, I just... I just had to get out of the house. I started walking and ended up here."

"Yvette lives about a half-mile from here," Myles said, his voice low. "Collin's mother was killed in a car accident this morning."

Geneva gasped, and her hand flew to her mouth. "Oh, my God. That's awful. I'm so sorry for your loss," she said to Yvette, then realized Myles had lost someone, too. Her hand went to his chest. "You, too. I'm so sorry."

"Thank you," Yvette said. "Whitney always said that if anything ever happened to her, make sure I get Collin to Myles. I took a chance on stopping by."

Myles explained to Geneva the little information they knew about Whitney's accident and that Collin didn't know yet. Geneva couldn't imagine how hard it would be to tell that little boy his mommy was gone. He couldn't have been more than three or four years old. Would he even understand at that age?

"I acted like a total idiot earlier," Geneva said, feeling like the lowest form of human life. She could be mad at Myles for not being forthcoming, but had she known what she was walking in on, she would've handled herself differently. "I am so sorry. Let me know if there's anything I can do."

"Thank you," Yvette said with a shaky smile. "I think I'm still in shock. My husband is on his way here. Then we'll head to Macon to claim my sister's bod..." Her voice caught, and she bit down on her bottom lip, swiping at the tears that suddenly appeared.

Myles put his hand on Yvette's shoulder. "Are you sure you don't want me to handle everything regarding Whitney?"

"No. No, Collin needs you. Besides, DeShawn will be with me," she said of her husband. "I'll call if I need anything, and I'll keep you posted on any new developments."

A buzzing sound filled the space, and Yvette pulled her phone from her jacket pocket. Glancing at the screen, she said, "DeShawn is outside. I better go. I'll be in touch." She glanced at Geneva and gave a small wave. "Bye. Nice meeting you."

Hunted

"You too. Take care of yourself."

"Hold on a sec, Yvette." Myles dropped his arm from around Geneva. "I'll walk you out."

"Okay, but let me say bye to Collin."

When she walked across the room, Myles grabbed his keys off the top of the refrigerator, then approached Geneva. She swallowed hard at the intensity in his eyes.

"Can you keep an eye on him for a minute?" Geneva wasn't sure what Myles saw on her face, but he quickly added, "I'll explain *everything* when I get back."

She nodded, and he glanced at Collin and Coco before quietly easing out the door.

Geneva took in the scene in the living room. When she first saw Coco at the pound, it was love at first sight. Journey and her parents had insisted that the last thing she needed was the responsibility of a dog. Geneva was so glad she hadn't listened. Coco was the calm in her life. Now, seeing how gentle she was with Myles's son, she was even happier to have the dog. Collin's world was about to be turned upside down, and maybe Coco could be a good distraction.

A heavy weight settled in Geneva's chest. Not only did Myles have a son, but now he was a single parent. Everything was different now.

"Where's Daddy?" The small voice shook Geneva out of her thoughts.

Collin was no longer sitting on the floor. Instead, he stood next to the sofa with his lips trembling while trying not to cry. Coco whined, nudging him with her nose. She was almost as tall as him, and thankfully Collin wasn't afraid of her.

Geneva walked across the room and sat on the sofa next to where Collin stood. He was such a cutie. His hair was cut close to his head, and he had smooth, tawny-brown skin and plump, kissable cheeks. His onyx eyes were definitely from Myles. Even as young as Collin was, his gaze held the same intensity as his father's.

A fat tear slid down Collin's cheek, followed by another.

71

"Oh, sweetie, don't cry. Your daddy will be right back." Geneva picked him up and sat him on her lap. Now that she was up close to him, he looked younger than she initially thought. "He's coming back, okay."

"Okay," he murmured and stared at the door.

Sadness pierced her heart. She had grown up with two loving parents. Even when she was hard to love, they were right there every day of her life. The thought of losing either one of them, even at her age, was unthinkable. Geneva couldn't imagine what it would be like for a small child. Collin's mom was gone. What would his life be like growing up?

Not wanting to get melancholy, she shook the thoughts free.

"How old are you, Collin?"

He fumbled with his fingers then raised two of them on one hand and one on the other hand.

Geneva smiled. "You're three?"

He nodded. Then his attention went back to the door.

"Do you go to school?"

He shook his head.

"What about daycare?"

"Yes."

"Do you know your ABCs?"

"Yes."

"Can you count to ten?"

"Yes."

So much for holding a conversation. So far, talking to him was like trying to communicate with his dad. The one-word responses weren't getting her anywhere, just like with his dad. But *damn* if he wasn't a cutie-pie like his daddy.

"What's your name?" Collin asked, surprising Geneva.

"My name is Geneva."

He scrunched up his nose as if smelling something bad. "Ja-nina?"

A laugh burst free from her, and she rubbed his back. "Not quite, but that's close. It's Ge-nee-va. Or you can call me Gen. Can you say Gen?"

"Yes." Instead of repeating her name, he asked, "Is that your dog?"

"Yes, her name is Coco."

"I know. My daddy told me." Collin released a long yawn and laid his head against Geneva's chest. "I want my daddy."

"I know, honey. He'll be back soon."

What a strange morning. At least the last half-hour had taken Geneva's mind off of her own issues. She had so many decisions to make about the salon. The insurance adjuster wouldn't be out until later that day. Geneva had no clue how long it would take to pull everything back together. The night before, she had contacted the staff and requested they all reach out to clients who had appointments coming up over the next week. Unfortunately, they'd have to cancel them without being able to set new appointments. It was an inconvenience to everyone involved, but none of that compared to what Myles was going through. Or what he would have to deal with going forward.

About what I said a couple of weeks ago.

His words from earlier came back to her. If only she would've let him finish whatever he was going to say. Of course, her impatience and need to have him buried inside of her took precedence. That was so her—interrupting someone in order to get what she wanted.

Had he planned to suggest that they keep seeing each other? The way he showed up for her at the salon the night before and his tenderness since then made her believe that they had something special. Or something that could be special if they ever got on the same page.

Everything was different now.

Myles didn't need a lover or a girlfriend. He needed a friend. Someone he and Collin could count on until they got through this difficult time.

Could she be that person?

Could she put their needs before her own?

Geneva glanced down, noting that Collin was drifting off to sleep. She held him close and continued rocking back and forth. Coco plopped her head onto Geneva's knee and stared up at her with those puppy-dog eyes.

"You did good, girl," she whispered, scratching behind the dog's ear. Her fur baby had handled the situation well. Unlike her, who had walked in on Myles and Yvette and had been ready to pummel Myles for not telling her he had a kid.

So much for first impressions. Yvette must have thought her a nutcase.

Collin's soft snores reached her ears, and Geneva debated whether to lay him on the sofa. He seemed kind of small for a three-year-old, but she really wasn't sure if he was small for his age or not. Her only interaction with kids lately was with her one-year-old niece.

Instead of laying Collin down, Geneva held him close. He was going to need all the hugs and love he could get now that his mother was gone.

Poor baby.

She tightened her hold and sent up a silent prayer that he and his dad could get through this.

The door opened and Myles walked in, his expression tight with worry. Who wouldn't be concerned? The mother of his child was dead. Geneva didn't know what their relationship was, but still, now he was a single parent. The firm set of his jaw and the stiffness in his spine made it seem as if he was carrying the weight of the world on his shoulders.

"Sorry it took me so long. He's asleep?" he asked, setting his keys on the dining table.

"Yeah, he zonked out a couple of minutes ago."

"I'll take him upstairs and lay him down."

"He's okay," she said without releasing Collin.

Myles studied her for a minute before sitting on the sofa next to her.

"Why didn't you tell me you had a son?"

He gave a slight shrug. "It didn't come up. Besides, I'm surprised Journey didn't mention it."

"She never said a word, but that's beside the point, Myles. *You* should've told me. We were dating. Well…kinda, sort-of dating. Anyway, you had more than enough opportunities to say, *hey, by the way, I have a kid*."

"Gen, remember our conversation when we first hooked up? No expectations. No commitment."

She remembered. They were just having a good time. At least until she stupidly fell for his ass. He never wavered on where he stood regarding their relationship. She was the one who had changed the rules, at least initially.

If his actions over the last couple of days were any indication, their feelings were mutual.

"We've been hanging out for what? Six weeks?"

"Technically, a month," she corrected. "The last two weeks don't count since you kicked me to the curb before heading to California."

"I didn't kick you to the curb. I mainly suggested we put some distance between us."

"Myles, that's the same thing."

He leaned forward with his elbows on his thighs. "Maybe it is, but… You were getting too close. *We* were getting too close. I wasn't ready, at least I didn't think I was ready, but while I was in Cali, I couldn't stop thinking about you."

"Yeah, I get it. I'm pretty unforgettable."

He shook his head and chuckled. "And you're a character. What am I going to do with you?"

"I have a few ideas," she cracked and wiggled her brows, hoping to loosen him up a little. She got the response she was looking for when a grin spread across his face. "Now, how about you tell me everything about you, Collin, and Whitney."

"How much time you got?"

"For you? I'll make time. Start talking."

Chapter Eight

"I know we don't know each other well, but you're not in this alone, Myles. Remember that while you're working things out in your head," Geneva said, covering his hand with hers and squeezing.

Myles brought the back of her hand to his lips and placed a lingering kiss near her knuckles. He appreciated her words, but right now, he felt more alone than he ever had in his life. Actually, maybe off-kilter was a better way to describe the unrest flowing through him.

He glanced to his left at his sleeping son. Geneva had laid him on one end of the black sectional sofa, and they sat on the other end. What did he know about raising a child on his own? Sure, he and Whitney had tag-teamed over the last three years, but she'd been an amazing mother. She was the one who was always right there for Collin.

Yes, Myles knew his sister Soul and her husband Micah were only a phone call away. They lived a few miles away with their one-year-old daughter. Myles knew the two of them, as well as his Supreme Security family, would be by his side every step of the way. But ultimately, he was the one responsible for Collin.

And then there was Geneva.

Myles returned his attention to her, admiring her flawless skin and how beautiful she was, even without makeup. He wanted more than anything to get to know her better but had never brought his child around another woman. Neither he nor Whitney had any intentions of getting married, but both agreed to limit introductions to people they were casually involved with. Like him, Myles had never known her to be in a serious relationship. Working for the CIA made it difficult to form strong bonds that could lead to marriage.

Myles shook the last thought free. He was getting way ahead of himself. He was crazy about Geneva, but marriage wasn't on his radar.

"I never planned to have children," he blurted.

Geneva didn't respond immediately. Eventually, she said, "So, Collin was an *oops?*"

"No, he was intentional, but not in the way that you're probably thinking," he hurried to say when she started to speak. Myles stood and extended his hand to her. "I'll tell you anything you want to know, but let's talk over breakfast."

Myles glanced at Coco, who had positioned herself on the floor near Collin. She hadn't left his side since Yvette showed up. It seemed Collin had already made a friend, which was something that pleased Myles. He and Whitney had entertained the thought of getting him a puppy but hadn't decided on when. They had also discussed loosening the reins and allowing him to spend more time with other children his own age. Collin had a few friends at the preschool he attended, but Whitney had never accepted any playdates for him. One of many things Myles needed to reconsider.

With her hand in his, Myles pulled Geneva up and held onto her as they headed to the kitchen. He had never been much of a hand-holder. Yet, it was another thing that was different with her. Not only did he want to keep her near, but he also couldn't help wanting to touch her.

Geneva squeezed his hand. "I'll be right back," she said and went in the direction of the half bath that was near the stairs.

Myles rinsed his hands in the kitchen sink, then proceeded to pull breakfast items out of the refrigerator. This unfamiliar feeling regarding Geneva was mind-boggling. He was a loner by nature, totally comfortable in his own little world. Sure, he spent a lot of time with Whitney, Collin, and some of the guys from Supreme, but mostly, it was just him.

Until now.

Until Geneva fell into his life.

Now he had to figure out how to care for his son while also weaving Geneva seamlessly into their lives. That was assuming she was still interested. Hell, there were moments when he wasn't even sure if that's what he wanted. Then again, after tormenting himself by spending the last two weeks away from her, Myles didn't want to go through that again. He had spent practically every waking hour consumed with thoughts of her.

He sighed in frustration and grabbed one last item, a pack of bacon, before shutting the refrigerator door. Now he knew how his friends, Kenton and Angelo, felt this past year. Considering all the people who were a part of the Atlanta's Finest team, he was the closest to those two. Closer than brothers, he had watched how hard they'd fallen for their women and vowed never to put himself through that.

Now those women were their wives. Kenton and Egypt had gotten married a few months ago at a church wedding. Angelo and his singing sensation wife, Zenobia, had eloped in Hawaii only weeks after that. Both men were more content than Myles had ever seen them, and he was happy for them.

"So, what are we preparing?" Geneva asked, interrupting Myles's thoughts as she strolled into the kitchen.

He glanced down at everything he had pulled out of the refrigerator. "Well, we have a few choices. Eggs, bacon, hash browns, fruit and," he opened the pantry, "and there's pancake mix in here. What do you have a taste for?"

When she didn't respond, Myles glanced over his shoulder. She was leaning against the kitchen counter, staring at him with hunger in her eyes.

He shook his head and chuckle. "You have a one-track mind."

Geneva shrugged. "Yeah, it's probably a gift and a curse."

Myles would be lying if he said he didn't like that about her. Her sexual appetite was in line with his, but they needed to have a talk before moving forward in any type of relationship.

"Tell me about Collin," Geneva said.

As Myles tried to figure out where to start the conversation, he watched as she opened one cabinet door after another. He didn't have much as far as dishes, pots, and pans, but he had the basics. Geneva eventually pulled out a mixing bowl. Then she grabbed the pancake mix.

Myles began cutting the cantaloupe into cubes. "My mother died giving birth to my sister."

Geneva gasped and pancake mix flew from the box, covering part of the granite countertop, as well as the floor. "Oh, my God, Myles. That's awful. I had no idea."

"Yeah, one of many things you don't know about me, but I hope to slowly change that."

Their gazes locked. Her eyes were huge and her mouth hung open, and Myles almost laughed at her comical expression. He wasn't the best at communicating when it came to sharing a bit of himself with anyone. He couldn't blame her for being surprised. Not just about his mother, but also that he intended to share more of himself with Geneva.

He was definitely stepping into new territory. He didn't know what he was doing. Unfortunately, he'd been unintentionally throwing out mixed signals. It was a wonder she hadn't just said the hell with him and moved on. One thing he knew for sure, though, was that he wanted Geneva in his life...in some capacity.

As they cleaned up the pancake mix from the counter and floor, Myles shared a little about his past. Hopefully, it would help her understand why he was so closed off at times.

"That all must've been hard on your father."

"It was. He was crazy in love with my mother. When she died, a part of him died, too. But he was never able to grieve the way he probably needed to because he had a baby girl to raise. Not to mention trying to also take care of my brother and me.

"Seeing him barely keep it together every day was hard to watch. He struggled in every capacity, mentally, emotionally, and physically." Myles shook his head as memories of his father came to the forefront of his mind. His dad was the strongest man he'd ever known. Yet, those first few years had been hard for all of them. "I hated he had to experience that type of loss, and I remembered thinking that I would *never* get married or have kids."

Geneva prepared the pancakes while Myles put several strips of bacon on the griddle. He went back to cutting up the cantaloupe. Usually, he didn't keep much food in his refrigerator, but he had stopped by the store the morning before.

"So, you never want to get married," Geneva said more as a statement than a question.

"Watching my dad after my mother died...I guess I just never wanted to feel that type of loss. I figured if I didn't let people get close, I'd never have to go through the pain of losing them. Of course, there's my family, who I'd kill for. Outside of them, though, I tend to keep my heart closed off and keep people at a distance."

Working for the CIA had only magnified those tendencies. Most spies had trust issues. That went for Myles, too, but he had always been like that. Not trusting easily was just a part of his nature. In some circumstances, he could even be considered paranoid. And just because he wasn't a part of the Agency any longer didn't mean he let his guards down. If anything, he was even more vigilant about his surroundings. He knew better than anyone how one's past could always come back in the form of a threat. That was one of many reasons why he used to live a solitary life while with the Agency.

Until Whitney came along.

A heaviness settled even deeper inside his chest. It still didn't seem real that she was gone. He'd experienced loss before, but this…this was different. This type of internal pain ranked up there with losing his mother when he was a child and his father passing away a few years ago.

Geneva's perfectly arched eyebrows dipped into a frown. "What?" she said. "What's that look for?"

Myles wasn't sure what she saw on his face, but instead of responding right away, he opened the drawer in front of him and pulled out a fork. He stabbed a small chunk of the cantaloupe and offered it to Geneva.

With her gaze steady on him, her frown disappeared, and her pretty brown eyes glimmered with a bit of mischief. A sly smile kicked up the left corner of her tempting mouth before she opened for him. As she slowly chewed the succulent fruit, Myles couldn't take his eyes off of her sweet, kissable lips.

Who would've thought feeding someone could be so sexy?

That heaviness he'd felt in his chest moments ago slowly eased as they shared a quiet moment. *This woman. This beautiful, sexy, exciting woman.* Geneva had the ability to drive him nuts, but she also could evoke a lightness inside him that no one else could.

"I know you tried to distract me by feeding me, but it's not going to work. Well, it might've worked a little, but tell me about you, Whitney and Collin."

Myles turned from the counter and went back to the griddle and turned the bacon. He then started on the eggs.

"It wasn't until I met Whitney that I started to open up some."

Geneva snorted next to him, and he couldn't help but chuckle.

"Okay, I started opening up a little."

"And to think there was a time when you were even more closed off than you are now. Hard to believe."

Myles grinned. "Yeah, you would've hated me back in the day. I didn't give a damn about much of anything, except my father and my siblings. So, I didn't have much to say to anyone."

Geneva added the last golden-brown pancake to the tall stack on the plate. "How did Whitney change you?"

Myles mulled over the question. He wasn't sure if she really did anything. He just noticed himself feeling at ease with her. Like he could let his guard down and know she wouldn't take advantage of him.

"We had a few assignments together over the years and slowly bonded. Whitney's social skills weren't much better than mine, and like me, she had trust issues. She blamed some of her problems on growing up in foster care and being shifted from one house to another until she was twelve."

"That had to be awful," Geneva mumbled.

"Yeah, it was, but she and I clicked. Our bond only got stronger as time went on. Toward the end of our CIA careers, we were partnered up on almost every assignment."

While Myles finished up the eggs, Geneva turned off the stove and leaned her hip against the counter. He didn't have to see her face to know that she was staring at him. He could feel the heat from her gaze.

"Were you two more than coworkers? Were you married?" she asked.

"No," Myles said. He usually didn't mix business with pleasure. *Ever.* "But she was one of my best friends. For two people who typically didn't let others get close, somehow we formed a friendship. But we never slept together."

Geneva's brows dipped, and a crease marred her forehead. "I don't understand. Collin looks just like you. What do you mean you never slept with her?"

No one knew the backstory of how Collin came to be, and Myles had planned to take that information to his grave.

But if he hadn't learned anything from Kenton's and Angelo's relationships with their spouses, he knew that secrets had a way of coming out. Both couples had almost died...because of secrets.

Myles carried the bacon and eggs over to the small round table tucked into the corner of the kitchen and set the items down. Geneva had already set out plates and utensils. Once they grabbed the pancakes, fruit, and coffee, they sat down to eat.

"I left the CIA shortly after Whitney did. Neither of us knew exactly what we wanted to do with the rest of our lives, me especially. I just knew it was time to move on, especially after that last assignment. It was a tough one. Anything that could go wrong did.

"Anyway, a few months after we were out, Whitney showed up in Atlanta wanting to talk. She'd been living on the east coast but never stayed in one spot for long. So, when she arrived in Atlanta, I knew something was up. She was acting a little squirrely, couldn't look me in the eyes, and it took her forever to ask me."

"Ask you what?"

"To be the father of her child."

Silence fell between them, and Myles could almost hear the wheels inside of Geneva's head churning. "I never slept with her, Gen. I was just her donor. Nine months later, Collin was born."

"If you didn't want kids, why'd you agree?"

Myles thought about the question. In his mind, his answer was different each time he recalled that day. "Growing up in foster care, one of the things Whitney wanted but never really had was a family. Sure, she had Yvette in her life since they were twelve, but she wanted a family of her own."

"Why didn't she just find a man and get married? Why have a donor?"

"Trust issues. She never let a man get close enough to establish that type of bond that would lead to marriage.

83

Growing up in foster care, moving from one house to another until she was twelve affects people in different ways. For Whitney, she kept people at a distance."

"Except for you," Geneva said. Myles didn't miss the judgment or something else he couldn't quite put his finger on in her tone.

"She had a couple of friends, but our relationship was special. We clicked. A little different than you and me, but we had a bond. A closeness that neither of us really had with anyone else. So, when she asked me to be the father of her child, I said yes. I knew she'd be a good mother, and I wanted her to have that family that she desired. I wanted to help."

Myles stopped talking when Coco trotted into the kitchen. She stopped in between their chairs and glanced from one to the other before plopping down on her haunches.

"She loves bacon, but I only give her a little bit now and then," Geneva said, breaking off a small piece of the meat and giving it to Coco. "That's it, girl. No more. Go eat your own food."

She pointed to the doggy dish near the door, but Coco remained where she was. When she realized Geneva was serious, she lowered her head and laid on the floor.

"What type of arrangement did you guys have before Whitney..." Her words trailed off, and that ache Myles felt before was back.

He glanced at his watch. Yvette should be in Macon soon. Myles needed answers. Maybe then he could wrap his brain around the idea that Whitney was really gone...that he'd never be able to talk to her again. Right now, though, it just didn't seem real.

Geneva squeezed his thigh. "I'm sorry. I shouldn't have mentioned—"

"No, it's fine. It's still a little weird knowing that she..." He shook his head. "Anyway, I've been one hundred percent active in my son's life. I might not have wanted a child at first, but there was no way I could father a child and not be a

84

part of his life. Collin is an amazing kid. Whip-smart. Funny. He's a ball of energy, and there's never a dull moment with him around. I see him practically every day, if only for a few minutes."

Geneva glanced in the living room. Where they were sitting, they could see part of the sofa where Collin was still sleeping. "You never brought him to any of the gatherings."

"No, but keep in mind, I don't attend a lot of them either. Some of the guys met Collin when I took him to Supreme one day after his doctor's appointment. Otherwise, they probably wouldn't know he existed either."

"Laz would've found out."

Myles laughed. "You're right."

Laz was relentless when digging for information. Actually, a few of the guys, like Angelo and Kenton, would've somehow found out, too. Their undercover and investigative backgrounds meant they dug deep into a person. Myles had never given either of them reasons to snoop into his life, but if they had reason to, they would have.

"I'm the only one who didn't know," she said as if talking to herself.

"I assumed Journey would've mentioned it."

"She never said a word."

Myles wiped his mouth and hands with a napkin, then draped his arm on the back of her chair. "Listen, I wasn't trying to keep him from you, but you and I were...well, we were just hanging out. Remember? No commitment."

Geneva nodded as she picked at the remaining pancake scraps still on her plate. "Right. I know. We were supposed to have a one-and-done type of set up." She turned her head slightly and smiled at him. The mischief he'd seen in her eyes earlier was back. "Well, at least I have an idea of why you pushed me away. At least you tried to."

Myles couldn't hold back the grin that spread across his face. "You're not the easiest person to walk away from."

"So I've been told," she deadpanned, then laughed. "What can I say? To know me is to love me."

She might've been joking, but there was definitely something about Geneva's infectious personality that had snagged his attention. Myles couldn't quite put his finger on it, but he was hooked. She fascinated him like no woman ever had, and that also scared him to death. To make himself vulnerable to another human being wasn't easy. Yet, he had just opened himself up to her, sharing something so personal that some parts of his story only his immediate family knew.

"I hope it goes without saying that this conversation stays between us," he said.

"My lips are sealed."

"Also, I need you to know that I'm treading through new territory here. I've never brought a woman around Collin before. I'm not sure how a relationship between you and me would work now that I have him full-time. But right now, I need to figure out how to tell a three-year-old that his mommy is never coming back."

"Oh, Myles."

Geneva cupped his cheek, her thumb brushing over his stubble. He shamelessly loved when she touched any part of his body. It surprised him that he was hoping his new situation didn't send her running for the hills. But if she wanted to walk away, he'd let her.

At least he would try.

"I can't imagine how you must feel losing not only your friend but the mother of your child. If there's anything I can do to help, just let me know. I'm even a good babysitter now that I have a niece."

"I appreciate that. Right now, I'm not sure what my next steps will be, but I might take you up on the babysitting offer."

He'd seen Geneva with Arielle, as well as Hamilton and Dakota's one-year-old son. She was a natural with kids, and Collin would be lucky to have her in his life. But was that a good idea? His and Geneva's relationship was a bit complicated at best.

"Earlier, when we were in bed, you started to tell me something. Something about what you said a couple of weeks ago. What were you going to say?"

Of course, she would ask now when he didn't know what the day or even the next few weeks would bring. Myles rubbed his forehead, the pressure of what Whitney's death meant weighing heavy on him.

"I was going to tell you that I was wrong about pushing you away. That I want us to keep seeing each other and maybe play this...whatever this is between us...by ear."

"So, what you're saying is that you want to date me."

Myles sputtered a laugh and stood with their plates. *Date* seemed like such an intimidating word, but...

"Yeah, I guess I do."

Chapter Nine

Dating. I'm actually dating someone, Geneva thought as Myles exited I-75 on route to Mason and London's home in Kennesaw. Sure, they'd only been an official couple for a week, but still, it was going to take some getting used to.

She glanced over at his handsome profile. Her mother would be thrilled and probably a little shocked that Geneva was finally in a relationship. She was always telling her she needed to settle down with a nice man.

What would her parents think of Myles?

That thought brought a smile to her face. Her mom would love him, but her dad would probably be suspicious, especially since Myles didn't talk much. As a former cop, though, her father was suspicious of everyone. But if she and Myles got married…

Whoa. Slow your roll, girl, she told herself and shifted in her seat. This was too new for her thoughts to head in that direction. Besides, it was only a matter of time before she screwed it up. That was her M.O., according to Journey. Always finding a reason to move on from a guy.

Geneva pushed all of that from her mind. She had a hot date, and she planned to enjoy every moment with Myles…and Collin. She had to remember—he had Collin now.

She glanced in the back seat at the little guy. He was asleep and had a death grip on his stuffed dinosaur that looked as if it had seen better days. Coco was lying next to him, as close as the booster seat would allow. The two had quickly become best of friends, and it seemed she'd have to start sharing her dog. Considering the little boy had just lost his mother, that was the least Geneva could do.

She returned her attention to Myles. After a few seconds, he glanced at her, and the corners of his lips lifted slightly.

He turned the music down. "What?"

"Nothing. I was just admiring your handsomeness."

"Is that right?" He grinned.

"Yeah." He really was good-looking. She'd always been attracted to dark chocolate brothers, and Myles fit the bill to a tee. "You look a little tired, though," she said.

"I am. It's been...it's been a tough few days. Actually, it's been a tough week."

Myles wasn't a sharer, at least not with his feelings or emotions. For him to say that much let her know that he was probably having a rougher time than he was letting on. He'd been quieter than usual as he drove, and Geneva's heart went out to him. Last week, after he told her about Collin, she made it clear that she would be there for both of them in any way she could. But Geneva wasn't sure how to comfort him.

Whitney's body had arrived in Atlanta days ago, and Myles had gone to view it.

It had to have been hard seeing his friend...his child's mother...dead...in a morgue. Myles's plan had been to view the body, then start making arrangements to have her cremated. That was delayed since the medical examiner was waiting for additional documents from authorities in Macon before she could sign the death certificate. The day before, he'd finally been given the green light.

It was good that Myles and Whitney had created wills before Collin was born, and they were each other's executors. It was interesting that neither of them wanted a funeral when they died.

That surprised Geneva. She had never heard of people not wanting a funeral. According to her sister, though, that wasn't as unusual as Geneva thought. At least Myles and Whitney had made plans, which was more than she could say for herself. She hadn't thought that far ahead. Maybe if she had children, it would be different.

Myles's arm rested on the center console, and she covered his hand with hers. He surprised her when he turned his hand over and intertwined their fingers. It seemed he was full of surprises lately. First, the whole dating thing, now the hand-holding thing. She liked it.

"I know I said it would probably be good for you and Collin to be around friends today, but maybe it's too soon." They were about twenty minutes out, and Geneva was starting to have second thoughts about them attending London's birthday party. "I won't be mad if you want to change your mind."

He didn't speak right away but then said, "I finally told Collin about Whitney."

Geneva's heart broke a little more for him. That had to be an awful conversation for both of them. "How'd it go?"

"About as well as you would expect with a three-year-old. He doesn't understand. He wanted us to go to heaven and get Whitney, then bring her home. It's safe to say I botched the conversation."

"Oh, Myles. I'm so sorry. I'm sure it's going to take time. Maybe later we can do some research and find ideas for the best way to explain death to him."

He nodded. "That sounds like a good idea, and as for the party, I think you were right about us attending. I want Collin to be around kids his own age, and Mason and London have a ton of them."

Geneva laughed. They had five children under the age of seven, with a couple of them being twins. Collin would probably have a ball with them running around that huge house.

"But what about you?" Geneva asked. "You gon' be okay with everyone expressing their condolences?"

Myles sighed. "I'll be fine. It's just...weird."

He was such a private guy. At first, he didn't want to tell any of their friends about what happened to Whitney. Geneva had offered to do it, and surprisingly, he'd been okay with that. She only called those he was closest to and knew they'd get the word out to the others.

"How about tonight you come over and I'll..." Geneva's words trailed off when she realized what she was about to say.

What was she thinking? Gone were the days of Myles spending the night on a whim. He had a child to consider in *every* decision he made going forward. That probably had always been the case, but even more so now that Whitney was gone.

"Never mind," Geneva mumbled.

Myles squeezed her hand. "I would love to come over, but I'm not sure if...or how... Heck, I'm not sure about much of anything right now; you and I will figure *us* out, all right?"

Geneva nodded and smile. "This is new territory for both of us, but I'm glad we're giving it a shot."

"Yeah, me too."

A few minutes later, driving through Mason and London's quiet neighborhood, Geneva admired the large homes. The couple had purchased land a few years ago and built what could best be described as a mansion. They had spared no expense and had recently added a guest house on the land.

Myles turned onto the property and stopped at the guardhouse. The first time Geneva visited, she'd thought it a little much to have security at the entrance. But then her sister had mentioned that it was the only way that London would agree to move out of the city. Growing up, her parents had been killed during a home invasion, and she refused to live in a stand-alone house, only preferring secure apartments and condos.

"What's up, Micah?" Myles greeted his brother-in-law, the buffed man stationed at the front gate.

Micah, a former police officer, joined Supreme Security shortly after marrying Myles's sister Soul, a world-renowned ballet dancer. She and Micah had been college sweethearts before their individual dreams sent them in different directions. Years later, they found their way back to each other and were proof that some did get second chances at love.

"What's up, bruh? I was wondering if I was going to see you today. Soul told me what happened. I'm sorry, man," he said, stepping out of the guardhouse and shaking Myles's hand. "If you need anything…"

"Yeah, I know. Thanks. So, you drew the short straw and ended up on guard duty, huh?" Myles joked.

Micah released a loud, hearty laugh that made his entire body shake. "Man, you already know the perks I get for being out here. I'd take this assignment any day, and it makes your sister happy."

As a personal security specialist, Myles and the others who worked for Supreme put their lives on the line every day. Geneva wasn't much of a worrier, but she wondered if that would change now that she and Myles were seeing each other.

"Yeah, I guess you gotta keep my sister happy," Myles said. "Is she here?"

"Nah, she and my mother took Mikera to visit my aunt in Savannah," he said of Myles's little niece. "Hey, Geneva."

She smiled and waved.

"Hi, Uncle Micah," Collin called out from the back seat, and Myles let the rear window down. Geneva hadn't realized that he woke up.

"Hey, little man." He gave his nephew a fist bump, which made Collin giggle. "How you doin'?"

Geneva smiled at how animated Collin suddenly became while introducing his uncle to Coco as if the dog were his. She was going to do whatever she could to keep that smile on his face.

It worked out tonight that London had asked her to bring Coco to the party. The kids were crazy about the dog, and Coco ate up the attention.

"All right, I'll let you guys get going. Have a good time." The barrier arm of the security gate went up before the eight-foot rod iron gate swung open. "Oh, and tell Aunt Carolyn to save me some food," he said, referring to Mason's live-in aunt. Aunt Carolyn might've been blood-related to Mason, but the rest of them had claimed her as their aunt, too.

"Will do."

Myles pulled onto the property and started the long drive up the winding tree-lined driveway. The picturesque landscaping with a manicured lawn, colorful flower beds, and a large, two-tiered water fountain had a park-like vibe and looked like something right out of a *Home and Garden* magazine.

The stunning French country-style home finally came into view, and the outside was just as breathtaking as the inside. The exterior, made up of brick and stone, had a rustic elegance with tall sloping roofs, huge windows, and double front doors.

Geneva couldn't see herself living in something so big. Then again, if she had five kids running around, she'd want plenty of space, too.

"Daddy, where we going?" Collin asked.

"This is my friend's house," Myles said, pulling in behind Kenton and Egypt's black SUV.

"Looks like most of the gang is already here," Geneva said, wondering what their friends would think seeing her with Myles. This would be the first time that they showed up together for one of the gatherings.

Geneva reached down and grabbed the gift bag that held London's present and started to open the car door.

"Sit tight. I'll come around and get the door for you." Myles was out of the car before she could respond.

Geneva's heart fluttered as she watched him help Collin and Coco out of the back seat. When he moved around the front of the vehicle, she took in his appearance. He was tall, dark, and powerfully built in a brown turtleneck beneath a camel-colored jacket with brown pants. It was as if they had intentionally coordinated their outfits.

The man was downright fine and really should've considered a career in modeling. The camera would love his deep espresso eyes, chiseled jaw, and juicy lips that were made for kissing.

He opened her door and extended his hand to help her out. As usual, the air crackled between them. This evening, everything about him seemed to be more potent, and Geneva's body tingled with awareness as their gazes clashed.

Myles slid his arm around her waist and pulled her to his side. "In case I didn't mention it, you look amazing."

Instead of the black leather pants and crop top she had initially considered wearing, Geneva settled on a dress. The short tan sweaterdress was one of her favorites, and she loved the way it hugged her curves and showed off her assets. She'd paired it with a pair of tall brown thigh-high boots.

"Thank you."

He placed a sensual kiss on that spot just below her ear, sending desire pulsing through her body. This was definitely not the time to get her all hot and bothered, especially when they couldn't do anything to cool her off.

As if he could read her thoughts, Myles flashed her a wicked grin. "I love it when you blush."

Geneva laughed. "I do not blush. Besides, my skin is too dark for you to even see me blush."

He smiled, and it was as if birds took flight inside of her, making her feel even giddier than she felt moments ago.

"I can tell," he said.

"Daddy, pick me up."

They both gazed down at Collin, who was holding Coco by her leash.

"You're a big boy. Why can't you walk?" Myles asked.

"I'm...I'm scared," Collin said in a tiny voice, his long lashes fanning his cheeks as he stared down at the white Converse Chucks on his feet. He looked so cute in the denim jacket, white turtleneck, and blue jeans. The baseball cap that he'd been wearing was now in his hands instead of on his head.

"There's nothing to be afraid of," Myles said.

Collin batted those sad eyes at his father, and Geneva almost laughed. The kid was too adorable to say no to.

She grabbed Coco's leash, and Myles lifted Collin up into his arms. With his other hand at the small of Geneva's back, he guided them to the front door.

The whole scene was odd on so many levels. As a serial dater, Geneva could count on one hand her relationships that had lasted longer than a month. And she never dated men with children. Myles having a kid should be a deal-breaker. Even so, the urge to bolt hadn't hit her yet.

If anything, watching Myles with Collin had Geneva thinking about things she shouldn't be thinking. Such as...what it would be like to spend every day with them? What would it be like if she and Myles had a child together?

Thankfully, moments after Myles rang the doorbell, the front door swung open. That halted those thoughts before they could get too far out of control.

Chapter Ten

"Hey, you guys. Come on in," Mason Bennett said.

Well over six feet tall with intense eyes, a bald head, and skin the color of mocha, he was a big man with broad shoulders usually found on a linebacker. His size might've been intimidating, but Mason was one of the kindest men Geneva had ever met.

With a glass of amber liquor in one hand, he pulled her close and placed a kiss on her cheek as she entered the house. He then greeted Myles with a one-armed hug, which was awkward, seeing that he was still carrying Collin.

Geneva stepped to the side while Mason offered his condolences to Myles, and conversation ensued. She inhaled deeply; the savory aroma wafting through the house tickled her nose and had her stomach growling. Knowing Aunt Carolyn was hard at work in the kitchen, Geneva couldn't wait to eat.

She stood in the open foyer under a magnificent Swarovski crystal chandelier and glanced around. The house might've been grand with crazy-tall ceilings, marbled floors, and elegant double-curved staircases, but it always felt warm and inviting. Probably because of the pops of bold turquoise on a couple of the walls and unique pieces of furniture everywhere you looked. There was a coziness about the home that made her feel welcomed the moment she walked in.

"Honey, who's at the door?" London called from the top of the stairs. Seconds later, she was on her way down.

Geneva smiled as her friend practically glided down the stairs, looking like royalty in a white pantsuit with silver accents. She definitely didn't look like a woman who had pushed out five babies over the last few years. London was petite, and it seemed her body bounced back into shape after each child.

"Oh, my goodness, I'm so glad you guys were able to make it," she said when she reached them.

"Check out the birthday girl lookin' all cute," Geneva said and set down the gift bag in order to embrace her friend. "Your hair still looks good, girl."

Geneva had done London's hair days before her shop had been destroyed. The short pixie cut was perfect for her face shape.

London patted the sides of her head as she grinned. "Girl, I love this cut. I've been able to just get up and go without much fuss."

Being reassured with another satisfied client immediately made Geneva think about her salon. She lived to help women look their best, and she couldn't do that with her beauty shop coated in soot. It would be a minimum of six weeks before she could get back up and running again. In the meantime, Myles suggested she start looking for a different place in a better neighborhood. If only it were that easy. She was already established where she was. Would her clients follow her to a new location?

There was so much to consider, but she didn't shoot down his idea—especially when he promised to help in any way he could.

Myles hugged London, wishing her a happy birthday while she offered her condolences. Hopefully, all of the attention wouldn't send him running for the hills. Like Geneva didn't want to be constantly reminded of her salon, at least for the evening, Myles didn't want to discuss his personal life.

Coco barked and moved around in front of London with her tail wagging, trying to get her attention.

"Coco, calm down," Geneva said, tightening her hold on the dog's leash.

"You might as well let her roam around," Mason said, "Because once the kids know she's here, they'll be all over her."

As soon as the words were out of his mouth, there was a loud thump above their head and what sounded like a herd of elephants running toward the stairs.

"Here they come," London said, rolling her eyes. "So, Collin, I'm glad you came to visit us. How old are you?"

Collin glanced at Myles.

"You're not shy. Tell her."

"Three," he eventually said, then hid his face in the crook of Myles's neck.

London laughed. "Well, he'll warm up soon enough when our crew finds out he and Coco are here."

Myles set Collin down just as some of the kids bolted down the stairs. The twins, who were identical boys, were the spitting image of their father, except they had full heads of hair.

"Coco!" They said in unison before sliding to the floor to roughhouse with her dog.

The last child pulling up the rear was Miracle, the second to youngest. She was closest to Collin's age, and Geneva's heart melted at the sight of her. She was petite like her mother and had two long ponytails hanging past her shoulders. Also, like London, she was dressed in all white with silver ballet slippers.

Except her white top had a red stain in the center of it.

She was too adorable, and Geneva couldn't help the smile spreading across her face when Miracle walked up to Collin.

"Hi," she said and reached for his hand. "Do you want to play?"

"She's our social butterfly," London whispered as Miracle held Collin's hand while they walked up the stairs. Coco and the twins were right behind them.

Mason squeezed Myles's shoulder. "Don't look so worried. He'll be fine. They're upstairs with the nanny, and I'll check on them throughout the evening."

Aunt Carolyn appeared in the hallway that led to the kitchen and walked toward them wearing one of her cute cardigan twinsets. She loved her bright colors. This set was hot pink, paired with black pants. It didn't matter when Geneva saw her, or whether the woman was cooking or baking something, she was always perfectly coordinated. Like this evening, with matching jewelry and hot pink flats.

"Welcome! Welcome," she said and made a beeline to Myles. "I have sweetness to share. Come get a dose."

They all laughed as she wrapped her arms around him and held on. Mason was her favorite nephew, but she was crazy about Atlanta's Finest, especially Laz. But it was evident every time Myles came around that Aunt Carolyn had a soft spot for him. She held onto him for a minute, then turned to Geneva and winked.

"My girl. Give me some love."

Geneva giggled and accepted the warm hug. She laughed even harder when Aunt Carolyn whispered in her ear, *"You did good. That dark chocolate goodness is a keeper."*

"Okay, it's good seeing you two," Aunt Carolyn said, releasing Geneva, "but I need to get back in the kitchen and check on my peach cobbler." She disappeared back down the hall just as fast as she had appeared.

"Y'all come on in and make yourself at home," Mason said, leading Myles toward the back of the house and probably to the walkout basement where the guys usually hung out.

"And *you*," London said, looping her arm through Geneva's and giving her a wicked grin, "got some explaining to do. The ladies are in the family room. Before we go in there, I want all the details about you and Myles, even the nasty stuff."

Geneva burst out laughing. "I *knew* you were a closet freak." She jabbed her finger at her friend. "That's why you got all those doggone kids. Always trying to blame it on Mase. Now the truth comes out."

"*Shhh.*" London waved to quiet her and glanced around conspiratorially. "Don't tell nobody."

Geneva laughed even harder. After the last few days she'd had, this was what she needed—girl-time with the women in her life.

Who knows, maybe they can give me some pointers on how to handle Myles.

*

An hour into the party, Myles was ready to call it a night. If it weren't for Geneva and Collin, he would've left fifty-five minutes ago. Actually, if it weren't for them, he probably wouldn't have attended in the first place. Not because he didn't enjoy being around his friends. No, it had everything to do with his brain working overtime.

Seeing Whitney lying in the morgue the other day had shaken him more than he thought possible. He still hadn't wrapped his mind around the fact that he'd never be able to talk to her again. But it was seeing her lifeless body that brought it all home.

She was gone.

He couldn't remember the last time he'd gotten choked up. Yet, seeing her like that had roused emotions he hadn't experienced in a long time. Even now, the tightness in his chest brought on by memories they'd shared was almost suffocating.

How was he going to make it without her? How was he going to raise a well-rounded child without her input? They were a team. They might not have ever been in a romantic relationship, but he loved her more than he could've ever expressed. He needed her as much as Collin did.

Standing at the entrance to the kid's playroom, Myles watched his son sitting at a small table across from Miracle, coloring. Since meeting downstairs, the two kids had been inseparable, and Coco was always close. Even when Mason's oldest son had taken her outside for a few minutes, the moment the dog entered the house, she was back at Collin's side.

Myles felt awful about Whitney, but he was glad Geneva and Coco were filling a void.

Thinking of Geneva, he turned from the door and headed back to the first floor. The women were laughing and talking in the family room, while the men occupied the basement, watching an NBA game and talking trash.

When Myles reached the bottom step, Geneva was exiting the kitchen with a small plate of food.

"Hey you," she said and walked up to him, kissing him on the lips as if it were the most natural thing to do.

When she started to pull back, he caught her around the waist and held her close. "I've missed you," he said, unable to stop the words before they flew from his mouth. He couldn't ever remember saying that to a woman. *Ever.*

A slow, sensual smile spread across her tempting mouth and had him wanting to carry her out of there. He'd give all the money in his wallet for some quality time with her.

If only they weren't in a house full of people...

Myles couldn't wait to get her alone, though he didn't know when that would be. How they were going to make a relationship work was a mystery to him. It was also wild that he wanted it to work. As a matter of fact, he couldn't think of anything he wanted more than he wanted her, and it was a good feeling.

"I missed you, too. I started to come downstairs a couple of times, but I stopped myself. I didn't want to come across as clingy," she whispered close to his ear, and her sweet-smelling perfume was doing wicked things to his body.

He placed a lingering kiss on the spot just below her ear that always got her revved up. "Feel free to be clingy anytime."

Geneva moaned and slipped her free arm around his waist, making the front of their bodies flush.

"If you keep kissing me like that, you're going to get something started," she crooned.

Myles released a long sigh. That's exactly what he wanted to do, but it wasn't the right time or place. He was still kicking himself for the other morning when they were in bed, and he stopped what was about to be some wild sex.

Never again. The next time either one of them got something started in the bedroom, they were going to finish it.

Geneva eased out of his hold and held up a small pastry. "Taste this. It literally melts in your mouth."

Myles wasn't much of a sweet-eater, but having her feed him was too tempting to pass up. He opened for her, their eyes not breaking contact as he savored the sweet treat. Chocolate and marshmallow burst onto his tongue. She was right. It practically melted in his mouth.

"That's amazing," he said just before she fed him the rest of it. He locked his mouth around her finger, causing her to gasp before she started laughing.

Slowly easing her index finger from his mouth, she said, "Oh, you're really playing with fire." She leaned in and kissed him, her lips as sweet as the treat he'd just eaten.

Yeah, he wanted her.

Someone cleared their throat, and they both looked over to find Laz shaking his head with a smirk on his face. How had he walked into the house without either of them noticing?

"Knock that shit off. *Or* better yet, take it somewhere else," Laz said and kept walking. No doubt he was going in search of Journey and their daughter.

"I love the way you think, brother-in-law," Geneva called after him, then returned her attention to Myles. "I need to get back in there and finish watching a chick-flick. But the moment it's done, I'm coming to find you, and we're going to pick up where we left off. Deal?"

"Deal."

Myles watched her walk away, not missing the extra swing action of her hips.

Oh, yeah, they were definitely going to pick up where they left off.

Chapter Eleven

Myles was heading back down the stairs when Laz caught up to him.

"You and Gen looked pretty cozy up there."

"Yeah, you all right with that?" Myles asked, even though it didn't matter what anyone thought. He did whatever the hell he wanted to, and Geneva was no different.

"Cool by me. She needs someone solid like you who ain't gon' take crap. Though I have to admit, I'm shocked that you kept her attention. You know I usually refer to her as the man-eater. Chews them up, then spits them out. Yet, you've lasted longer than most. That's impressive. I just hope you both know what you're doing, especially with your current situation."

Myles nodded in agreement. He had talked to Laz late last night and filled him in on what little he knew about Whitney's accident.

Myles knew he had no business starting a relationship with Geneva, especially now. All his focus should be on raising Collin. Problem was, Geneva was in his system, and he couldn't shake her. Not that he wanted to. If anything, he wanted to be with her morning, noon, and night. A first for him. He was crazy about the woman and was actually looking forward to seeing how things played out between them.

Myles followed Laz to the buffet table that was set up near the patio door. Aunt Carolyn had prepared enough food to feed an army. She had a nice spread on every floor of the house.

"I need to holler at you about something," Myles said.

Laz grabbed a paper plate. "All right, you can talk while I get something to eat. I've been waiting all day for this."

Myles looked around the basement, trying to figure out where they could talk in private. Like the rest of the house, the space was huge. There was a game room where a poker table and pool table took up much of the area. A theater room was tucked away at the far end of the basement and was large enough to seat twenty people. Some of the guys were in there, still watching the NBA game.

A few feet away from where he and Laz were standing, a seventy-two-inch flat-screen television hung on the wall, and some of the younger security specialists were playing the latest Madden. To say they were loud was an understatement.

"How about we talk outside on the patio?"

"Works for me. Grab me a beer, would you?" Laz said around a mouthful of food and headed to the door that led to the covered patio.

Once they were outside, Myles turned on one of the heaters, and they sat at one of the patio tables. It was colder than usual for an October evening, but the quiet atmosphere was enjoyable. The patio overlooked a fenced-in Olympic-sized swimming pool and beyond that was the guest house. The property sat on two acres, and Myles was curious to see what else Mason and London had planned for the land.

"So, what's on your mind?" Laz asked between bites.

Myles took a long drag from his beer before speaking. "Why'd you get Geneva a gun?"

Laz huffed out a breath but didn't seem surprised by the question. "What was I supposed to do? She came to me and told me she was having trouble with some punk kids and wanted a gun."

"And you didn't think to talk her out of it?" Myles snapped and glared at his hazel-green-eyed friend, who resembled the actor Theo Theodoridis. Sometimes he just couldn't figure the guy out. "A convicted felon comes to you because she's having trouble with some thugs, and you give her a gun? What type of sense does that make? Heck, you could've even gotten Ham to put someone on her," he said of their boss, Hamilton Crosby. Geneva was part of the Supreme Security family, and they always took care of family.

"I suggested that, but Geneva said it wasn't serious enough to have a security detail."

"Not that serious? Yet, she needed a gun." Myles gritted his teeth to keep from saying something he might later regret as anger boiled inside of him.

Laz and Geneva were two of a kind—hotheads that didn't always think before doing something stupid.

"Does Journey know?"

"Of course not. She would've killed me. You know Gen is like a little sister to me." He shrugged. "I wanted to help her out. She asked for a gun. I gave her one."

"Even though it could land her in jail," Myles said as a statement more than a question as he tried to hold onto his temper that was slipping.

"That wouldn't have happened."

"You don't know that."

"I know people, and I would've gotten—"

"Dammit, man!" Myles pounded his fist on the table, making their beer bottles rattle. "You might know people, but you can't control everything, especially the justice system."

Myles could admit that Laz was well connected. As a former police detective, he knew people on both sides of the law. And when he put his mind to anything, legal or not, things happened. Laz was a force to be reckoned with, and Myles was glad they were on the same team. His friend wasn't a man he'd want as an enemy.

"Why didn't you tell me Geneva was having trouble?" Myles asked.

"Dude, why would I?" Now Laz was the one glaring. "Your ass said that there was nothing going on between you two. Y'all was just kicking it. I think those were your exact words. But then Journey said that she had a feeling something more was developing between you two. I figured I'd test her theory."

"And you set me up," Myles finished, thinking about how Laz had asked him to stop by Geneva's shop and help her lock up. He was glad he had because there was no telling what those thugs would've done to her.

Laz shrugged again and finished off the chicken wing he'd been chomping on. "What can I say? I'm married to a brilliant woman. I would've bet money that you and Gen were just hanging out. *Clearly*, I would've lost that bet."

Myles didn't say anything as he stared out into the night. What could he say? He and Geneva hooking up had caught him off guard months ago during Kenton and Egypt's wedding reception and even more so now that they were dating exclusively.

"Any news on the investigation?" Laz asked, changing the subject and referring to Whitney's accident.

"Not much. I called Ashton earlier to see if he could dig around for me. The police department handling the investigation is not very big. I don't know how long it's going to take to get more details.

"What I know so far is that they found an envelope on her containing five hundred dollars in cash. Though they probably think she was into something shady, I'm assuming that was payment for an assignment. She didn't carry cash like that around, and she was meeting with a client that morning."

When Whitney first mentioned doing P.I. work, Myles didn't like the idea and told her so. She insisted that she was very careful in choosing assignments, and so far, she hadn't had any problems. He hoped the accident was just that—an accident—but his twisted mind always took thoughts farther.

What if the car crash had something to do with the case she was working on? Or a past case?

Myles shook the thought free. They weren't with the Agency anymore. He didn't have to view every situation as a possible threat the way he had while with the CIA. He needed to wait until the cops knew more instead of jumping to conclusions.

"She looked bad," Myles said, more to himself than to Laz. "Her face was bruised. The medical examiner said the bruises were from the airbag and shattered glass from the windshield. I've seen my share of dead bodies, but this…"

"Damn. I can't imagine. I'm sure it had to be rough." Laz was about to shove a forkful of beans and rice into his mouth but stopped. "Since you have Ashton digging for information for you, do you think the crash was more than just an accident?"

"You know how we are. Of course, the thought crossed my mind. So far, no one seems to think foul play was involved. Or they're just not saying."

Laz went back to eating. "It's an active investigation. They can't share much yet. Do you know if the detectives talked to the client she met with?" he asked between bites.

Myles shook his head. "That police department is small and moving at a snail's pace. I'm not sure if they even have detectives on the case or just police officers."

"You don't have to worry about that. Either way, they'll still operate like a larger department. Their officers should be capable of doing a proper investigation."

"I hope so. Anyway, last I heard, they hadn't spoken with the client, and they're not sure where Whitney was coming from."

Laz nodded. "Ashton will get answers. If not, I'll make some phone calls."

"I appreciate that."

The patio door swung open, and Kenton Bailey stepped out, carrying Hamilton's one-year-old son as well as Arielle. The kids looked even tinier than they were in the big guy's arms. Well over six feet tall and as wide as a door frame, Kenton was one of the biggest guys on their team.

"Laz, I think one of these belongs to you," Kenton said as he crossed the patio. The moment the little girl saw her father, she started fussing and wiggling to get out of Kenton's hold.

"Hey, baby girl," Laz cooed, scooping her into his arms and immediately going into baby talk.

Myles chuckled. As big and bad as his friend was, he was like mush when it came to Journey and Arielle. Some days it was amazing to watch how gentle and low-key he was with his girls. Any other time, he was like a fearless warrior daring anyone to step to him the wrong way.

But maybe that's how they all appeared to each other because, like Laz, there was nothing Myles wouldn't do for those he loved.

"It still blows my mind that he has a kid," Kenton said of Laz, who was pretty much ignoring them now that his baby had his full attention.

Myles stood with his half-full bottle of beer and grabbed Laz's empty plate. "Scary, isn't it?"

"Yeah, it is, and she's so darn cute."

Arielle had Journey's darker skin tone, but everything else, including the hazel-greenish eyes, stubbornness, and head full of hair with streaks of blonde, were all Laz.

"I feel for any little boy who tries to step to her." Kenton laughed and repositioned Hamilton's son in his arms when he started fussing.

"That's not going to be a problem because I'm planning to teach her how to chase little knuckleheaded boys away," Laz piped in. "Ain't that right, angel face?" Arielle shrieked as if understanding what he was saying. "She also won't be allowed to date until she's thirty," Laz said with a straight face, ignoring the way Myles and Kenton were laughing.

"Well, I figured if Laz can take care of a kid, then I'll have nothing to worry about when Egypt and I start a family."

Myles had a feeling that was going to be sooner than later. Egypt loved kids. She'd had a rough childhood after witnessing a murder, and her turbulent adult life wasn't much better. With no family, Egypt had commented often about her and Kenton having at least three kids, and the big guy was all for keeping his wife happy.

Myles headed to the door of the house. "Pretty soon, these parties are going to turn into events where the kids outnumber the adults."

"Heck, at the rate Mason and London are pumping out kids, we're almost at that point," Laz cracked, and they all re-entered the house laughing.

Despite the events of the last couple of days, Myles was beginning to feel better about his situation. Geneva had been right. It was good to be around friends.

After tossing Laz's paper plate in a nearby trash can, Myles lifted his beer bottle but stopped inches from his lips. His heart kicked inside his chest, and heat soared through his body.

It never failed. The sight of Geneva always got his motor running, even now. At first, all he saw were her long legs encased in thigh-high boots, but then the rest of her luscious body came into view.

Damn, the woman was fine.

She reached the bottom step, and their gazes connected. Geneva had the power to make him forget that they were surrounded by people. Everything about her made her stand out from any other woman, but it was her self-confidence that really made her shine.

She headed his way. Her long strides ate up the space between them, and it was like everything and everybody disappeared. Lust radiated in her gorgeous eyes, and something so sensually intense passed between them.

Myles slammed back the rest of his beer and set the bottle on the bar before meeting her halfway. He gently grabbed hold of her hand and guided her away from the main area and prying eyes. Geneva didn't speak, nor did she protest as they headed to the back of the basement where no one was hanging out.

Oh yeah. They were definitely picking up where they left off because right now, Myles needed her like an addict needed his next hit.

And there was no better time than the present to check out the closest bathroom.

Chapter Twelve

When Geneva decided to go in search of Myles, she didn't really have a plan. But the moment she made it to the middle of the staircase and laid eyes on him, she knew she had to have him.

Once inside the brightly lit bathroom, Myles backed her to the locked door and covered her mouth with his. Their sweet kiss quickly spiraled out of control, and each lap of his tongue had Geneva craving for more. In no time, their heavy breathing filled the bathroom, and her desire for him multiplied.

God, she wanted him. All night she had wanted them to have some alone time. It wasn't even just about getting intimate with Myles. Geneva also wanted to make sure he was doing all right.

But now that he was kissing her senseless, thoughts of offering him comfort flew from her mind. In its place were naughty thoughts of how good it was going to feel when he was buried deep inside of her.

From day one, they'd had an intense sexual connection that could only be described as unbelievable. The more time they spent together, learning each other's body, the harder it was to control her need to be near him.

Tonight was no different. It was mind-blowing how the intensity of their kisses could go from zero to sixty in a heartbeat. Their hands were pawing at each other as moans of pleasure ricocheted through the room. Myles ground his hard body against hers, and the heady scent of his cologne turned her on even more, sending her senses reeling.

Geneva tore her mouth from his. "Myles. I want you," she panted. "*Now.*"

He chuckled and eased her away from the door to a nearby wall. "You're so impatient."

His lips grazed her cheek and worked their way down, kissing, sucking, and nipping at her neck. He was bound to leave a mark, but Geneva didn't care. He was right. She was impatient compared to his ability to take his time in whatever he was doing. Sometimes slow and thorough was a good thing, but right now, her body was on fire for him. She wanted this quickie to be hard and fast.

While he peppered her skin with kisses, his hands traveled along her body, skimming down her sides until they glided over her hips. He didn't stop there, and Geneva's pulse amped up when he reached under the hem of her dress.

"Damn, you're so wet," Myles said gruffly against her lips before lifting his head. "I can't wait to be inside of you."

"Yeah, me too. So hurry up."

Geneva unfastened his belt. Next was his zipper. When he kept torturing her with feathery kisses along her neck while he palmed her ass, she had to take matters into her own hands. Literally.

She slid her hand down his pants and gently cupped his package. Caressing, squeezing, she loved the way she could make him moan. Gliding her hand up and down his length, she increased the pressure, eliciting a curse from him.

"Okay. Okay. Gen, you're going to make me come," he gritted between clenched teeth and stilled her hand. Once he caught his breath, he guided her hand out of his pants. "Take your panties off," he choked out and fumbled for his wallet to grab a condom.

Geneva shimmied out of her panties and kicked them to the side. Their gazes bore into each other as he ripped open the foil packet with his teeth and quickly sheathed himself. Within seconds, Myles's mouth was covering hers again, and he kissed her with an eagerness that rivaled hers.

Geneva was suddenly glad she had her tall boots on. Their bodies were lined up, and she was at the perfect height for him to enter her in one smooth move.

Which he did.

"Oh, yes," she breathed against his mouth, her arms tightened around his neck as he drove in and out of her like a man possessed.

He was giving her exactly what she wanted, what she needed. Her heart pounded harder and faster with each thrust as he pushed her closer to her release. She pulled her mouth from his as their passionate moans mingled.

"Myles," she whimpered, her breaths coming in short spurts.

When the pressure inside of her started growing to explosive proportions, Geneva dug her nails into his shoulders. She was barely hanging on. She was so close. So...

"Myles!"

He quickly covered her mouth with his, drowning out her scream of passion. Heat rippled beneath her skin, and an orgasm spiraled through her body, sending her tumbling over the edge.

Myles gripped her butt tighter as he pumped his hips faster, going deeper with each thrust. Geneva held on for the ride until he lost it and groaned his release. Collapsing against her, he pressed her against the wall. Aftershocks shook his body, which ultimately shook her since her head was on his shoulder. She was bone-weary, struggling to breathe but basking in the intensity of what they'd just experienced.

She loved quickies.

Still panting, Myles brushed a kiss against her cheek and rested his forehead against the wall over her shoulder. They stood like that for the longest time, neither saying a word as their heart rates slowly went back to normal.

"I will never get enough of you," he said quietly against her ear and gathered her into an embrace.

"Me either," Geneva agreed and placed a kiss against his skin that was damp with perspiration.

"But next time I have you, it will be in a bed. I'm getting too old for quickies in the bathroom."

Geneva laughed, then sighed with contentment. She didn't care where they made love as long as they were together.

*

A short while later, after they were cleaned up and had pulled themselves together, Myles kissed Geneva long and hard. They were still in the bathroom, and he could honestly say that he had never met a woman like her.

Yes, the sex was off the charts, but it was more than that. It had everything to do with the way she made him feel—and not just physically. Geneva reached something deep inside of him. Something that had never been touched by another, and it made him want her in every way a man could want a woman.

"How about we grab Collin and then head out?" he said with his hand on one of her hips and the other braced against the wall behind her. He wasn't ready to call it a night with her, but he wanted to get Collin into bed before it got too late.

Thinking about his son, Myles didn't know how he would juggle being a single dad and dating. He wasn't sure he could pull it off. Who would've thought he'd ever be in this predicament?

Dating. Such a foreign concept, but if Myles was honest with himself, he was looking forward to spending more time with Geneva. He just had to figure out how to do that without sacrificing his time with Collin. He'd always had a keen respect for single parents, especially after being raised by one. He just never thought he'd be one.

"That sounds good, but I'm not ready to go home yet," Geneva said.

Myles nodded. "Yeah, and I'm not ready to take you home, but—"

"But we need to think of Collin. I get it," she said, offering a small smile that didn't reach her eyes. "I've never been with a man who had a child, Myles. I don't know how this works, and before you say anything, I know this is new for you, too."

Myles cupped her face between his hands and stared into her eyes. He brushed the pads of his thumbs over her soft cheeks. "I'm sorry. I know you didn't ask for any of this. If you want to take a step back, I'll understand. It'll be hard to let you walk away, but—"

"That's not what I want. We said we'd give dating a try, and that's what we're going to do." She covered his hands with hers. "But first, how about we figure out how to get out of this bathroom without drawing too much attention to ourselves."

Myles chuckled. "Good point."

He eased the door open, glad to see there was no one hanging out in the short hallway. They left the bathroom hand in hand and strolled into the central area of the basement. The first person they saw was Ashton.

The detective glanced up from piling food onto a plate. His gaze met Myles's, then bounced to Geneva before returning to him. His left eyebrow inched up. "I was wondering where you were since I saw your car outside," he said, humor in his voice.

Ashton didn't miss much. By the amusement in his eyes, it was safe to say he knew exactly what they'd been up to. Then his expression turned serious.

"You got a minute for us to talk?" he asked Myles and set his plate on the table.

Myles immediately went on alert. He didn't know what his friend found out about the car crash, but his taut expression said it wasn't good.

Geneva squeezed Myles's hand. "I'll go and check on Collin. Come find us when you're ready to leave."

He nodded and watched her head up the stairs. "What's up?" he asked Ashton.

"I heard back from my contact at the police station in Macon."

Myles shoved his hands into the front pocket of his pants and braced himself. "And?"

"And it was more than a car crash. Whitney's brake line was tampered with. The *accident* is being ruled a homicide."

Chapter Thirteen

Myles stood frozen. Even if he thought about the possibility of her car crash being something more, he wasn't prepared for this news. Whitney was dead, and someone killed her.

How? Why? Questions rattled around in his head as he tried to wrap his mind around it all.

"*Homicide,*" he said quietly and ran a shaky hand over his mouth and down his chin.

Her brake line was tampered with.

This couldn't be. Whitney was the sweetest person he knew. Who would want to kill her?

"Are they sure?" he asked Ashton, already knowing the answer but still trying to come to terms with the information.

"Positive. The line wasn't cut all the way through, but enough to lose most of the brake fluid."

"*Damn.*"

Murdered.

Someone killed her. No matter how he said the words in his mind, they meant the same thing. She was dead and had died at the hands of someone. Someone he planned to hunt down and make suffer.

"The detectives on the case are gonna want to talk to you."

Myles reared back. "*Me?* Why?"

"Standard procedure. Now that the accident is being ruled a homicide, they're going to question everyone who was close to her. As well as those she's been recently in contact with, including the client she met with that morning. They talked to her about an hour ago."

"What did she say?"

Ashton glanced around, then nodded for Myles to follow him to the back of the basement. It was an area near the hallway that led to the bathroom that he and Geneva had just vacated. Considering how much fun Myles had with Geneva, it was being overshadowed by this revelation.

"I know it goes without saying, but this conversation stays between us," Ashton said. He held up his hand when Myles started to speak. "This is an active investigation. It's okay to share some of the details with Atlanta's Finest if needed, but that's it. No one else."

Myles nodded. He trusted his team more than anyone and knew they'd use discretion once he asked for their help, which he definitely planned to do. They were all well connected, each with specific skills needed to find Whitney's killer. Assuming the cops didn't find the person first.

As he studied Ashton's solemn expression, a sense of foreboding stirred inside of Myles's gut. He couldn't remember the last time he'd felt so on edge.

"The client's name is Margaret Anders. She hired Whitney a few weeks ago to determine whether her husband was cheating on her."

Myles listened as Ashton recounted his conversation with the detective. The morning of the crash, Whitney and Margaret met at a diner just outside of Macon, Georgia. They hadn't stayed long, only long enough for Whitney to share her findings and for Margaret to pay her.

Myles tried to pay attention, but he was barely holding it together. Those last minutes with her client were the final minutes of Whitney's life.

Emotions warred inside of him, but shock and anger were winning. How dare someone take such a precious life. How dare someone take her from him and Collin. It was bad enough knowing that she was dead, but to learn that she'd been murdered ignited something lethal inside of him. He would make it his life's mission to find the person who did this.

"Whitney not only confirmed the husband's infidelity," Ashton was saying. "She also learned he had a drug problem."

"What was the client's name again?"

"Margaret Anders. You know her?"

Myles shook his head. "No, just wondering."

Whitney occasionally asked his opinion about a case, but rarely did she divulge her client's names. Myles knew Ashton wouldn't give the husband's name, but he'd find it. He didn't know if the guy had anything to do with Whitney's death, but he would find out.

"Did authorities talk to the husband?"

"Not yet. The wife confronted him right after leaving her meeting with Whitney, and no one has seen him since. You probably think that he might be behind the crash, but right now, it could be anyone."

"But he'd be a good person to start with," Myles ground out, unable to hide his anger. His fists were balled at his sides. Normally, remaining calm wasn't a problem for him, but knowing someone took the life of a person he loved made him see red. "What's his name? What's the husband's name?"

Ashton shook his head. "I don't know, and I'm probably wasting my breath when I say this, but Myles, let the authorities handle this case."

Yeah, he was wasting his breath, Myles thought. There was no way he could just sit back and do nothing while the cops tried to piece everything together. Especially when he had the means to investigate her death himself.

"Margaret also said that just before they left the restaurant, some guy asked their server to deliver a note to Whitney."

Myles straightened. "Note? What did it say?"

"She didn't know. Whitney didn't read it while she was in the restaurant. Margaret teased her a little, suggesting that maybe it was from an admirer. She said Whitney didn't seem to think so. As a matter of fact, she looked a little uncomfortable, according to Margaret."

"Uncomfortable how? Like she knew the guy? Like she was afraid?"

"She tensed up, glancing around the diner. The client didn't think much of it until the cops showed up at her house, asking about her relationship with Whitney."

"Did she or Whitney see the guy?"

Ashton shook his head. "The server couldn't find him. Only said that he'd been sitting at the counter minutes before he slipped her the note. By the time she made it to their table, the guy was gone. She said that Whitney asked the server for a description, but all Margaret could remember was that he was a good-looking guy almost six feet tall, olive skin, and wearing a cap."

Irritation clawed through Myles. That description wasn't much to go on. Maybe the man really was someone admiring her, but his gut told him it was more than that—especially in light of the crash. And if the husband had been at the diner, Whitney and maybe even the wife would've seen him.

"Just as a heads-up, if you don't hear from detectives tonight, they'll be contacting you tomorrow. And if I was working this case," Ashton said slowly, as if making sure Myles was paying attention, "tonight I'd be getting a warrant to search Whitney's home."

Myles nodded his understanding. If the cops searched the house, for any reason, Myles had no idea what they'd find. He and Whitney might've owned the place together, but as far as he was concerned, the house was hers. She and Collin lived in it, not him.

Now that he knew the cops would need to search the place, Myles needed to go there tonight to poke around before they got there. He didn't have a clue to what he'd be looking for, but working so many years for the CIA, it didn't matter. If there were something to be found, something that could give him a hint to whoever might've been after her, he'd find it.

Myles sensed there was more, something Ashton wasn't telling him. "What else?" he said forcefully, unable to hide his anxiousness.

"There was a small piece of paper found between Whitney's driver's seat and the center console. The detectives think it might be the note from the mystery man."

"Damn, Ashton! You should've started with that. What did it say?"

"The paper was crumbled, and they could only make out a small part of it. So—"

"Just tell me what it said!"

"It said...*you will pay for destroying my family.*"

*

Hours later, after dropping Geneva and Collin off at his loft, Myles stood in the doorway of Whitney's home office and glanced around. A sliver of moonlight shone through the two windows, casting shadows throughout the space.

The last thing he wanted to do was touch any of Whitney's belongings. At least not yet. He and her sister, Yvette, agreed to give it a couple of weeks before they boxed up the house. But no matter when they did it, it would be one of the hardest things Myles would ever have to do.

They both still needed time to come to terms with the knowledge that Whitney was really gone. Yvette assumed he would move into the house for Collin's sake, but Myles planned to put it on the market as soon as possible. There was no way he would move in. He loved his loft. Besides, the house reminded him too much of Whitney.

He pushed away from the door jamb and flipped the light switch. The lamp on the desk came on instead of the overhead light, giving the room a serene feel, a calmness that he hadn't felt in hours.

Myles strolled across the dimly lit space, his footsteps silent on the plush carpet. After closing the blinds on the window that overlooked the side of the house, he then went to the one that gave a view of the street. His hand was on the wand to shut the blinds, but he stopped. A parked car, a few houses down, caught his attention. It was the same vehicle he had seen the other day when picking up some of Collin's items.

The car probably wouldn't have stood out, but someone was sitting in the driver's seat, like the other day. A nearby street light illuminated just enough to see the figure's outline, but not enough to identify if it was a man or woman. Whoever it was, appeared to be looking at Whitney's house.

Myles shut the blinds and hurried back to the door, almost bumping into Kenton in the hallway. Kenton and Laz agreed to help him look around the house, and they were the perfect people for the job. Both could go through the place without making it look as if it had been searched.

"I'll be right back," Myles told him. "I want to check something out front. A car and driver I saw sitting out there the other day."

He started down the stairs.

"Wait, I can check it out for you," Kenton said, following behind him.

"Nah, man. I got this. It's probably nothing. I'll holler if I need you."

Instead of going out the front door, Myles left through the back. He hopped a fence that separated Whitney's yard from the neighbors and did the same thing with the next house.

When he reached the street, he planned to sneak up on whoever was in the dark four-door sedan. He quickly made a note of the Georgia license plate: *PXG9311*. The car was running, and there was a sliver of light coming from the inside of the vehicle. Maybe something from an electronic device like a phone or a tablet. Whatever it was, he was thankful it was distracting the driver.

Myles crept closer. Maybe this was just someone waiting on a person from another house, but just in case...

Before he could get to the driver's door, the guy glanced into his mirror. Startled dark eyes met Myles's gaze. Seconds before Myles reached the window, the man gunned the accelerator. He roared away from the curb like his butt was on fire and almost ran over Myles's foot in the process.

Dammit. He barely got a look at the person. White with dark eyes, a thin mustache, and scruff on his cheeks. The wool cap and the high-collared jacket didn't give him much more. Hopefully, they would get a hit on the plates.

When he walked back into the house, Kenton met him near the door with a finger at his lips, signaling for him not to say anything. He pointed to his ear, and Myles cursed under his breath.

The house was bugged.

They both went out the back door, and Myles ran a hand down his face once they were standing just beyond the patio. He hadn't considered that the place could be bugged, and the thought had his blood boiling.

"How the hell did someone get in?" he said more to himself.

Kenton's cell phone rang, and he held a finger up to Myles to give him a minute while he took the call. While he did that, Myles went back to check the door that they'd just exited. There were no broken windows and no sign of forced entry at the front or the back door.

How did they get in?

Whitney was a stickler for security, to the point of being obsessive about locking doors and having the alarm on even when they were in the house.

Maybe the person used a bump key, Myles thought. That would've been a way to unlock the door and then lock it back. That still didn't answer the question of how they got past the alarm system.

He strolled across the yard to where Kenton was just finishing his call.

"Where'd you find the listening device?" Myles asked. "Or is it more than one?"

"So far, Laz found one in the living room. There was a small stack of mail on an end table. When he went to turn on the lamp, that's when he found the listening device. Whoever is listening doesn't know we found it."

"Where's Laz now?"

"He has a spy bug detector at home, and he lives closer. He went to get it. He was going out the front door just as you came through the back."

Myles nodded and pulled out his cell phone. "Okay, good. In the meantime, I'll contact Wiz to see if he can trace the signal, as well as determine if the alarm system has been overridden at some point. Even though I can't imagine Whitney not having it on at all times."

"If she was half as paranoid as you usually are, I figured the person had to have somehow sabotaged the alarm."

Myles didn't take offense to the paranoid comment. He could admit to being extra careful in every aspect of his life. It was just the way he was made, and after spending so many years as a spy, being a little distrusting was ingrained in him.

He told Kenton about the car parked out front, and he agreed to forward the plate number to Ashton while Myles talked to Wiz. It was good having friends in law enforcement and the rest of the Atlanta's Finest team, whose skills and abilities in situations like this were second to none.

Myles stayed outside and called Wiz. Cameron "Wiz" Miller, a part-owner of Supreme Security-Chicago, was their go-to person for any type of technology needs. The computer guru was a former Navy SEAL and a master hacker. If anyone could help Myles in this area, it was him.

"Hello."

"Hey, man. It's Myles. I need a favor."

Myles explained everything, and after being assured Wiz would look into the situation, he re-entered the house. Now he and the guys had to pretend they didn't know the house was bugged.

"I'm sorry about what happened to Whitney," Kenton said when Myles returned to the office. He was searching the closet.

"Yeah, thanks. It's still hard to believe she's gone," Myles said, playing along. His friends had already expressed their condolences.

He and Kenton exchanged small talk and moved quickly around the room, trying to determine if there were any more bugs or even cameras that had been planted. They wouldn't know for sure until Laz returned, but they could at least look.

Kenton checked the heat vent, the area around the small flat-screen television, and the bookcase. Myles checked all around the desk, surprised he didn't find anything.

"Do you think you want to keep this?" Kenton pointed to the back of the shelf, then pointed to his ear.

"I'm not sure," Myles said through gritted teeth as irritation stirred inside of him. He wondered just how many were in the house.

Payback was a bitch. How many times had he and Whitney planted listening devices during an assignment? During his CIA years, that was as natural as putting on a pair of socks. It came with the job. But now that they were dealing with someone spying, he was mad enough to spit bullets.

At some point, some stranger had been inside the house, invading Whitney's privacy. Questions bombarded his mind. When were the devices installed? What had Whitney discussed in these rooms? What had he and Whitney discussed during his visits? Just how much did this person know about her...about him...or Collin?

Myles would love to get his hands on the person who had the audacity to come after his family.

When his cell phone vibrated in his pocket, he pulled the device out and glanced at the screen. *Laz*.

Open the front door. Also, the outside is clear.

Myles jogged down the stairs and glanced out before pulling the door open.

"Hey, thanks. Sorry it took so long, but I couldn't find the beer you usually get," Laz lied and held up a familiar bag.

"No worries. I'm sure whatever you bought is fine."

"We're in the office. Come on up."

The moment they stepped into the room, Laz pulled out the equipment. The device actually belonged to Supreme Security. On occasion, when they wanted to ensure a client's home wasn't bugged, they'd use the device to sweep the place. It was almost a hundred percent accurate in finding bugs.

Kenton pointed to the bookcase, showing him that they'd found at least one on the second floor, and Laz nodded. He silently started searching the closet.

Whitney made sure Myles knew where she kept personal items, including spare keys to the desk and lateral file cabinet. He pulled open the false electrical outlet near the office door and removed the spare keys. She had a number of concealed hiding places throughout the house, just in case.

Usually, she was always prepared for worse-case scenarios. It didn't matter that they'd left the CIA years ago. In some cases, she still operated like she still worked for the Agency. There was even a go-bag for her and Collin if she ever needed to leave town at a moment's notice. Myles had taken that duffel to his house the other night, knowing that it contained cash. It also had some of her passports, aliases from when she was an agent.

He dropped down heavily into Whitney's desk chair, his chest tight with emotion. No amount of planning could have prepared him for all of this. Even with the type of work they used to do, dying wasn't a topic of conversation, the exception being preparing their wills. Even then, though, it was just a precaution, mainly for Collin's sake. They wanted to make sure everything was in place to ensure he'd be taken care of in case of their untimely death. With Whitney's insurance policy, as well as investments, he and Collin would be set for years to come.

Myles needed to focus on the task at hand. He unlocked the file cabinet, as well as the desk drawers. Earlier, before leaving Mason's house, Ashton had mentioned that when the cops searched the place, they'd mainly be looking through files. Anything that would give them some insight into Whitney's clients and what type of jobs she took on.

Whitney was extremely organized and had the latest client's files at the front of her desk's bottom drawer. Instead of taking them with him, Myles took pictures of the content. He'd start reviewing everything in the morning. Hopefully, they'd give him some clues of who or what they were dealing with.

His cell phone buzzed with another incoming text message. This one was from Wiz.

Someone definitely overrode the system, then reset it. They're good. Very good. I added a safety feature remotely to prevent it from happening again. Change the password before leaving. My team will do the monitoring until further notice.

Myles sat back in the chair. At least he knew that Whitney had still been vigilant in setting the alarm. Whoever they were dealing with was not only a murderer, but they had serious tech skills. Supreme Security had installed a top-of-the-line system. For someone to have been able to hack into it was disturbing, and for Wiz to admit that the person was good was saying a lot. As far as Myles was concerned, Wiz was the best.

Thanks, Myles typed back, then added, **What about the listening devices? Are you able to trace the signal?**

Myles looked up as Laz walked out and headed to the next room. And when his phone vibrated again, he read the text from Wiz.

I'm working on it. More time needed. Stay vigilant.

Myles sent him a thumbs-up and went back to taking pictures. In case the cops decided to remove any of the information from Whitney's files, he wanted to have copies. They could search the house and investigate all they wanted, but he wasn't leaving it up to them to find her killer.

"What do you want to do with the junk that's in here?" Kenton asked casually, holding up Whitney's handgun safe. They were careful with their words for the benefit of whoever was listening in.

"Let me see."

Myles picked up the key ring from the desk and found the one that would unlock the box. He hoped her pistol was in there. Once he confirmed it was, he breathed a sigh of relief, not realizing he'd been holding his breath. If she wasn't traveling with her weapon, chances were she didn't feel threatened. That answered one of the questions he'd been thinking about. She didn't know someone was tracking her.

After relocking the box, Myles handed it back. "I need to go through all of that stuff."

"I'll just leave it here." He returned it to the top shelf of the closet. The plan was to leave everything as it was for when the cops searched the place. Whitney had a permit for the weapon; as long as it hadn't been fired recently, it wouldn't raise any red flags.

Myles rubbed his tired eyes. Exhaustion was settling in. The last few days had been like scenes from a nightmare. But he couldn't stop. He needed to go through as much as possible in case he didn't get a chance to before the authorities reached out to him tomorrow.

As he logged into her laptop that was sitting on the desk, he thought about what he knew so far. The last person to see Whitney alive was her client. Her brakes were tampered with, and she received a threatening note from an unknown enemy. Now they found out that someone had overridden the alarm system and bugged the house.

The more he thought about it, the more he wondered if it really was one of her clients that had killed her. Tampering with brakes and hacking weren't your everyday skills. Could someone else have targeted her? What if her murderer wasn't a client at all? What if the client had hired a killer?

Just stop, he told himself. He was going to drive himself nuts. He knew from experience that the answers would come. He just had to be ready for whatever he found.

Myles spent the next hour going through computer files, specifically the client folders. When he was done with that, he reviewed Whitney's internet browsing history. In the note app on his cell phone, he typed in a few search words and sites she had visited, then paused.

Gunrunners.

South Sudan.

Arms trafficking.

What the heck? Gunrunners? She promised not to take on any dangerous cases. Was one of her clients into arms trafficking? That subject alone could get a person killed.

What the hell did you get yourself caught up in, Whitney?

Chapter Fourteen

Geneva ordered a car service to take her to Brookhaven, a suburb of Atlanta. She couldn't wait to hang out with her girls. She was planning on having an early dinner with her sister and a few of the spouses of Atlanta's Finest. Sure, she'd seen some of them the other day at London's birthday party, but they hadn't been able to talk freely with so many other guests present.

The moment Geneva stepped into the eatery, known for its award-winning pizza, she inhaled deeply. The tantalizing scent of fresh-baked bread and herbs wafted past her nose and had her mouth watering in anticipation. She loved food, period. But pizza was absolutely her favorite meal.

"Hi, just one for dinner?" the hostess asked and grabbed a menu.

"Actually," Geneva glanced behind the woman into the mostly full restaurant, "I'm meeting a few people who should be already...oh, wait, there they are." She pointed to where Dakota waved her over.

"Okay. Well, enjoy your meal," the hostess said with a smile, and Geneva headed to the table.

The restaurant was buzzing with conversation as she gracefully maneuvered around a few tables. When she walked near the long mahogany bar, a few heads turned in her direction. Geneva knew she looked good.

Some might think she was arrogant or full of herself, but that wasn't the case at all. She was just confident. Her style—sexy/chic—was always eye-catching, and rarely did she leave the house without being totally put together. This time, she had chosen a fitted beige sweater that revealed a bare shoulder, and she paired it with off-white pants and matching high-heeled ankle boots.

As she neared the end of the bar, Geneva caught the attention of a man with pretty eyes, perfectly groomed facial hair, and he was nicely dressed. He was handsome and well put together in a CEO-kind of way.

He had just lifted a glass of beer to his mouth but didn't drink from it as they made eye contact. He smiled, and she did as well, acknowledging him with a nod. The man was definitely her type and had she still been single, she would've stopped to talk. Instead, she kept it moving.

"You're a trip," Dakota said, laughing. She stood and greeted Geneva with a hug. "Got these men up in here drooling over your sexy ass."

Geneva shrugged. "What can I say? I can't help it if I'm beautiful."

They both laughed, and Journey rolled her eyes. She pointed to the vacant chair next to her. "Just sit down. You always have to make an entrance," she said with mock disgust. "Been like that since we were kids."

Geneva grinned and blew her sister a kiss. "*Whatever.* Where's Egypt and Zenobia?" she asked, referring to Kenton and Angelo's wife.

"Egypt had to work late," Journey explained. "She said she'd catch us next time."

Egypt was not only Kenton's wife, but she was the heartbeat of Supreme Security. As the office manager and the assistant to Mason and Hamilton, she knew the business's inner workings and practically ran the company single-handedly.

132

"And Zenobia had some kind of gig tonight. For a person who claims to no longer be performing, she's had back-to-back singing engagements over the last few weeks," Dakota said.

Zenobia—or as her fans called her, "Zen"—was a singing sensation whose career took off after her first album. Soon after, though, she realized she didn't like the spotlight. When she and Angelo got married a few months ago, Zenobia vowed she was done with the limelight. Since then, she was mainly a songwriter for several famous singers.

After the server took their drink and food orders, Geneva turned to Dakota. "So, how's the mommy-to-be?"

Her friend smiled and placed her hand on her barely-visible baby bump. As a dojo owner with a black belt in karate, the former stuntwoman was in incredible shape. No one would ever imagine that she was eighteen weeks pregnant.

"All is well. I still can't believe I'm pregnant again. Junior is barely fourteen months," she said, excitement building in her voice. "I'm a little impatient for this little one to make *her* appearance."

Geneva and Journey gasped.

"Oh, my God!"

"You're having a girl?"

They said at the same time, squealing loud enough to cause people at nearby tables to look over. Geneva was thrilled for her friend, especially knowing she was having a girl.

Their daughter would be Dakota and Hamilton's second child together. They were also raising Hamilton's twelve-year-old son. Time was going so fast. It seemed like only yesterday that Dakota almost died at the hands of someone who was after her father. That was how she first met Hamilton. He'd been assigned to protect her, and now, years later, they were happily married and growing their family.

Conversation flowed easily between the women, and they acted as if they hadn't seen each other in months instead of days. Geneva was close to all of the women of Atlanta's Finest, but not as close as she was with Journey and Dakota. These ladies were her confidants, people she could talk to about anything, anytime. And the older she got, the more she appreciated the power of a sisterhood bond.

Meeting up with them was exactly what Geneva needed to take her mind off of Myles. She hadn't seen him since the morning after London's party, and she was missing him, which was just crazy. She didn't sit around waiting for guys to call. They sat around waiting for her. Yet, last night, that's precisely what she'd done, then got angry at Myles when he didn't call until a few hours ago.

Geneva knew he had his hands full. He'd learned the night of the party that Whitney had been killed, which was shocking and awful. He sounded sure the murderer was someone affiliated with one of her clients, but the cops were still investigating. But Geneva knew Myles well enough to know that he was probably looking into the case himself. Meaning that would be even more time away from each other, and that pissed her off. In turn, her anger made her disappointed in herself.

Journey often called her selfish, and Geneva usually ignored her, until lately. She could admit to being self-absorbed sometimes, and she really wanted to change that about herself, especially knowing that Myles had a child. It wasn't going to be easy for him to split his attention between her and Collin. She needed to come to grips that he had other obligations than just being with her. Besides, Collin was so precious. She had already fallen in love with him. He deserved as much of his father's attention as possible. But still, what about her?

After London's party, Myles had dropped her, Collin, and Coco off at his loft while he spent much of the night at Whitney's place going through her belongings. The next morning, he drove her and Coco home, and she hadn't seen him since. Granted, it had only been twenty-four hours or so ago, but still, she missed the jerk.

"Hey!" Journey snapped her fingers in front of Geneva's face to get her attention.

Geneva frowned. "What?"

"I asked if you've heard anything else about your car or the salon."

"Oh." Geneva glanced down at the table and hadn't even realized the server had brought the spinach and artichoke appetizer that they'd ordered. She scooped a spoonful onto her small plate, along with pieces of the garlic toast.

"The mechanic is still waiting for the car windows to come in. They had to be special ordered, and he's thinking maybe another week or two. As for the salon, the cops haven't given me any good news. They haven't caught the guys. So Laz is reaching out to some of his old contacts." And by old contacts, she knew he meant some of the confidential informants he used when he was a police detective.

"If anyone can get answers, it's my husband," Journey said between bites.

"I still think it was those delinquents from the other night. I just don't have any proof," Geneva said.

She stopped talking when the server returned with the large barbecue chicken pizza. He set it on the stand in the center of the table.

"Can I get you ladies anything else? Maybe something else to drink?" he asked.

Geneva and Journey had barely touched their margaritas and echoed Dakota's request that he bring them glasses of water.

"As for the shop, after I pay the deductible, my insurance will cover the repairs," Geneva continued as she placed a slice of pizza on her plate. "Myles thinks I should look for a new location for the salon. He wants me someplace safer. But I'm concerned that my clients won't follow me."

"Girrl, do you know how hard it is to find a good hairstylist? Trust me, if you move, your clients will follow,"

Dakota said and moaned when she bit into her pizza. "I know I will. As a matter of fact, I'll probably be at your house in a few days for you to touch up my edges."

"Myles is right," Journey said. "You've been talking about finding a bigger place. And it wouldn't hurt to be somewhere safer considering the danger you've lived through. I hate that those punks tossed the Molotov, but maybe this was the push you needed to grow your business."

Geneva listened as they gave their opinions about going bigger and better. Dakota even gave suggestions on neighborhoods Geneva should consider. The more they discussed it, the more she seriously considered making a move to a new location.

"Now, let's go back to Myles," Dakota said. "What did I miss? I knew you guys got busy in Journey's guest bathroom after Kenton and Egypt's wedding, but—"

"Do not ever bring that up again," Journey snapped at Dakota but was glaring at Geneva. "I still can't believe she christened my bathroom with all of those people there."

"And I can't believe y'all knew about that," Geneva said, not embarrassed at all. "Besides, everyone was outside."

"Whatever. Next time you two come to my house, my bathrooms are off-limits. Heck, I might not even let you in the house."

Thinking about sex in the bathroom, Geneva recalled what she and Myles did at the party. Seems the girls didn't know about that. She smiled, secretly pleased to keep that info to herself.

"Are you and Myles officially dating?" Journey asked with a knowing smile. Clearly, she already knew, but Geneva confirmed it anyway.

"It's still new," she said. "But it feels like I've known him forever. We're as different as grapes and bananas, but we click. The idea of us together is wild, exciting, and a little scary all rolled into one. I never really thought about settling down, but lately, that's all I've been thinking about."

"*Finally*," Journey said. "It's about time you found someone worthy of you. Someone who can make you forget about all other guys."

"Someone who completes you," Dakota added. "When the right man comes along, you just know. I knew it the first time I laid eyes on Ham that he was the one for me."

"Yeah, you practically scared the man half to death chasing him down," Journey said with a laugh. "Ham didn't know if he was coming or going messing around with you."

Dakota shrugged with a Cheshire cat grin. "What can I say? Me and Gen have that in common. We always go after what we want."

Geneva smiled. That was true, except this time, she was out of her element. She didn't know what the hell she was doing with Myles. More than anything, she didn't want to mess this up.

Geneva ran her finger down the stem of her glass as she listened to them talk about how great it was to be with that special someone. In her heart, that's what Myles was to her, but the unknown made her uncomfortable. She didn't know what she was doing when it came to being in a committed relationship. It was scary how strong her feelings were for Myles, but when they were together, everything seemed perfect.

"I want to be with Myles more than anything, but he's got a lot going on right now, and he has Collin. Which, by the way, I can't believe neither of you told me about."

"I knew he had a son, but Myles doesn't come around often," Dakota said. "So, the few times I saw him at any of our gatherings, I never thought about his son. It's not like he brought him around or talked about him and the child's mother."

"Same here," Journey said. "Laz mentioned once that he had a son, but he didn't share any details about him. I didn't even know how old Collin was or if Myles was in his life until the other day at London's."

"You know those guys stick together," Dakota added. "And they all know how private Myles is. It's not like they go around discussing his personal business."

Geneva knew they were right. She wasn't surprised that they hadn't known details about Myles's relationship with Collin or Whitney. He was the best person to tell a secret to because he would never share it.

"Besides all of that," Journey pointed her finger at Geneva, "I don't know if I would've thought to mention Collin to you since you and Myles were just 'hooking up.' At first, I figured he was just like the other men you spent time with and then kick to the curb. It wasn't until the last few weeks that I started thinking you had feelings for him, right before he took that trip to California. And it wasn't just me who noticed. Laz had a feeling that Myles was more invested in you than he was letting on."

Geneva's heart squeezed, and a warm, fuzzy feeling engulfed her knowing that Myles was as into her as she was into him. With him not being a big sharer, it was hard to tell at times. At least it had been until recently. Now she knew without a doubt that he was seriously interested in her. But now there was Collin.

"I feel guilty always wanting to be in Myles's face when I know his son needs him more than anything," she said to her girls. "He's his top priority, as he should be, but I'm not used to being second in anything. Yet, I want Collin to have as much time with his father as possible. What if I get in the way of that happening?"

"The fact that you're concerned about that little boy's needs speaks volumes," Journey said. "It means you're growing up. *Finally*. But seriously, though, I think Myles and Collin are lucky to have you."

"Don't overthink all of this, Gen," Dakota added. "None of us knew what we were doing when we got into our relationships. We just did what came naturally. Trust your instincts, follow your heart, and love on those two guys the best you can, especially now with all that's going on."

Geneva nodded. All she could do was her best, and she was crazy about both Myles and Collin.

Her cell phone rang, and she dug it from her purse and smiled when Myles's name showed on the screen.

"Well, we don't have to ask who that is. She's damn near drooling on her phone," Dakota cracked.

Geneva laughed and excused herself from the table. Suddenly, she was feeling more encouraged than she'd felt all day. She, Myles, and Collin were going to be fine. But thinking about what Dakota said, regarding her and Geneva always going after what they wanted, Geneva was about to make plans with her man.

And I'm not taking no for an answer.

*

Myles disconnected the call from Geneva and smiled. The woman was funny without trying to be, and he loved it when she got all alpha on him. He had called to invite her out, maybe have a drink or a late dinner. At first, she didn't give him a chance to ask anything. She had already decided when she answered the phone that they were getting together, whether he had the time or not. When she finally let him talk, he suggested they go play pool at a local bar.

Typically, he wasn't interested in aggressive women, but that trait on Geneva was sexy as hell. Everything about her made him want to know her even better. For years, he'd managed to stay clear of romantic attachments, and it had been relatively easy to do. At first, it was because he never wanted to get close enough to a woman and then lose her the way his father had. He'd been determined not to go down that road.

Also, working for the CIA had made staying clear of relationships easy. He'd always feared that his dangerous job could possibly reach his personal life and the people he cared most about. But now that Geneva had come along, it was as if he had no control. His desire and need for her was impossible to ignore. It had been a long time, if ever, that a woman held his attention the way she did. The timing couldn't have been worse. Yet, she had a way of making him look forward to every moment with her.

Now all I have to do is figure out how to juggle my time with her, my son, and work.

Myles leaned back in the desk chair. Much of his day had been spent with Collin. They had started with breakfast at McDonald's, his son's favorite place. Then they ended up at Georgia Aquarium, where they stayed much longer than Myles had initially planned. When they finally arrived home, they streamed and watched the latest Disney movie.

Myles enjoyed every minute but was secretly glad when Yvette called to see if she could spend some time with Collin. A couple of hours ago, he dropped his son off at her house, then stopped by Supreme Security to do some research. Not only was the office a few miles from Geneva's home, but it also gave him a chance to use the company's computer equipment, as well as provided him access to a database that he wanted to check out.

A quick knock sounded at the door before it swung open, and Kenton strolled in. "I'm glad Egypt told me you were here. I was planning to call you after I took her home."

"Yeah, I was in the area and figured I'd stop in for a few. Were you able to get any information?"

The other day, when Myles copied Whitney's computer files, he hadn't known what he would find. But he stumbled upon a file that didn't totally make sense to him. For the last couple of months, Whitney had been adding a mishmash of information to a document. The last entry stated that she thought she was being followed but then chalked it up to being paranoid.

Myles wasn't sure if the document had been intentional or accidental placed in a folder labeled *Collin's Baby Pictures*. He couldn't help but think that it was for him to find if anything happened to her. Now, he just had to make sense of it all. He also had to decide if or when to share his findings with the detectives on her case.

The two men had shown up at Whitney's house the day before, just like Ashton predicted. Even though they roamed around the house, the detectives hadn't found the listening devices. That didn't surprise Myles. Their primary focus had been in Whitney's office, specifically, her files. They were convinced her death was tied to one of her clients.

Myles wasn't so sure.

Kenton folded his large body into the chair in front of the desk. "I made a call about the case names or the names you think are case names," he said, referring to the information found in Whitney's document.

As a former FBI agent, Kenton still had contacts he could reach out to. It wasn't something he liked to do considering how devastating his career ended with the agency, but Myles appreciated him making an exception.

"Most of the information didn't come up in the system, but they might be operations from other agencies like *the CIA*," he said pointedly. "Or even NSA or DEA. However, my contact did get a hit on one of the names. The GEA Assassination was an FBI operation dated back a little more than seven years ago. You couldn't find anything on it because it's listed as classified, and the case is closed. He did say that it had to do with gun trafficking."

Myles nodded, finding that interesting. "Guns and gunrunners were some of the last subjects that she searched online," he said absently.

An unsettling sensation, a stirring in his gut, had him clenching and unclenching his hands. The more he dug for information, the more he was convinced that there was something even more sinister at play in all of this. Knowing Whitney was involved in something serious enough to get her killed was disturbing on so many levels.

Why hadn't she come to him? Or said anything? He might've been able to help. She could've still been with them, but instead, she had died at the hands of some asshole, and Myles had to find out who and why.

He glanced at the computer screen. There was no way this was tied to any of the cases she was working on. He knew without a doubt that she wouldn't take a job involving gunrunners, but then why was she digging for information?

"You know…the public can access some FBI records," Kenton said, and he pulled a pen from his jacket pocket and scribbled something on the notepad near the computer monitor. "Who knows, you might be able to find information on this website that can help." He slid the note pad over to Myles.

They talked a few minutes longer before Kenton stood. Myles had to get going, too, but he had hoped to sift through a few more of Whitney's files. But what he needed more than anything was a break, some downtime to help him regroup. He couldn't think of a better person than Geneva to make that happen.

"Oh, I almost forgot. What'd you hear back about the mystery car outside of Whitney's place the other day?" Kenton asked.

"Definitely nothing as sinister as I expected," Myles said. "It turned out to be a high school kid waiting on his girlfriend. Seemed the girl had a history of sneaking out after curfew and having him pick her up several houses away."

Kenton shook his head and chuckled. "Wow. This generation of kids…man. I'm sure having the cops show up at their houses went over great with their parents."

Myles could only imagine. The car sitting outside the house wouldn't have been a big deal if there wasn't an active investigation going on for Whitney's death.

"Well, I'm glad it was nothing else. Hopefully, Wiz can narrow down the signal for the listening devices."

"Yeah, he's a little baffled but also impressed by this guy's tech skills. Supposedly, there's a maximum signal range. Yet, this bastard somehow exceeded it. Whatever Wiz is looking at has triangulated an area that's miles long and wide."

"If anyone can figure it out, it's Wiz," Kenton said. "I'm sure he'll have a neighborhood or an address for you soon."

"Yeah, I hope so," Myles said and logged out of the computer. He not only wanted to nail this mystery guy but more than anything, he wanted to know what Whitney had stumbled onto. Was her death really connected to one of her P.I. cases? Or worse…did this have anything to do with one of her CIA operations?

That was a stretch, but the sinking feeling in Myles's stomach sent a strong signal that whatever was going on wasn't over.

Chapter Fifteen

Geneva glanced at the slim platinum watch on her wrist and cringed. She needed to hurry. She had just enough time to freshen up and let the dog out to handle her business before Myles showed up, and he was never late.

She opened the door, and Coco pranced around happily before running outside into the fenced backyard. Geneva closed the door and headed to her bedroom.

When Myles called while she was at the restaurant to ask her out, of course she said yes. Geneva loved the idea of them doing something fun, and shooting pool was one of her favorite pastimes. She wouldn't have him for the whole night since he had to pick Collin up from Yvette's house later, but a couple of hours was better than nothing.

She finished touching up her makeup and let Coco back inside just as the doorbell rang. "Dang, he's early."

Barking, the dog made a mad dash to the front of the house, with Geneva following behind. When she swung the door open, the excitement of seeing Myles quickly turned into disappointment.

"What are *you* doing here?" she asked.

Reuben stood on the other side of the threshold, looking at her and salivating as if she'd been offered up as his last meal. His long, high-pitched whistle pierced the air, irritating her even more.

"Wow, you look *hot*. Did you dress up for me?"

"Of course not. What do you want?" She put her hands on her hips and sighed impatiently. "And since when do you start dropping by my house without calling first?"

"Since you stopped returning my calls. I wanted to see how you were doing, especially after what happened to your shop," he said and entered the house as if she had invited him in. "What's up with you?"

A low growl from Coco caught Geneva's attention, and she pointed to the family room where the doggy bed was located. "Go," she said, and after a slight hesitation, Coco trotted away.

Before closing the door, Geneva glanced around outside, glad that Myles hadn't shown up yet. Considering how he behaved the first time he'd seen Reuben, this time would probably be worse. It was no secret that he didn't like the guy. She needed to make this visit quick.

Still, it would be nice if Myles got to know her old friend. Reuben might've been a pain sometime, but deep down, he was a good guy. He had always been a gentleman with her, even claiming once that they would be perfect together if she'd only give him a shot.

She strolled into the family room where he stood near the mantel, holding a framed photo of her, Journey, and their parents. She ran across the picture a few weeks ago when she was looking for something else and decided to display it.

"Nice photo," he said and set it back in place.

"Thanks. Now, what do you want?"

Reuben flashed that smile that probably made most women melt on the spot, but Geneva was immune from his charm. "You," he said simply. "I want you."

"That's not going to happen."

He walked toward her. "Come on, Gen. Why not?"

"Because I'm seeing someone else." Even if she weren't, she wouldn't hook up with Reuben again. He was a part of a past that she'd worked hard to leave behind.

"And in *seeing someone* do you mean that you're just kicking it? Or is this something more?"

Geneva was slow to respond, not because she didn't know the answer, but the words lodged in her throat. Why? She wasn't sure. All of this was so new to her. It felt strange saying that she had a boyfriend. Myles was more than that, though. She just didn't have a word for what she truly felt for him or what he was to her.

"It's serious," she said.

Reuben stared at her for the longest time, then burst out laughing. "Serious, huh? Gen, come on. It's me you're talking to. You don't do serious. You take what you want and need from a man, then you kick him to the curb and keep it moving."

Dang, was that how he saw her? He made her sound as if she just used men—which she didn't. Any hookups she'd been a part of were mutually beneficial, and they always knew the deal going in. No ties. No commitments.

"We used to be so good together. If you were ready for something more serious, why didn't you tell me?"

What he meant was they used to be good together between the sheets. She hadn't wanted anything more than his body back then, and at the time, she assumed he felt the same way.

Now...she wanted more from a man...but not from him.

"That was a *very* long time ago, and I've changed. I'm ready for something lasting. Something real."

Reuben laughed. "Come on, baby. Tell it to someone who doesn't know you. On a serious note? You're not the marrying type if that's what you're getting at. I'm not sure who put these thoughts in your head, but—"

"Get out." Geneva pointed toward the front door. "Go. Just get out. Now!"

Reuben was still smiling when he looked at her, but then the smile dropped. "Oh, so you're serious? I thought you were—"

"I'm not saying it again. Get out and make this the last time you stop by here on a whim. As a matter of fact, lose my number. Whatever we shared back in the day will *never* happen again."

He lifted his hands out in front of him. "Okay. Okay, I'm sorry. I didn't mean to offend you. I'm just...shocked." He reached out to touch her cheek, but Geneva turned her head.

"Reuben, I'm seeing someone, and I *really* care about him. I'm not trying to mess up what I have with him by screwing around with you. You need to leave."

Instead of touching her face, he fingered one of her large curls. She mostly wore her hair in a messy ponytail or a bun on top of her head. Today she was wearing it down, letting it hang past her shoulders in layers. It was a look that made her feel sexy, as well as sophisticated.

"You really want to walk away from what we had?"

She grabbed his wrist, forcing him to release her hair. "Yes. We've had this discussion before, and it's been, like, forever since we've hooked up. What you and I had back in the day was fun, but I'm not that same person, Reuben. I've moved on. It's time you do the same. That means no more showing up unannounced. Now, if you'll excuse me, my date will be here in a minute."

Just then, the doorbell rang, and Geneva had to keep herself from groaning. Myles was always prompt, and of course, tonight was no different. If only she could've cleared out her unwanted guest before he showed up.

Her dog barked, then zipped past Geneva. It was as if Coco knew Myles was outside, considering the way she whined and pranced back and forth in front of the door.

"It's time for you to go," she repeated to Reuben.

She walked across the room and opened the door. Her heart did a little jig. It didn't matter how often she saw Myles or how much time she spent with him, the sight of him always had a visceral effect on her.

Geneva didn't know how long they stood there staring at each other, but the trance was broken when Coco darted out the door. The dog barked her greeting and danced in front of Myles with her tail wagging like crazy.

"Hey, girl," Myles said, bending slightly and rubbing Coco behind the ear. "I guess you missed me, huh?" Myles then turned his attention to Geneva. "I think you get more beautiful each time I see you. Hi."

For a man who didn't talk much, he sure knew the perfect thing to say to make her heart melt.

"Hi yourself," she said and stepped into his arms.

Geneva always felt cherished when he held her. And when his mouth covered hers, the heat sparking between them was almost enough to make her forget that it was chilly outside.

Crushing her to him, Myles deepened their kiss, and the way his lips caressed hers sent a shock wave of desire soaring through her body.

She would never get enough of this...of him. If anything, Geneva wanted to spend the rest of her life just like this: in his arms, sharing a passionate kiss, and savoring every moment of it. She just kept falling deeper and deeper for this man, and it didn't scare her.

When the kiss ended, they stepped into the house. Myles was barely across the threshold when he slowed. He hadn't even looked Reuben's way, but it was as if he somehow knew they weren't alone. He moved farther inside and turned to where Reuben stood, exactly where Geneva had left him.

"What are you doing here?" he asked Reuben, then glanced at Geneva. Myles opened his mouth to say more, but she stopped him when she placed a hand on his torso. Hopefully, her touch would keep him from starting a fight with Reuben.

"He was just leaving," she said quickly and looped her around Myles's waist.

"You're the guy from the other day at the shop," Reuben said and spared a glance at Geneva. "So, this is the guy, huh?"

"Yes, and remember what I said. No more calls or just dropping by."

He folded his arms across his broad chest with a smirk on his face. "You ain't gon' introduce us?"

"Nope, because you're leaving." She went to the door and opened it. "Goodbye, Reuben."

He didn't budge. Instead, he said, "You didn't give me a chance to tell you why I stopped by. I know who smoke-bombed your shop."

"Smoke bomb! Hell, those assholes set fire to my place. Stop screwing around and give me a name!"

"A couple of neighborhood kids. Nothing you have to worry about, though. I got you. I'll handle—"

"Oh, hell no," Myles barked. There was a lethal edge to his tone, and Gen could sense the deadly aura surrounding him. He was like a snake lying in wait, preparing to strike at any moment, and Geneva and Reuben stood straighter.

"You don't have to do shit for her." Myles got in Reuben's face. "Just give us the names. We'll take it from there. Or let the cops handle it."

Reuben shook his head and chuckled. "It don't work like that on the streets."

"Oh, so you are still hanging with the Devils, huh?" Myles said of Reuben's former gang, the Minauros Devils. Geneva knew that remark was for her benefit. Myles insisted that Reuben hadn't changed and that he was still hanging with lowlifes.

"I didn't say that," Reuben snapped, glaring at Myles. The man seemed to grow a few inches right in front of them. He was a little taller than Myles and had a good twenty pounds on him. Reuben was also the type of man who fought dirty to come out on top. But Myles had a fearlessness about him, along with brains and stealth. Geneva would put her money on her man any day and every time.

"What are you saying then?" Myles asked.

"I'm saying that no cops are needed, and you know as well as I do why." Reuben's gaze bounced between her and Myles.

Yeah, they all knew that there was no telling what would happen to those boys if the cops got their hands on them, but Geneva still believed in the legal system. To a point. She and Vanessa could've been killed that day, and that's what she told Reuben. The time for trying to handle anything themselves was over. She wanted the delinquents arrested and charged.

"You either give us some names or... Better yet, just leave." Myles went to the front door and opened it as if knowing Reuben wasn't going to snitch.

"Fine. I'm outta here." He stepped outside, then glanced over his shoulder. "Geneva, take care of yourself, and I'll be in touch."

"Don't bother. I told you, lose my damn number!"

Myles slammed the door the moment the words were out of Geneva's mouth. Then he turned to her. "You ready?" he asked, his coolness throwing her off balance.

Geneva narrowed her eyes at him. "I was ready, but are you sure you don't want us to go get Reuben and torture the information out of him? We could try flogging, maybe. Oh! Or we can attach jumper cables to his nipples until he tells us everything."

Myles's eyebrows pinched together, and he looked at her as if seeing her for the first time. "Sometimes, you scare me. You're like a female version of Laz because that sounded exactly like something he would say. Hell, I think he *has* said that before."

Geneva laughed and gave a little shrug. "I'll take that as a compliment." She grabbed her jacket from the hall closet. "So, you're not going to read me the riot act for letting him in? You're not concerned that we might've done a little somethin'-somethin' before you arrived?"

"Did you?" he asked simply, his dark stare nailing her in place.

"Of course not, but I'm surprised that you didn't freak out the way you did the other day at my shop."

"What good would it have done? You do remember how well that went over, right?"

"Yeah, but..." He was right. Had he come in there acting like he owned her or something, she probably would've lashed out. "I can't figure you out."

He slipped his arm around her waist and pulled her against his hard body. "The feeling is mutual." He lowered his head and kissed her with so much passion Geneva was tempted to suggest they spend a few hours in her bedroom instead of a pool hall. She didn't. She liked the idea of them actually going on a date.

When the kiss ended, she slowly opened her eyes. "That was nice, and I'm glad you weren't mad."

"I didn't say I wasn't mad." He dropped his arms to his sides. "I don't like any man near you, especially one I don't trust. If I find Reuben here again, I'm going to kill him. Now, are you ready to go?"

Geneva didn't move, trying to determine whether he was serious. She was sure he wouldn't kill anyone over her, but he might make Reuben's life difficult. She'd learned that the men of Supreme Security were very resourceful.

"You do trust me, right?" she asked.

"Yeah, sure, but Geneva, I don't trust him. By letting him into your house, you're putting yourself at risk. He made it clear that he's still in with the Minauros Devils, and we both know that they're trouble. They're dangerous people who you don't want to get caught up with. So just stay the hell away from that guy."

She couldn't argue with that. Reuben had told her that he was done with that life, but she honestly didn't know if that was the truth. He had just started coming back around, and since she hadn't spent any length of time with him, Geneva honestly didn't know what he was involved with. All she had to go by was his word. In the past, he'd always been straight with her, but who knew if he was telling the truth?

"I've been done with him. It's just you and me, babe."

Myles smiled and took her hand. "Good, because I don't like sharing. Now let's get out of here."

Chapter Sixteen

Myles gripped the steering wheel tighter as he hopped onto Highway 285 to head to Whitney's house. He and Geneva hadn't gotten far when he received a call from Wiz. Whitney's house alarm had been tripped a few minutes ago. The cops were on their way there, and Myles wanted to make sure everything was all right.

"I'm sorry about tonight." He reached over and grasped Geneva's hand. "Hopefully, this won't take long, and we can stick with our plans."

"No problem. I mainly just wanted to spend time with you."

She gave him a sweet smile. It was such a contrast to her sometimes combative, badass demeanor. Myles appreciated her many layers and couldn't help but think about how lucky he was to have her in his life. Even throughout the last couple of hours, knowing he'd be spending time with her had loosened him up after leaving Supreme.

That was until he found Reuben at her house. The guy was like a nasty rash that refused to go away. Myles wouldn't even be surprised if he had somehow been involved in the Molotov fiasco. It was clear Reuben was into Geneva. Maybe he thought by orchestrating the incident that she would be scared enough to run to him. It hadn't gone unnoticed how he happened to show up immediately after the salon caught on fire.

Myles didn't know for sure if he was involved, but Laz mentioned a couple of days ago that the trouble Geneva was having with the teens might be a gang initiation. Her shop was in Devil's territory, so it was possible. If anyone would know, it would be Laz. As a former detective, he knew the streets of Atlanta better than most. His rationale for thinking the Devils were behind Geneva's attack was that other neighboring businesses were experiencing break-ins, but none had endured any physical attacks. The gang might've initially targeted the strip mall since it was in the Devils' territory. But the moment Geneva showed that she wasn't afraid of them had probably ignited the chain of events that followed, starting with her car.

Myles hadn't discussed any of his with her. Yet, after the run-in with Reuben tonight, he was more convinced than ever the incidents revolved around the man's old crew.

"Does Whitney's home alarm go off often?"

"No. That's why I want to go and see what's going on. Hopefully, it's nothing. The other day, Wiz updated the system, so maybe there's a glitch or something," Myles said, hoping the problem was a simple electronic glitch. Yet, there was a part of him that feared it was something more. If he had time, he'd drop Geneva off at home before going, but he already knew she wouldn't cooperate with that idea.

Myles had only shared the basics with her regarding Whitney's death. All she knew was that the brakes were cut on Whitney's car, and the cops were trying to piece together who killed her. Geneva hadn't asked too many questions about the investigation, and Myles wanted to keep it that way.

"I always liked the Dunwoody area," Geneva said as Myles drove through the Atlanta suburb.

"Yeah, we were planning ahead and picked it because of the good school district."

"Then why are you putting the house on the market? Collin only has a couple of years before he starts school. It might be better for you to move in, then you won't have to look for another place in the district."

"I can't. Too many memories. It'll be better to start fresh, and..." Myles's words trailed off when he saw two uniformed officers walking toward the back of Whitney's house. Their weapons were holstered, but they each had their hand resting on their guns.

At first, he didn't hear the alarm, but as he got closer and parked his BMW behind the squad car, he heard it. It was faint but still loud enough to cause a disturbance.

"Beautiful home," Geneva said as they both peered out at the red brick colonial. "Should I stay in the car?"

From the front of the house, nothing seemed out of order. Myles hoped it was a false alarm, but he wouldn't know for sure until he checked things out inside.

"No. I'm not comfortable with you staying out here."

He wasn't necessarily comfortable with her going inside either, especially not knowing what they'd find. At least with her by his side, he'd be able to keep an eye on her.

Myles reached across her and removed his gun from the glove compartment. He could feel Geneva's eyes on him as he stuck the weapon in the back of his waistband. The weapon would be easily hidden under his leather jacket.

"Myles," Geneva said slowly. "What's going on? Why do you need a gun, especially with the cops here? What if they search you?"

"They won't. They don't have a reason to. They're just here to respond to the alarm going off."

She *tsk*ed. "Oh, please. They'll stop and search a black man for any reason. I don't think it's a good idea to carry it."

"Says the woman who had a 9mm stashed under her car seat," he mumbled. He didn't bother adding the part about her being a felon with a weapon. He was still ticked that Laz gave her a gun.

Instead of commenting on his last statement, Geneva said, "You didn't answer my question about why you're

Sharon C. Cooper

taking a gun inside. Is something going on that you're not telling me? Why would you need—"

"Sweetheart, I doubt if I'll need it. I just want to..."

The cops reappeared, one coming from each side of the house, and they glanced at them in the car.

"Come on. Let's go," Myles said, and they climbed out. "Is everything okay, officer?" he asked the cop who was closest to him.

"Is this your place?"

"Yes, it is," Myles said and took in their surroundings.

The house was on a quiet block, and no one was outside, but he was reasonably sure the next-door neighbors had heard the alarm, if they were home.

"The security company called me," Myles told the policeman. "We got here as fast as we could. Was there a break-in?"

"Doesn't appear to be. We just finished walking around the perimeter. We can stick around until you turn off the alarm and check inside."

"Okay." Myles assumed they wanted to see if he was telling the truth about owning the house.

Holding Geneva's hand, he headed up the five concrete steps. The door appeared fine and was locked, but that was the case the other day. Yet, someone had gotten in. Even after changing the locks on both doors the day before, Myles couldn't be sure that the person who had entered the other day hadn't tried again.

Once they were inside, he disarmed the system and glanced around. Nothing appeared out of place, but the alarm was beeping every five seconds. That was new, but it was also a new system. Myles wasn't sure what Wiz was doing or had done on his end after the alarm was tripped. He'd give him a call once the cops left.

He strolled down the hallway, past the kitchen, and to the back door. It was locked. Myles backtracked, looked around the main floor, then went upstairs. When he returned, the police officers and Geneva were standing near the front door.

"Must've been a false alarm," he said.

The cops nodded. "Okay. If everything looks all right, we'll head out," the cop that Myles had spoken to outside said.

"Yes, everything appears fine. Thanks for stopping by."

Myles walked them out while trying to ignore the unease swirling inside of him. Before he locked the door after them, he glanced up and down the street. There was no movement. Not even a car passing by, but his gut was still unsettled.

The alarm didn't have a glitch. Whoever had gotten in before had tried again, but why? Why come back when Whitney was gone...when they had already killed her? Was there something in the house that they were looking for? If so, what?

Myles eased back into the house and locked the door. When he turned around, Geneva was standing in front of him with her hands on her hips. "You care to tell me what the hell is going on? I can feel the tension coming off of you in waves. Something is happening or has happened, and I want to know what," she snapped.

He definitely wasn't dating an ordinary woman. Most days, he loved her fierceness and how direct she was. Today wasn't that day. Myles wasn't sure how much to share, but whatever he decided to tell her, it needed to be somewhere in a part of the house that didn't have ears.

He stretched his hand to her. "Come with me."

Once they were in the back hallway, near the alarm's control panel, Myles pulled her into his arms and held her close. Surprisingly, Geneva didn't fight him. Her arms went around his waist, bringing them chest to chest.

God, she felt good. She snuggled against him, and her sweet-smelling perfume floated to his nose, causing him to lose focus on why he'd brought her back there in the first place. He was the epitome of focus, except when she was around.

Myles couldn't explain it. He couldn't figure out why his response to her was different than with any other woman. Not that he was complaining. He could honestly say he had never been with anyone who made him feel so…so complete.

He lowered his head and moved his mouth over hers, consuming its softness. A shock wave of need pumped through his body as he explored the interior recesses of her luscious mouth. Myles wanted to tell her about the listening devices, but the intimacy of the kiss had his senses reeling. Yet, if he didn't slow down, he wouldn't be able to stop at just a kiss. And now wasn't the best time to explore the rest of her magnificent body.

He reluctantly pulled his mouth from hers, needing to get himself back under control, but he found he wasn't ready to release her. He moved his lips over her jaw, peppering kisses down her wonderfully scented neck, and worked his way back up. When he reached the erogenous spot behind her ear, he lingered.

He nipped and kissed her soft skin before whispering, "The house is bugged."

Chapter Seventeen

"Bugged?" Geneva whisper-yelled, her eyes wide with shock. "Then un-bug it or whatever the hell you security specialists do. Wait. Why is the house—"

Myles covered her mouth with his hand and backed her to the wall. They didn't find any devices near the back door, but he still wanted them to be careful.

Geneva narrowed her eyes at him and jabbed him in the ribs, forcing him to drop his hand from her mouth. Myles laughed, unable to help himself. That was something else he appreciated about her. She made him laugh. By nature, he was usually serious, rarely smiling much. Yet, Geneva could make him laugh or smile over the simplest things she said or did. She definitely brought out a lighter side of him. A side that he was starting to like himself.

When she started to speak, Myles put his finger to *his* lips, hoping she'd get the message to be quiet. He assumed she was about to ask questions, but he didn't have time to go into details of why they wanted to keep the devices in place for a little longer. Instead, he pulled her back into his arms.

"It's a long story. I'll tell you later. Just try to act normal," he said, then chuckled at that thought. "Or as normal as you can."

"You're not funny," she said, sounding offended, but her lips twitched as if trying to keep from smiling.

"Let's keep the conversation as general as possible while we're here, especially in the living room and kitchen," Myles said seriously. "I'm going to walk through the house one more time; then I need to call Wiz. It shouldn't take long. Once I'm done, we'll head out. In the meantime, make yourself at home."

A few minutes later, Myles was standing in front of the alarm system's control panel. It was three times as big as a typical system Supreme Security would install into homes. With the number of buttons and sounds it made, it looked as if it should control a spaceship instead of protecting a house.

Wiz, who worked out of the Chicago office, had invented and designed a number of security products over the years. Some were patented. This device was currently being beta-tested, but Wiz had ordered its installation the day before, saying that Whitney's home would be the perfect opportunity to test it out.

The guy was a genius, and Myles trusted his judgment a hundred percent.

"Okay, push the input button and the green button at the same time and hold it for twenty seconds," Wiz instructed.

When Myles realized he would need both hands for some functions, he pocketed his phone and started talking through his smart watch.

"Okay, you can release the buttons. I'm using the equipment as a conduit to help triangulate the signal in order to…"

Myles half-listened to the why and waited for instructions on what Wiz wanted him to do next. All the while, he wondered what Geneva was up to.

A short while ago, he'd heard the television in the living room blaring. Clearly, she was watching something funny. Her hearty laughter could be heard throughout the house, and that warmed him. He loved having her around. Even in the short time that they'd been together, the differences in them could easily be identified.

Geneva was complex. One minute she could be ready to beat someone down, and the next, she might be comforting them. While her personality was fun and easygoing, Myles was more serious and controlled. He was focused and all about getting things done, whereas Geneva could accomplish a task in a timely manner, but she was going to have a good time in the process.

Thinking about their individual traits, Myles thought about how Whitney often called him out on being too rigid and inflexible. But like his and Geneva's relationship, he and Whitney balanced each other. They clicked.

"Now the red and orange lights should be lit up. Are they?" Wiz asked, cutting into Myles's thoughts.

"Yeah, they are, and the green one is no longer blinking."

"Okay…okay, that's good. This actually might work; an alarm system that may also be able to help with long-distance sound vibrations," Wiz said, sounding as if he was talking to himself.

The excitement in his voice matched what Myles imagined most tech geniuses experienced when they were designing or testing inventions.

"Man, I'm sorry this is taking a little longer than I initially thought it would. Now…I need to see if I can reverse the radio frequency…" he mumbled, sounding as if he was thinking out loud.

Myles let him talk. Wiz's goal was to create some type of long-distance conduit or…something or another that could help pick up the signal for the listening devices.

Myles couldn't make heads or tails of his idea, and he definitely didn't have a clue to what the technical terms meant. Even still, he wanted to do whatever possible to help. If Wiz could come up with a way to get him an address or even the name of the person who might still be listening in, Myles was all for it.

He wanted more than anything to find this person and make them pay. But Myles would be the first to admit that trying to hunt down an unknown killer while juggling the rest of his life was no easy feat. Everything seemed important at the moment. Yet, the sooner they found this person, the sooner he could figure out the next steps in his and Collin's life.

Geneva strolled into the back hallway while glancing down at her phone. When she looked up and met his eyes, a smile kicked up the corners of her ruby-red lips.

What a beautiful distraction.

Damn. He had it bad.

"Hey, you," she whispered and moved closer. "Where are your keys? I left something in your car."

"Hold on a minute, Wiz," Myles said and pushed the mute button on his watch. He wasn't sure if the man was even listening, but Myles could hear him pecking away on his computer keyboard.

He dug the keys from his front pocket and handed them to Geneva.

"Thanks. I'll be right back." She turned to leave, but Myles had a sudden urge to kiss her again.

He tugged on the back of her sweater before she could walk away, causing her to glance over her shoulder at him. Confusion marred her gorgeous face. Without a word, he pulled her close and kissed her soft lips. He would never get tired of savoring her sweetness, and kissing her was becoming his new favorite pastime.

When the kiss ended, Geneva graced him with a sexy smile. "That was nice," she said, wiping lipstick from his lips with the pad of her thumb. "Feel free to kiss me anytime...anywhere."

Myles grinned. "I plan to, and I'm sorry about tonight. I'll make it up to you."

"Oh, yeah. You definitely owe me. I'm talking dinner, dancing, a little somethin'-somethin' and anything else I can come up with. *And* I'm expecting you to pay up *real* soon."

Myles placed another quick kiss on her lips. "Sweetheart, I love being in your debt. It sounds like a win-win for both of us."

As she walked away, Myles heard Wiz calling his name, and he unmuted him.

"Yeah, I'm here."

"Okay, now press the red and green button down at the same time. Then you're going to hear three short beeps."

Myles followed his instructions, and he heard the beeps, but seconds ticked by without Wiz saying anything.

Myles glanced at his watch. The call hadn't disconnected, but he didn't hear anything. He lifted his wrist closer to his mouth. "Hello? Wiz? You there?"

"Yeah. Yeah, I'm here, but something's going on," he said slowly. Again, the sound of his fingers tapping on the keyboard came through loud and clear. "Ahh, hell. Myles, where are you?" Wiz asked in a hurry.

Myles brows drew together. "What do you mean? I'm standing in front of the control panel by the back door. Did I push the wrong buttons?"

"No, but I'm picking up some interference nearby. Did you or the cops clear the house when you got there? Are you sure no one got in?"

Myles pulse amped up. "Positive. No broken windows and the doors were locked. Tell me what's happening."

He moved away from the control panel and strolled through the kitchen. As he slowly moved through the house, he wasn't sure what he was looking for, but he had a feeling he'd know it if he saw it.

He glanced in the living room and dining room combo. Nothing.

"Talk to me, Wiz. What am I looking for?"

Myles no longer cared if anyone was listening to what was occurring inside the house. So what if the person knew if they were on to him? If it made the asshole come out of hiding, all the better.

He slid his gun from this waistband and held it at his side as he eased up the stairs.

"The signal is strong, but..." Wiz's words trailed off, and Myles heard several people talking at once in the background. "It doesn't appear to be strong enough to be inside the house, but it's close by. Someone's on the same frequency as the listening devices. Whoever is on the other end of them is nearby."

Wiz's voice took on an ominous tone, and Myles's heart rate kicked up. His gut stirred with trepidation as he roamed around upstairs, opening closet doors, looking under the beds.

"Myles, are you armed?"

"Yeah," he said, his pulse racing with each step he took.

"Good. Take a look outside. See anybody sitting in their car? Anyone hanging out down the street? The signal is getting stronger."

Myles rushed out of Whitney's room and headed to the stairs.

"Where's Geneva?" Wiz asked.

"She's outsi... Oh, hell!"

He bolted down the stairs, taking some two at a time. He didn't know if some bastard was out there, but...

"Geneva!" Myles yelled from inside the house, not caring that she probably couldn't hear him. He leaped over the last three stairs. Breathing hard, he yanked open the front door, ignoring the cool blast that slapped him in the face.

It was dark except for the outside house light and a streetlamp a few yards away. Both gave just enough illumination for him to see Geneva standing in the middle of the walkway with her phone to her ear, laughing.

Just then, he noticed a car creeping up the street. Myles couldn't tell the make or model. Nor could he tell if the driver was a threat or if they were lost. But as it grew closer, a chill slithered down Myles's spine.

He wasn't taking any chances.

The moment he rushed outside and hurried down the concrete steps, the car sped up, burning rubber in the process.

"Geneva!" Myles yelled. Before she could turn completely toward him, he tackled her hard to the ground, landing with a thud.

Shots rang out.

Bullets pinged off his car. The two massive clay flower pots that sat on the front stoop exploded behind them. Chards of clay fell like a torrential downpour, cutting into his neck and arms.

Myles returned fire while keeping his body on top of Geneva.

They were pinned down. He couldn't risk them trying to run for cover. Instead, he continued shooting at the passing car. When one of his bullets hit the vehicle's side window, the driver sped off.

Myles couldn't let him get away.

He leaped up and ran down the street after the vehicle, shooting out the rear window in the process. The driver gunned the accelerator and screeched away. Myles kept chasing until he started falling farther behind and finally stopped.

"Dammit!" He punched the air with his fist, then flinched when he felt a pinch in his left shoulder. He turned to head back just as a few neighbors started pouring out of their homes.

"Myles!" He heard Wiz yelling his name over and over again. "Myles! If you can hear me, help is on the way!"

Ted, the neighbor who lived two doors down from Whitney's place, was walking in his direction. "Myles! You all right, man? Do you know who that was?"

Myles eased his gun into his back waistband and pulled his shirt over it.

"I called 911," Ted said when he was a few feet away.

No soon as the words were out of his mouth, Myles heard the sirens. "Yeah, I'm okay," he finally said and walked a little faster toward the house. But his steps grew heavy when he glanced at Whitney's front yard. Neighbors were on their knees and huddled together. Voices raised. Arms flailing. A frantic energy pierced the air.

Myles's throat tightened.

His hammering heart nearly blasted out of his chest as his gaze bounced from one person to another.

Geneva. Where's Geneva?

He picked up his pace. Before he realized it, he was sprinting down the middle of the street.

Oh, God. No. No. No.

"Geneva! Geneva!"

Chapter Eighteen

Heart racing. Pulse pounding. Cyrus tore through the neighborhood like his ass was on fire. Weaving around cars, turning corners on two wheels, and plowing through stop signs, he couldn't get out of there fast enough.

Stupid! Stupid! Stupid!

What the hell had he been thinking? That wasn't supposed to happen. He had a plan. He was supposed to stick with the plan.

He drove like a man possessed in the opposite directions of the sirens that could be heard screaming in the distance. He couldn't slow down. Not until there was space between him and that neighborhood.

It wasn't until he was at least a mile away before he was finally able to take a breath and took notice of the car's condition. He glanced at the hole in the windshield. At least the window hadn't shattered the way the rear one had. That hole could've been through his head. Instead, he'd gotten lucky.

He clenched his teeth and gently touched his right ear that stung like it was on fire. Pulling his hand away, blood coated his fingers. One move to his right when that bullet soared through the car, and he would've been a dead man. Instead, the round had only grazed him.

What the hell was wrong with him? Shooting at the woman and Norris Dixon wasn't part of the plan, at least not tonight.

Wait. No. Not Norris Dixon.

The man's real name was Myles. Myles Carrington. Not Norris.

It had taken Cyrus so long to track him and Samantha down. It was hard to keep their real names straight. They were Whitney and Myles. Not Samantha and Norris. Those had been their undercover names. Aliases. But that was beside the point. He might've ruined everything, and what if someone had seen him?

He pounded his hand on the steering wheel as he drove and glanced around his surroundings.

I should've stuck with the damn plan.

The moment Myles had barreled out of the house, rage took over Cyrus's common sense. His first instinct had been to shoot and get the hell out of there. But now, he wasn't even sure if he had shot either of them. Myles, that son of a bitch, had leaped and shoved his girlfriend out of the way.

"I had to have shot him," Cyrus mumbled under his breath.

He was a good shot. Granted, it was difficult shooting, driving, and dodging bullets at the same time, but he had practically emptied his gun. No way did he miss both of them. Hopefully, Myles took a bullet, but Cyrus didn't want him dead. At least not yet. Not like that.

He growled into the quietness of the stolen vehicle. He showed his hand too soon. He wanted Myles to die a slow, painful, agonizing death, and Cyrus wanted to watch. Now it might be too late. Myles would figure out that he, too, was being hunted. He had more resources at his disposal than Cyrus first thought, but that was okay. At some point, like Whitney, his enemy would soon share the same fate.

And what about the woman? It wasn't until recently that he had learned about Geneva Ramsey. She was the assistant district attorney's sister, and her father used to be a police detective. Cyrus didn't have a beef with her, except she was guilty by association. He'd seen what happened to her little business. Seemed she had her own problems. But he imagined the pleasure he could get watching Myles lose yet another woman in his life. Cyrus had even considered taking out the son, but he couldn't stomach killing a kid.

"But I can kill his father."

Cyrus glanced in his side-view mirror, studying the cars driving behind him. He had taken several turns, and it didn't appear anyone was following him. Still, he needed to stay off of main streets and ditch the car. The last thing he needed was for some Good Samaritan to call the police about a vehicle driving with a shattered rear window.

"If only I could've stuck with the plan." *Get inside the house and stay put until Myles showed up.*

Instead, he blew it. Nothing had gone as planned. He had hoped to get into the house and wait for Myles to show up again. Something went wrong. He had tried overriding the security system like he'd done the other two times, but it hadn't worked. Nothing had worked.

Had Cyrus not heard the faint beeping sound when he opened the back door, the cops would have caught him. As it was, he had barely got out of there. Good thing he had parked around the block. They would've questioned him if he had been out front when they arrived.

What happened?

Why hadn't his computer program worked?

Cyrus shook his head, getting more frustrated by the moment.

I could've been face-to-face with the man responsible for destroying my family. Instead, I'm running away.

He wanted to see the fear in Myles's eyes when he took his life. That's how Cyrus had wanted it with Whitney, but most of the time, she had the kid with her. As a last resort, he had to sabotage her car to kill her.

"I need to figure out what went wrong," he murmured.

Had they figured out that he'd been able to hack the system? Did they also know about the listening devices? The Myles guy did work with a security firm, and the few times people had been in the house, not a lot was said. Then again, those detectives had been there. They searched the place, never once mentioning listening devices.

But, still…

Nah, no one knows. There's no way they knew. He could still use their ignorance to his benefit. He'd keep listening in.

But, *damn.* If only he hadn't gotten caught up in the moment and abandoned his original plan. Hopefully, he hadn't ruined everything by acting on impulse. The moment he realized he couldn't get into the house, he should've left. But learning that they might have bested him pissed him the hell off. That's why he stuck around.

Decisions made in anger always lead to bad decisions, his father had often said.

Thinking about his dad only made Cyrus more frustrated. He was determined to avenge his parents' death. Myles and Whitney might not have directly killed them, but they were the ones who started the snowball of lies with their inaccurate reports. For that, he wanted them both dead.

One more to go.

He'd come up with a new plan, but first, he needed to ditch the car before a cop pulled him over.

*

"I will *not* calm down!" Myles roared. "She could've been killed! That son of a bitch opened fire on us…on *me!*" he choked out, slapping his hand to his chest as rage ripped through his body. "He was gunning for me."

That realization—and the fact that Geneva could've been killed—hit Myles like a roundhouse kick to the face. Someone was after him. Someone wanted him dead. And that someone didn't give a damn who they hurt in the process.

His breaths came in short spurts as he stamped up and down the small room. Journey, who'd been acting as his lawyer, had somehow commandeered the space when police arrived to question him.

"And you're sure you were the target?" one of the officers asked.

"Yes! The shooter was gunning for me. He didn't start firing until I stepped out of the house," Myles said, irritation dripping from each word.

"Okay, guys. I think you've asked enough questions. I'll fill you in on the connecting case out in the hallway," Ashton said, referring to Whitney's murder case, and ushered them out of the room with Journey following behind them.

That left Myles with Kenton and Parker, both standing across the room, each with their cell phones plastered to their ears. They were talking to various members of the Atlanta's Finest team.

Myles dropped down on the sofa. The elephant-like weight that had been pressed down on his chest was finally starting to ease. The last two hours had been a nightmare-on-steroids. He had experienced every emotion from fear to anger and everything in between.

I could've lost her.

Geneva could've been killed. She could've died because some deranged bastard was gunning for him.

And it would've been my fault.

This was why he didn't do relationships. His past life as a spy wasn't conducive to long-lasting connections. Myles had no idea who was hunting him, but he was sure it had to do with whatever happened to Whitney. And considering what she'd been researching before her death, he would bet his life's savings that all of this had to do with something from their CIA days.

Myles stretched out on the plaid sofa that was at least six inches too short for his tall frame. He didn't care that his legs hung over the arm of the furniture. He closed his eyes and covered them with his forearm, forcing himself to take long, even breaths.

Geneva was going to be okay. She had a concussion and was currently getting a CT scan to ensure there was no swelling or bleeding in the brain. The doctors claimed she appeared to be all right. Geneva even insisted that she was fine. But Myles wouldn't be totally convinced until she was able to walk out of the hospital.

Settling against the sofa cushions, the events of the night came to the forefront of his mind. He was grateful that Wiz had been on the phone during the shooting. The computer guru's quick action saved a lot of headaches.

Wiz had sent out a 311 alert to all of Atlanta's Finest who were not on duty. The code was initially meant to be used as a safety protocol for when one of them didn't report in, or didn't respond to calls.

Now the code was used as an emergency alert system. A message got distributed to all of the team's phones simultaneously, letting them know that one of them was in trouble. The sophisticated system was similar to an Amber alert, and it had definitely come in handy tonight. Hamilton had shown up at Whitney's house at the same time the cops and EMTs arrived. The ambulance had taken Myles and Geneva to the hospital closest to Whitney's home, and by the time they made it to the emergency room, Parker and Kenton were there waiting.

If Myles had any doubt that his team wouldn't have his back in the time of trouble, tonight they'd proved their loyalty. The last couple of hours had been a whirlwind and a nightmare, rolled into one. And there was no way he could've survived it without them.

"Are you sure you're all right?" Kenton asked, breaking into Myles's thoughts. "You sure you don't need some pain meds?

The doctor had already started him on an antibiotic. Myles turned down the pain meds offered. He wanted to stay alert until he and Geneva were someplace safe. "I'm all right," he said, thinking that later he'd take something for the pain.

Thanks to the adrenaline that had been pumping through his veins at the time of the shooting, Myles hadn't realized he'd been shot. The bullet had only grazed him, leaving what looked like a two-inch burn mark just below his shoulder. Outside of Whitney's house, his shoulder had stung like he'd been branded, but the pain hadn't registered, especially when he found Geneva on the ground unconscious.

Even now, that suffocating sensation from earlier crept back in, and his chest tightened as memories of that moment surfaced. His heart had plummeted to the pit of his stomach at the sight of her motionless body. He thought he had lost her. Thought she was dead because he hadn't been able to protect her. His heart ached after losing Whitney, but that feeling of loss was nothing compared to what he experienced hours ago when he thought Geneva had been killed.

In the ambulance, she'd been in and out of consciousness. It wasn't until thirty minutes after they'd arrived that Myles started to believe that she might be okay. It was around that time Geneva started raising hell, insisting that she hated hospitals and wanted to leave.

"All right. I'll tell him," Myles heard Parker say.

Myles opened his eyes and glanced at the security specialist who used to be SWAT before coming on board at Supreme Security. He was now sitting in one of the upholstered chairs across the room, and Kenton was at the small table near the window, looking at something on his phone. The space wasn't overly big, but it was larger than Myles originally thought.

"Ashton had to leave, but he said to tell you that the teens who tossed the Molotov into Geneva's shop have been apprehended," Parker said to Myles. "Turns out they're affiliated with the Minauros Devils. Some type of gang initiation."

"How'd they find them?" Myles asked.

"Anonymous tip. Three in total were arrested, and they believe one of them is the third kid who bolted after vandalizing Gen's car."

Myles wasn't sure what to say. He was glad they caught the punks, but he didn't know how he felt about Reuben possibly playing a role in wrapping that case up. And it probably shouldn't matter to Myles as long as they were caught, but it did. He didn't want either himself or Geneva to owe someone like Reuben. But right now, he couldn't think about that.

"Thanks for letting me know. I'll tell Geneva."

When the door to the room opened, Myles bolted upright, thinking it was her, and regretted the sudden move. He placed his feet on the floor and gripped his head with both hands until the room stopped spinning.

Damn. Must've moved too fast, he thought.

As Laz walked in, Parker walked out, promising to return shortly. That left Myles with Laz and Kenton. Hamilton and Mason had insisted that he and Geneva have two people with them until they figured out who and what they were dealing with.

"You look like crap," Laz said, dropping a duffel near Myles's feet, then sitting on the sofa next to him.

"Whatever. Were you able to get Coco situated?" Myles asked as he dug around in the bag for a clean shirt. The EMTs had cut off the sleeve of his shirt to tend to his wound.

Immediately after talking to the police, Myles had told his friends about the shooter targeting him. All of his team leaped into action. Myles's primary concerns had been making sure Geneva was all right, getting his son someplace safe, and picking up Coco from Geneva's place. Neither of them would be able to return to their homes until after all of this was over.

Hamilton had jumped into action, making security arrangements for all of Myles's family. Mason had been tasked with picking up Collin from Yvette's place. Myles had been concerned that his son would be scared and upset, but luckily Collin had been asleep when Mason showed up.

Laz leaned back against the sofa, stretched his long legs out in front of him, and then put his hands behind his head.

"Coco is at Mason's place with Collin, who was asleep when Egypt and I dropped off clothes and other stuff you said you guys needed."

"That's good. Thanks." Myles closed his eyes against the exhaustion that was deeply rooted in his body. Physically, he was tired enough to sleep for a week, but his mind was still racing.

"Where's Egypt now?" Kenton asked of his wife.

"In the hallway with Journey, Hamilton, and Dakota," Laz said, then nudged Myles, who looked at him. "Mason and London's guest house is all set for you guys. Now we have to find the asshat who opened fire on you and Gen. Any ideas?"

You will pay for destroying my family.

Those words had been rattling around inside Myles's mind off and on since they arrived at the hospital. That's what the note said, the one the authorities had found in Whitney's car.

Myles had no doubt her death and the shooting tonight were connected. He just didn't know who their enemy was.

"I don't have any ideas yet," he finally said to Laz. "But first thing in the morning, I'll start reviewing some of the CIA assignments that Whitney and I did together."

If her death and tonight's attack turned out to be related to their spy days, Myles's biggest fear would've come true. There'd been a reason he kept his distance from people and stayed clear of romantic relationships. He often feared his past would come back to haunt him and put those he loved in danger.

What if that was currently the case? Geneva could have died.

What if that had happened because of something or someone from his past? Myles would've never forgiven himself.

As it was, he was starting to rethink his decision of having her in his life, knowing that something like this could happen again.

It might be time for him to take Collin and disappear...but not before he hunted down the bastard responsible for tonight.

Chapter Nineteen

Myles is avoiding me.

Geneva didn't know that for sure, but that's how it felt.

Sitting on the leather sofa in the living room, she folded her legs beneath her and sipped from the hot cup of chamomile tea her sister had prepared. It had been two days since the shooting. One of the scariest times in her life, but she had survived.

After her CT scan came back normal, a couple of Atlanta's Finest had escorted her and Myles to Mason and London's guest house. Located behind the main house, the place had all the luxuries of a five-star hotel.

The two-bedroom, two-bathroom dwelling had a cottage-like feel to it, warm and cozy and slightly larger than her home. She couldn't have asked for a more inviting place to recuperate...and to stay safe. Myles insisted that he wanted her and Collin to stay put under the protection of Atlanta's Finest, who seemed to be everywhere on the property. They were probably better protected than those living in the White House.

Geneva's only complaint was that she hadn't seen much of Myles. Sure, he checked in on her every few hours, but he was obsessed with finding the person behind the shooting. According to Journey, Geneva's strong, powerful, sinfully sexy man had lost his shit at the hospital. She couldn't imagine him losing control; especially the way Journey had described.

Geneva took another tentative sip of the steaming hot liquid and snuggled deeper into the overstuffed sofa. Staring into the fireplace, it was almost peaceful listening to the snap, crackle, and popping of the firewood. Red, orange, and yellow flames danced around, creating a zen-like moment for her.

Her thoughts returned to Myles. Had it not been for him, she would be dead. He had responded quickly when shots were fired, while she hadn't even seen the car coming. The one thing Geneva remembered was Myles yelling and then knocking her to the ground. She vaguely recalled being put into the ambulance and him saying over and over: *Don't die on me. Don't leave me.* Her heart ached, knowing that she had scared him like that.

"She's finally asleep," Journey said of Arielle as she strolled back into the living room. "I made a pallet on the floor in the room Collin is using. Hopefully, he and Coco will stay at the main house a little longer. Because once they come running back in here, she'll wake up and be ready to play with them."

Geneva smiled at that thought. Her niece was just learning to walk, but already she was trying to keep up with the big kids.

Journey lifted the large mug from the table. "I need to warm up my tea. Want anything?"

"No, I'm good." Geneva watched her stroll out of the room again. The open floor plan allowed her to see into the small dining room and the kitchen. "I'm really glad you and Arielle stopped by," she said.

"Yeah, me too. We've all been worried about you. Mom and Dad called, talking about cutting their trip short, especially Dad. You know how he gets when either of us is sick or hurt."

"I know. I hope you talked them out of coming home."

"I did, but don't be surprised if they show up."

Geneva was a daddy's girl. She was also the son he wanted but didn't have. Growing up, she followed him around like a puppy dog. They did everything together, from watching sports to building a treehouse in their backyard. She was also the one who gave them hell when she became a teenager. Wrecking the family car, staying out past curfew, and even sneaking beer into her bedroom—she'd done it all. Yet, she and her dad were tighter than a bowline knot despite her childhood escapades.

"I hope they don't," Geneva said. "I told them I'm fine. I'll admit, the last couple of weeks, between the fire at the shop and the shooting the other night, have been unusual. But I feel good. I'm alive, and I can't ask for much more than that."

The bruise on the side of her head that she sustained when hitting the ground was a little sore, but nothing like it had been. Right after it happened, she couldn't even lay on that side. Now, it wasn't as painful, and it didn't hinder her sleep. The swelling had gone down, and besides the occasional headache, she honestly did feel like she was back to normal.

"So, you think Myles is avoiding you?" Journey asked as she strolled back into the living room, steam billowing from her mug.

"I know he is. I'm just not sure why." Geneva had started sharing her concern about Myles right before Arielle began dozing off. "Whenever I ask him what's wrong, he says 'nothing' or he'll say he has a lot on his mind. He says he's trying to find the person who tried to kill us."

"I'm sure he is, Gen. You didn't see him when he thought you weren't going to make it. You know how cool and calm he usually is. Not that night. There were a couple of moments I thought Kenton was going to have to restrain him. Especially when the doctors took so long to tell us anything about your condition."

That would've been interesting. Kenton was built like a Mack truck, but Myles wouldn't have conceded without a fight.

Geneva sighed, feeling awful that he'd had to go through that, especially after what happened to his mother and Whitney. Maybe that's what was going on. Perhaps he was afraid that he could've lost her, like he had lost them.

She recalled the conversation they'd had the day she learned about Collin. Myles kept his distance from people for fear of losing them. What if, in his twisted mind, he blamed himself for what happened the other night? At the hospital, he'd been afraid that he'd lose her...that she'd die.

"But I didn't die, and I'm fine," she said more to herself than to Journey. Which meant they should be able to just pick up where they left off before the shooting. "God, I wish he would just talk to me."

Journey laughed and shook her head. "Aren't you the one who once said that he didn't talk enough? You knew going into this relationship that he was reserved. Don't expect that to change."

But he has *changed,* Geneva thought.

He was talking and laughing more. Even though he was obsessed with finding out what happened to Whitney and trying to make sure Collin was adjusting to their new normal, Myles had been opening up more. No, he didn't jabber on and on the way she did, but at least he was expressing himself more.

"How's Collin doing?" Journey asked after taking a sip of her tea.

"He and Coco have been having a blast since we got here. They spend most of their time at the main house with London's youngest kids. I've missed my fur baby, but I'm glad I have her to share with Collin. Usually, when you see one of them, you see the other."

"I noticed. It's actually kind of cute. We're even thinking about getting a puppy for Arielle to grow up with."

"You could just have another baby," Geneva said, grinning. "I would love to have more nieces and nephews."

"Well, you better adopt some or marry Myles and have a few kids yourself."

Marry Myles.

That would be wild…and highly unlikely anytime soon. They were still navigating this thing called dating. But if she was honest with herself, she could see spending the rest of her life with him. He was everything she never knew she wanted…or needed. That was something he had said to her on the phone one night—that she was everything he didn't realize he wanted or needed.

"Myles has a go-bag," Geneva blurted. That fact had been on her mind for a few days, but more so since the shooting.

Journey's perfectly arched brows dipped into a frown. "A what?"

"A go-bag. A bag that has clothes, money, ID, and other stuff he might need if he had to leave town in a hurry. I saw it in his closet that night he found out that Whitney had actually been murdered. He dropped Collin and me off at his loft before going to her house to…to investigate, I guess."

"What? You snooped through his stuff? And how do you even know what a to-go bag is?"

"It's a go-bag, and I did not snoop. I ran across it when I was looking for something to sleep in. *And* I didn't go through the whole bag. Just the stuff on top. I saw this spy movie once, and the main character had a bag like it. It was for if he ever had to suddenly disappear."

"So, because Myles was a CIA agent, you think he has a get-out-of-town-quick bag in case he wants to disappear?"

"He used to be a spy, Journey. And you know the guys always tease him about moving around like a ghost. The man can disappear in a heartbeat. Now you see him, and then you don't. What if he disappears on me?"

"He won't. Besides, he has Collin to think about. He wouldn't leave all of us. We're his support system. He needs us...and he needs you."

Geneva wasn't so sure about that. Myles did whatever the hell he wanted to do. If he thought leaving would protect her or his family, he'd cut out at a moment's notice.

But I'll be right behind him. Ride or die, baby.

*

It was after midnight by the time Myles slipped quietly into the guest house. He half expected Coco to greet him at the door, but with Collin around, the dog couldn't care less about him and Geneva.

Myles smiled at the thought as it reminded him of the bond he had with his childhood dog, Pepper. He might've wanted his nice, simple, quiet life back, but at least his son was slowly getting adjusted to his new world.

In the meantime, Myles was still reeling. He was a single parent, dealing with the death of his best friend Whitney, and trying to come to terms with almost getting his woman killed. Kenton had told him he was looking at that last part all wrong, but that's how it felt. Had it not been for him, Geneva wouldn't have been at Whitney's house that night. She wouldn't have gotten shot at, and she wouldn't have ended up with a concussion. The morning after the incident, she'd told him that she was too resilient to be taken out by a bump on the head.

That was his woman. Always able to make light of the most serious of situations. He appreciated that about her, but that wasn't him.

Myles didn't bother turning on any lights as he moved down the hall that led to the bedrooms. There was just enough illumination from a couple of night-lights plugged into a few electrical outlets.

He quietly entered the room where Collin was sleeping. Coco lifted her head, and Myles wasn't surprised to see her on the bed. She knew she was supposed to be on the floor, but his son insisted the dog sleep with him.

"Come," Myles whispered, coaxing her off the bed. Once she was on the floor, he bent slightly and rubbed her behind the ears. "Hey, girl. You know you're not supposed to be on the bed, but thanks for looking out for li'l man."

Myles turned his head just in time, barely missing one of Coco's sloppy wet kisses across the mouth. Instead, she caught him on the chin, and Myles chuckled. He was crazy about the dog, and apparently, the feelings were mutual. He rubbed her a little longer before walking her to the doggy bed near the closet door.

When Myles returned to Collin, his heart thumped a little harder as he covered his son with the blanket. He never knew he could love another human being as much as he loved his child. Agreeing to be Whitney's sperm donor had been the best decision he had ever made. Myles couldn't imagine his life without Collin.

He stood there a few minutes longer, then bent down and kissed his son's forehead. He made sure the baby monitor was on before leaving the room. When he reached the bedroom he was sharing with Geneva, he stopped and leaned against the doorjamb.

The large space was dimly lit with a sliver of moonlight peeking between the slats of the blinds. Geneva's soft snores met his ears. She was a heavy sleeper, which worked to his advantage the last couple of days that he'd come in late.

He moved farther into the room, closing the door behind him. He hated that he had to put distance between him and Geneva, but he had no choice. Well, maybe he had a choice, but until he decided for sure what his next steps would be, he didn't want them to get any closer.

The fear of what happened the other day was mind-numbing. He couldn't go through that again. If he broke things off now, he wouldn't have to worry about his past touching Geneva.

He just didn't know if he could do it. He didn't know if he could walk away.

Myles moved over to the bed, wanting to kiss her or at least touch her. He did neither. Instead, he gazed down at the woman who had worked her way into his heart.

How the heck was he going to be able to let her go? To move on with his life without her in it?

He sighed and sat in the recliner next to the bed and remove his boots. The moment he laid his head back and closed his eyes, exhaustion set in. It felt good just to sit back and relax. Physically, that is. He just couldn't shut his brain down.

Wiz had called him earlier with an address. He'd finally been able to trace the signal from the listening devices. Myles, Kenton, and Parker took a ride to the Midtown area, only to find out that the address was of an apartment complex. The problem was, there were two buildings with over a hundred units. Myles had been able to obtain a list of all the tenants, but during his initial review of less than half, no names had seemed familiar to him.

He yawned and stretched his legs out in front of him. Tomorrow he planned to start digging into the life of every tenant on the list. He didn't care how long it took, but soon he'd find the coward who tried to kill them.

That was his last thought when sleep overtook him.

Chapter Twenty

Myles jerked his eyes open, and his gaze went immediately to the bed. He thought Geneva had been the one to wake him. Instead, it was his cell phone vibrating in his front pants pocket.

Standing and heading to the bedroom door, he dug the device out and saw Laz's name on the screen. His friend wouldn't call that time of night—or in this case, morning—if it wasn't important.

Maybe he has news.

Laz was the most resourceful person he knew. If anyone could get Myles answers, it was him.

"Yeah," Myles answered once he was in the hallway.

"I got something," Laz said by way of greeting. "Well, actually, I know someone who knows something, but he's only willing to talk to you."

"Who is it?"

"Can't tell you. Otherwise, you might not show up."

Myles frowned. "Show up where?"

"Supreme."

"So, let me get this right," Myles said as he strolled to the kitchen, suddenly thirsty. He grabbed a bottle of water from the refrigerator. "You found someone who might have a lead on the asshole who might be hunting Geneva or me, but you're not gonna give me a name? What type of bullshit is this?"

Laz chuckled. "It's straight up. These are his terms. Not sure what that's about, but I'd trust the information."

His specific words didn't go unnoticed. *I'd trust the information.* In this context, that was code for the info was probably solid, but he didn't necessarily trust the person. It also probably meant the person was nearby. Meaning they were already at Supreme's offices, since Laz was on duty tonight.

Egypt, under orders from Mason, had worked out a schedule that had at least a few security specialists at the office 24/7. People needing protection called on their services all times of the day or night, and the executive office wanted to make sure staffing was always covered.

"Whose idea was it to meet at Supreme?" Myles asked and took a huge swig of water.

"Mine. How fast can you get here?"

"Give me forty-five minutes," Myles said. He probably could've shaved ten or fifteen minutes off of the time, but he needed to get someone from his team to ride with him.

When Mason insisted that Myles, Geneva, and Collin stay on his property, he also said he didn't want Myles traveling around town alone.

It wasn't about control or favoritism. Mason would do that for any one of his people. Atlanta's Finest was more than just a team of security specialists. They were family. Myles had witnessed over and over how everyone looked out for each other, which was why he had joined Supreme full-time a few years ago.

Like most of the people he worked with, he started off doing a few jobs here and there for the company. It was a chance for Mason to see how he operated and an opportunity for Myles to determine what type of company Supreme really was. Signing on full-time had been one of his best decisions, and that was proven every day that he was employed.

"I'll see you in a few."

*

Myles rode in the back seat of one of Supreme Security's SUVs. He hated leaving Geneva and Collin at the house in the middle of the night, even if they weren't alone. There were security specialists posted at both entrances of the guest house, and the property was secure. Yet, Myles worried about the two most important people in his life.

He shook his head as he stared out into the night. How had he let this happen? What had he been thinking by allowing Geneva into his solitary life?

"So, who's the person you're meeting with?" Angelo asked from the driver's seat.

Angelo González, one of Myles's best friends, had been on an assignment for the past couple of weeks. Myles hadn't seen him and hadn't known that he was on duty tonight. Not until Kenton told him that he and Angelo was Myles's shadow until further notice. According to them, Mason wanted at least two people with Myles at all times, and he wanted him to be treated like a client.

Myles was used to operating alone. He didn't like drawing attention to himself, and he definitely didn't want any special treatment. They all were coworkers and friends, and that's how he wanted to be treated.

"Laz didn't say," he finally answered. "I'm assuming it's one of his old CIs."

When Laz was a detective with the Atlanta Police Department, he'd had quite the reputation. He was one of the best in his field, always solving his cases and catching the perp. From what Myles had heard, some of his friend's methods had been questionable. Considering some of his assignments with the CIA, Myles would be the last person to judge anyone on how they got their job done.

Angelo turned onto the dark street in Midtown where Supreme was located. The huge converted warehouse was nondescript and took up most of the block. He drove around to the back of the building, where the employees parked. As he pulled up to the ten-foot-tall security fence, the heavy gate eased opened for them to enter.

"Just let me out at the door," Myles said as he unfastened his seatbelt. Angelo did, but before Myles could open the back door, Kenton had it open.

Myles glared at him, not missing the way the big man's lips twitched. They knew Myles hated the extra attention.

"Don't even think about walking me inside," Myles grumbled and shoved past him.

"No need. Parker and Laz will be shadowing you while you're inside. Just holler when you're ready to head home," Kenton said, closing the back door and climbing back in the passenger seat.

Myles was still grumbling when he entered his security code. After he placed his thumb on the clear panel, an extra security measure, the door unlocked. He strolled into the building, and sure enough, Parker was right there.

"How's it going, man?" Parker asked and fell in step with Myles.

"I'd be doing better if I didn't have you knuckleheads following me everywhere I go."

Parker chuckled. "It's for your own good."

"I'm perfectly safe here. Go back and do whatever it is you were doing, but first, where's Laz?"

"Conference room B," Parker said of one of the smaller meeting rooms.

Myles headed down the long hallway toward the front of the building, the soft soles of his Timberlands quiet against the travertine floor. He stopped at the second door on the right and walked in, but froze when he saw the person sitting at the long conference table.

"What the hell is he doing here?" he growled, his gaze shifting from Reuben to Laz.

Laz was leaning against the wall with his arms folded across his chest. He looked as if he didn't have a care in the world, but Myles knew better. His friend might appear cool and disinterested, but the former detective was always alert, ready for anything that might happen. Across from him, sitting at the long table, Reuben appeared just as uninterested.

"What's going on here?" Myles asked Laz and didn't bother addressing Reuben.

Laz pushed away from the wall. "I knew you wouldn't show up or listen if I told you who the source was." He pulled out the chair in front of him. "Hear the guy out."

Myles remained near the door. "Why? Why the heck should I listen to anything he has to say? It's not like I'm going to believe him."

"Fine by me. I'm out." Reuben stood but stopped when Laz lifted a hand.

"You're going to want to hear what he has to say."

Myles huffed out a breath. Laz had never steered him wrong, and if he believed the guy, that meant Myles would, too. He just didn't like it.

He strolled to the table. Reuben reclaimed his seat, and Laz dropped down in the chair that he had pulled out. Myles sat next to him, which put him directly across from Reuben.

"What was so important that you're here in the middle of the night insisting we meet in person?" Myles asked.

Reuben tapped his fingers against the mahogany table, then frowned. "If it weren't for Geneva, my ass wouldn't be here trying to give you a heads-up."

Myles stiffened, and his anger simmered just below the surface at the mention of Geneva. Usually, he didn't get riled that quickly, but he wasn't his usual self when it came to her. It didn't help that he knew Reuben had a thing for her, something the man hadn't kept a secret. It was in his eyes each time he looked at her, and that just pissed Myles off even more.

"Don't let her name come out of your mouth when I'm around," he said, his tone deadly. "You either tell me what this is all about, or I'm out."

"Fine. Go. I don't give a damn about you. I'm only here because I don't want her to get killed while someone is hunting for you. You know what?" He stood suddenly, practically knocking the chair over. "Maybe I should just keep the information to myself."

"Dammit, Reuben. Sit your ass down and tell him," Laz snapped.

Reuben dropped back into the chair. "Word on the street is that you pissed the wrong person off."

"Who? Just tell me who."

"Some military dude out for revenge. He's the one that shot up your car and tried to kill you and Gen." He glared at Myles as if he wanted to rip his heart out. "She could've died. You try to act all big and bad. Yet, *my girl* got hurt on your watch. Just know, if she'd been with me, she wouldn't have gotten a scratch on her, and the son of a bitch who ran you guys down would be dead."

Myles tried to remain calm. On the outside, he might've looked as if he was in control, but on the inside, that anger from earlier was veering into rage territory. He hated this man. The reasons were many, but hearing him call Geneva *his girl* had Myles seeing red.

It didn't help that Reuben had hit a nerve. Myles should've protected her better. He shouldn't have let her out of his sight in the first place. But the fact that Reuben thought he could take care of her better than he did made Myles want to strangle him. Even if he decided to leave town...leave Geneva, he'd be damned if she ended up with this asshole.

Laz bumped his leg, bringing Myles back to the conversation at hand.

"Does this military guy have a name?" Myles asked, trying to control the frustration in his voice. Was Reuben setting him up? Or was he really doing this to help protect Geneva?

"Cyrus. His name is Cyrus, but I don't have a last name. All I know is he's taking out people who know you, and he started with that CIA lady. You know the one. Your baby's momma."

Myles stilled. His pulse amped up as unease clawed through his veins. Nothing about Whitney was in the news, nor was it public knowledge. And there sure as hell wasn't anything out there about Collin. At least that's what Myles thought. They'd been so careful at shielding him.

Apparently, not careful enough.

Reuben chuckled and leaned back in his seat with his arms folded across his chest. "Don't look so surprised. I know people. My reach is long and wide, and when you started hanging with Gen, I had you checked out. Don't worry, though. Your secrets are safe with me, at least most of them."

Myles lunged out of his seat and slid across the table with such force, he knocked Reuben out of his seat. Myles's hands were around his neck when they thudded to the floor. If the former gangbanger's wide eyes were any indication, Myles had totally caught him off guard.

"Dammit, Myles! Let him go," Laz ground out as he tried pulling Myles off of the man.

"If you ever come near my family, and that includes Geneva, I will kill you with my bare hands," he snarled in a low, threatening tone and tightened his grip. Reuben clawed at Myles's hands, then went for his face, but Myles dodged his jab.

"Let him go!" Laz roared.

The conference room door flew open, and Myles heard Parker curse before he felt several hands on him. He gave the man's neck one more squeeze before releasing him.

Myles backed away and cringed as his shoulder wound throbbed like it had a damn heartbeat. Yet, the pain was no comparison to the anger roaring inside of him. He hated this man more than he hated anyone, and it was taking all of his restraint not to go after him again.

Coughing and gagging, Reuben stumbled to his feet with his hand on his throat. His watery eyes glared at Myles. "You know what?" he wheezed. "I was trying to help your crazy ass because of Geneva, but I hope the guy blows your brains out.

191

Know why? Because when you're gone, Gen will be all mine, and you better believe that I'm going to tap that—"

"Enough!" Laz roared and got in the man's face. "Let's go. You're out of here." Laz shoved him toward the door

"All right. Okay. I'm going," Reuben said and glanced over his shoulder at Myles. "Watch your back, CIA man. Watch your back."

When they left the room, Myles gently rubbed his shoulder, trying to work out the ache without touching the wound. He reclaimed his seat at the conference table while his mind raced frantically, going over and over all that Reuben had said.

It was already disturbing knowing there was some guy out there, possibly named Cyrus, who could've been responsible for Whitney's death and the shooting. But what bothered Myles just as much was how much Reuben knew about his personal life. He didn't give a damn how long the man's reach was in that city. He didn't like anyone knowing his business unless he shared it himself.

Laz sauntered back into the conference room, carrying two cups of coffee. He set one of the mugs in front of Myles, then took the seat that Reuben had vacated.

"I figured you'd probably want all of your brain cells intact and wouldn't want alcohol. So, I opted for coffee instead."

"Thanks." Myles brought the large mug to his mouth and took a careful sip of the steaming brew. He studied his friend across the table before asking, "How did Reuben know so much about me?"

"I have no idea, but like he said, dude is well connected. The gang he used to be a member of—"

"*Used to be?*" Myles ground out, getting pissed all over again. "You're telling me that you don't think that bastard is still running with the Devils?"

Laz sighed heavily. "As far as I know, he's no longer affiliated with them, but some of his boys are still part of the crew. Minauros Devils operate more like organized crime than just a neighborhood gang. Not only are they one of the most dangerous gangs in the city, but they have their hands in a little bit of everything. It's possible he got his information from them."

"How'd you and Reuben hook up today? Did he come to you, or did you go to him?"

Laz took a long time to respond. So long, in fact, Myles thought he wouldn't answer the questions.

His friend huffed out a long breath before saying, "Reuben used to be one of my informants...off the books. He helped me with a lot of cases, and after he got out of the joint, I kept up with him."

Myles wouldn't be surprised if Laz were the reason Reuben was still alive. Loyalty was big for gang members. If the Devils knew one of their own was a snitch, they would've handled Reuben. Whether behind bars or on the street, they would've killed him and then fed him to the sharks years ago.

"You think he's reformed?" Myles asked.

"I think he wants to be, but that life is not easy to walk away from."

"Damn. What's this world coming to?" Myles asked. "A gang member who is also a CI, and his ass is a snitch. That's a dangerous combination."

"Yeah, maybe." Laz slouched in his seat and put his hands behind his head. "Let's talk about this Cyrus dude. Does the name ring a bell? Any idea who he might be?"

"No clue. I'm not even sure I believe Reuben. For all we know, he could've been the one shooting at us that night."

"He wasn't," Laz said confidently. "He knows Geneva is family, and he knows what I would do to him if he even acted like he wanted to hurt her. Like I said before, I trust the information. If he says the man's name is Cyrus, then I believe him."

Myles didn't speak for a long time. He brought the coffee mug up to his mouth and glanced over the rim of it at Laz. Most of the guys at Supreme Security had a story. Most had been through crap that they preferred not to discuss, especially Laz. The man was complex and dangerous, but what he lacked in morals, he made up for in loyalty.

"If Reuben's right about the man—this Cyrus—we should be able to cross-reference his name with the list of tenant names we received earlier."

"Yeah, but that's going to take forever."

Myles felt a burst of renewed energy. "Well, I guess we should get started."

Chapter Twenty-One

Geneva ignored the warmth from the sun peeking through the blinds and heating her face. She also tried to block out the smell of breakfast food, specifically bacon, that teased her nostrils. Instead, she nestled deeper into the most comfortable pillow she'd ever laid on. That is until she opened her eyes and realized she had an audience.

Collin and Coco were sitting on Myles's side of the bed, staring at her.

What the heck?

Geneva lifted her head slightly and squinted at them. Collin looked as if he'd been up for hours. With his face washed and hair brushed, he was dressed in a football jersey and blue jeans. She must've been more tired than she realized. She hadn't even heard them enter the room, let alone climb onto the bed.

Her attention went to her fur baby. "Down, Coco," she said groggily, feeling as if she could use a couple of more hours of sleep. "You know you're not supposed to be on the bed. Get down. *Now.*"

The dog whimpered, then scooted closer, snuggling up to her while giving her those puppy-dog eyes, the ones she couldn't resist. The damn dog had too much sense. Sometimes she wondered if the animal wasn't part human.

Geneva couldn't help putting her arm around Coco and scratching behind her puppy's ear. "You're not slick. You know you're not supposed to be on the bed."

"She don't want to lay on the floor," Collin said, gently rubbing Coco's back. "Right, girl? You want to sleep with me, right?"

Geneva smiled and almost laughed at the inflection in his voice. He sounded so much like her and Myles, imitating the way they spoke to Coco. That reminded Geneva that she was going to have to watch her language around him.

The dog barked and nudged Collin's chin as if agreeing with him.

"Oh, so that's how it is? You guys are ganging up on me, huh?"

Collin's face scrunched in confusion, and he tilted his head as if trying to figure out what she was talking about. Before he could respond, Myles strolled into the room.

God, the man was a sight for tired eyes. Dressed in a black T-shirt that stretched across his taut muscles and jeans that hung low on his hips, he looked good enough to eat.

Or at least kiss. Or both.

"What are you two doing in here?" he asked, strolling further into the room. "Collin, I told you to let Gen sleep."

"I did," Collin defended and scooted to the edge of the bed, then turned onto his stomach and climbed down. "She opened her eyes by herself."

This time, Geneva did laugh. Over the last few weeks with Myles and Collin, her life felt more fulfilled than it ever had. Having a family hadn't been at the forefront of her mind, though she hadn't ruled it out. Now she couldn't stop thinking about it, especially if it included them.

"Can we go over to Miracle's house?" Collin asked, giving Myles the same look that Coco had just given Geneva.

Unbelievable. She wasn't sure who was teaching who when it came to those two.

"That's why I came in here." Myles ruffled his son's short, curly hair. "Aunt Carolyn called to see if you wanted to come over and make cookies with the other kids."

Cookies, Geneva thought. What time was it? She glanced at the clock on the nightstand, surprised to see that it was after twelve. And God bless Aunt Carolyn. She was a master at keeping the kids entertained and busy.

"Yay!" Collin cheered and ran to the bedroom door with Coco trotting behind him.

"Wait. You can't leave here without me," Myles said as he moved closer to Geneva's side of the bed. "Get your jacket and Coco's leash and meet me by the front door."

When Collin left the room, Myles sat on the edge of the bed. "Hey, baby." He brushed a feathery kiss across her lips.

"Hi yourself," she said, searching his eyes. Since he wasn't a big talker, that was how she gauged his mood. Right now, though, she wasn't sure what that was.

"How do you feel?" he asked.

A slow, wicked smile spread across her mouth. "Horny. You want to help me with that?"

Myles grinned, probably remembering the last time she'd said that to him. "I'm starting to think you only want me for my body," he joked.

"And you would be right." She laughed before turning serious. "I've missed you. I've missed us."

His steady gaze bore into her, and Geneva couldn't decipher his expression. But the gentleness in the way he caressed her cheek with the pad of his thumb almost had her whimpering.

"I've missed you, too," he finally said. "More than you know."

After a short hesitation, Myles lowered his head and covered her mouth. His large hands cupped her face and when his tongue parted her lips, Geneva's pulse quickened. The kiss started tenderly but soon stoked the fire inside of her that had been smoldering during his absence.

Myles's hand slid behind her neck and pulled her even closer, deepening the lip-lock. Suddenly, the kiss turned more demanding. Geneva succumbed to the domination of his lips, loving when he reminded her of his alpha side.

She wanted to be wrong, thinking he'd been avoiding her, but the way he kissed her, there was something akin to desperation in every lap of his tongue. Like it might be the last time. Like he was saying goodbye.

Women had a sixth sense about some things, and Geneva was no exception. Something was going on with him. More than just hunting a killer. Was he getting ready to break her heart? Was this the calm before the storm of him walking out of her life? Or maybe she was overthinking everything.

All she knew for sure was that she had fallen in love with him. And whether he admitted it or not, Geneva had a feeling Myles felt the same about her.

She couldn't bear the thought of losing him. Not now. Not ever.

"Daddy, we're ready," Collin's high-pitched voice carried into the bedroom.

Geneva smiled against Myles's lips. "You've been summoned," she said, giving him another lingering kiss before they pulled apart. "While you're walking them to the main house, I'll freshen up and get dressed."

Myles leaned back slightly. With his fingertip, he brushed her hair away from her face. The concern in his eyes couldn't be missed.

"You sure you don't want to stay in bed a little longer? You still look a little tired."

A slow grin spread across Geneva's mouth. "Is that code for *I want you to stay in bed until I get back so that I can have my way with you?*"

Myles chuckled and stood. "I'm convinced. You have a one-track mind. Relax, I'll be back in a minute."

He left the room, and Geneva debated her next move. They needed to talk. She knew that. Yet, if she was honest with herself, that was the last thing she wanted to do.

Sighing, she climbed out of bed and padded to the attached bathroom.

If he's thinking about leaving, I'm not letting him go without a fight.

*

After brunch, Myles stayed in the kitchen longer than necessary. He had already loaded the dishwasher and wiped everything down, but he wasn't ready for the conversation he needed to have with Geneva. He was still thinking that it was time for him to move on…time for them to go their separate ways.

They had talked during breakfast. Not about their relationship, but about anything and everything else. Even with the distance he'd tried to put between them, they still clicked. Conversation flowed effortlessly, and being with her felt natural. Like they were right where they were supposed to be. Together. That realization only made his decision harder.

Myles was still trying to convince himself that he was doing the right thing—breaking up with her before they got in too deep. He never should've gotten involved with her in the first place. Then she wouldn't have gotten hurt the other night. If he was right about Whitney's death, the shooting, and this Cyrus guy connecting to Myles's days in the CIA, he knew he and Geneva couldn't be together. That would be proof that unknown enemies or enemies of his past could get to him and those he loved. It was bad enough his son's life might always be in danger, but that didn't have to be the case for Geneva.

That was his reason for needing to leave, needing to walk away from what they were building together. It made perfect sense in his head, but Myles couldn't get his heart to cooperate. He didn't want to let her go, but he couldn't risk putting her life in any more danger.

But then there was Reuben. If Myles walked away from Geneva, that asshole would be right there, ready to step in and take his place. Myles knew it was selfish of him, but he didn't want her with any other man, especially Reuben.

Thinking about the guy had Myles rotating his shoulder. It didn't hurt the way it had the night before after his encounter with Reuben, but this morning the area around the wound ached.

It was interesting how he hadn't thought about his injury while having breakfast with Geneva. She had a way about her that made him tune out everything but her.

Damn. I have to stop thinking about how much she means to me and focus on catching a killer.

Myles yawned and poured two cups of coffee, one for Geneva and one for him, which would be his third for the day. Last night, he and Laz went through most of the tenant names from the apartment complex where he wanted to believe Cyrus lived. So far, there were no matches, and Wiz still couldn't narrow down a specific unit number.

Myles was trying to stay optimistic. Due to the late hour, he'd had to knock off and head back to the guest house. He wanted to make sure he was home before Geneva and Collin woke up. confident that they'd get it before the day was over. He wasn't sure how yet, but once they did, they'd pay the man a visit.

Myles carried the coffee into the living room. Geneva was curled up at one end of the sofa watching a sitcom.

"One sugar and a dash of cream," he said, handing her the large mug before sitting next to her.

She graced him with the sweetest smile, and Myles's heart banged against his chest. The woman was irresistible, and being near her had a way of screwing with his head…and his heart.

"I'm so stuffed, I don't even know if I can drink my coffee. I still can't believe you know how to make crepes. They were amazing. Is there anything you can't do?"

Myles wanted to laugh at that, but the weight of what they needed to discuss was heavy on his heart. He set down his coffee.

There was one thing he knew he couldn't do, and that was to be the man she deserved. A man who could offer her a long, safe life. Not one where she might end up dodging bullets again.

"We're alone. What should we do with ourselves?" Geneva asked. She placed her coffee mug on the end table and snuggled closer to him.

On reflex, Myles put his arm around her and pulled her against his side. She rested her head on his chest as if it was the most natural thing to do.

"You've been more reserved than usual all morning. What's going on? Where were you last night?" she asked.

"I went to Supreme for a little while."

"Why? I thought you took time off of work."

Myles didn't respond right away, debating on what to tell her. No way in hell was he discussing the visit from Reuben. Maybe if he didn't mention the guy, she'd forget he even existed. One could only hope.

"I was following up on a possible lead into the shooting, but… Gen, we need to talk," he finally said.

Removing his arm from around her, Myles leaned forward and propped his elbows on his thighs. He wasn't sure where to start.

*

Geneva didn't miss the way his back stiffened or how he ran his hands down his face. Whatever was bothering him was weighing heavy. When he closed his eyes and pinched the bridge of his nose, she rubbed his back, hoping to offer some comfort.

Either he was suffering from a very bad headache, or what he wanted to talk was something he really didn't want to discuss. It was safe to guess that it was the second one.

For a change, Geneva kept her mouth shut. She wanted him to work out whatever battle was going on inside his mind, and she was trying something new. Patience. The only thing was, she wasn't sure how long it would last.

After leaving the hospital, Myles had catered to her every need. The first night in the guest house, he hadn't left her side. That was when she had noticed that the cool, calm, and collected man she'd grown to love had disappeared. In his place was a man who'd wore concern…or maybe it was fear on his face each time he looked at her.

Geneva didn't know how to help ease his worries. Sure, she'd been terrified when he tackled her to the ground, and even more so when she realized she was in an ambulance. Yet, she couldn't let those moments define how she spent the rest of her life. She refused to walk in fear. Now, if only she could get him to come to that same realization.

She sat forward, imitating his stance by placing her elbows on her thighs. Then she glanced at him. "What do you want to talk about?"

There was a long hesitation, and she wasn't sure he was going to respond until he said, "I don't think this is going to work. You and me."

Geneva wasn't completely surprised by his words, but they still stung. Her relationships with the opposite sex never lasted for long. But what she and Myles had was different. Different enough to where she had no intention of giving up easily.

"Once we catch this bastard," Myles continued, a bite to his words, "I'm taking Collin, and we're going away for a while."

"To where?" she asked, anxiousness suddenly swirling inside of her.

Geneva would fight to keep what they had, but like she told Journey, Myles had the ability to disappear. It probably wouldn't be as easy to fall off the grid with Collin. But if anyone could do it, it was Myles. She wouldn't put it past him to cut out in the middle of the night without a word.

Anger swelled inside of her. She bolted out of her seat and began pacing in front of the living room table. "Let's get something clear right now. I'm not letting you go."

"Geneva…"

She stopped abruptly and sat on the table directly in front of him. "You can't make me fall in love with your ass, then cut out!" she snapped and jabbed a finger at him. "You don't get to crash into my life, turn it upside down, then just…just disappear. No, that is *not* how this works!"

Myles released a long sigh and brushed his hand over his mouth and down his chin, something he often did when he had a lot on his mind. It was the weariness in his dark eyes that had her tapping down her anger. Seeing him like this was like a gut punch, followed by a slap. She didn't know how to reach him. She didn't know how to shake some sense into him.

"Myles, I get that the other night knocked you off your game. I really do get that, but you can't let the fear of losing me or anyone send you running to God knows where."

Geneva knew this sudden desire for him to cut out wasn't just about her. It was everything. Losing Whitney. Becoming a single father. Learning that his baby's momma had been murdered. And then the shooting. All within a couple of weeks.

Add that to the fact his mother died when he was a child, and he put up a barrier to protect his heart—a barrier to protect him from experiencing that type of pain again. Yet, the moment he opened his heart and let people get close, it happened all over again.

"Babe, I almost lost you," he said quietly, emotion muffling his words. "I never would've forgiven myself if you had… If you had died, it would've *killed* me."

"But I didn't die, Myles. I'm right here, and I'm mad as hell. I can't believe you're trying to break up with me."

A flicker of regret lit his eyes, but he didn't say anything.

"You tried that shit before, remember?" Geneva continued. "Remember how you kicked me to the curb before you left for California? How'd that feel, huh? You missed me. You knew almost immediately that I had gotten to you. That I had penetrated that steel cage around your heart."

She was trying to lighten the moment, but tears pricked her eyes. All of what she had just said might've been true about him, but she'd felt the same, too. Never had she been with a man who she thought about all day and night. She had finally found someone who made her want to be a better person. Someone who made her feel alive and desired, and not just for her body. Myles liked her for her, no matter how crazy she acted sometimes. He understood her.

Now he was trying to ruin everything.

Geneva blinked away the moisture pooling in her eyes and wasn't surprised that Myles still hadn't spoken. But she could see his guard going down a little. He was a thinker. Sometimes he'd get inside his head and be able to tune everything and everybody out.

The last time when he gave her that BS speech about how they needed to take a break from each other, she hadn't been ready. He had caught her off guard.

This time, though, she was fighting for what she wanted.

"Besides all of that, you and Collin need me," she continued, getting a little ticked that she had to explain any of this to him. "Just because things get hard or scary, you can't just disappear. Relationships don't work like that, Myles. You have to put in the work. Take the good with the bad, the scary with the sane."

Still, he remained quiet. He just looked at her with those gorgeous dark, intense eyes that stirred something desperate inside of her. She couldn't let him leave. Not because she was stubborn, but because she couldn't allow him to walk away from what they had.

But what else can I say?

Frustration spun inside of her, and some of the fight seeped out of her pores. She moved from the table and sat on the sofa.

"I know I can't make you stay," she murmured, then laid her head back and stared at the wall that held the flat-screen TV. "But while you're making your decision," she continued, "I want you to know something."

The rest of her words stuck in her throat. She wasn't used to making herself vulnerable for anyone...not even Myles.

Maybe she'd said enough. Maybe it was time to just cut her losses.

"What else do you want me to know?" Myles asked.

Geneva's eyes snapped to him.

So caught up in her musings, she hadn't realized he had scooted back on the sofa, their shoulders a few inches apart. It always amazed her how he moved so quietly through the house. Whatever skill that was, it also worked in tight spaces. She hadn't felt him move at all, and they were sharing the same sofa.

Turning her head more, she met his gaze, and the overwhelming feeling of love churning inside of her was almost suffocating.

She loved this man. She was crazy in love with him, and it didn't freak her out.

"What else do you want me to know?" Myles asked again. His tone was lighter, and the tension that had been palpable when they first started talking had eased.

Geneva licked her suddenly dry lips and maintained eye contact. "I *need* you," she said quietly and cleared her throat. "I need you and Collin as much as you guys need me. So, while you're thinking about your next move, remember that."

Geneva huffed out a breath and diverted her gaze as she swiped at her eyes. This was so not like her. What the heck? She didn't get all mushy, weepy, and sentimental. For one, it was too exhausting. Secondly, it didn't feel natural. It wasn't her.

Geneva sat up straighter and turned fully to Myles, pissed that he had her acting out of character. "You can leave if you want to," she snapped, and that fire from earlier was back inside of her. Pointing her finger at him, she glared at him. "But just so you know, I will find you. The way you're hunting down the son of a bitch who shot at us, that's exactly the way I'm going to hunt your ass down! And you better believe that when I find you, I'm going to make you sorry you ever left me."

The silence in the room was as thick as a cinderblock when suddenly Myles burst out laughing. It wasn't one of those *ha ha ha, you're funny* laughs. No, it was a full-on, body-shaking, tears-streaming-down-his-cheeks laugh.

Geneva's heart thumped a little harder and faster. All she could do was stare at him. There was no way he could laugh like that and still be considering leaving. At least she hoped. Maybe she had finally gotten through to him.

"You laugh, but I'm serious," she added.

He started up again, and she let him. Hearing his laughter was like a healing balm for her tattered nerves. If nothing else came of the conversation, at least he knew how she felt about him and their relationship.

Myles wiped at his eyes and shook his head. "We haven't even known each other all that long, and I can't imagine my life without you in it. Your cursing problem and all." He reached over and cupped her cheek, and Geneva leaned into his touch. "But damn...I love you. God, I love you," he said softly.

Geneva's heart stuttered. No man, except for her father, had ever spoken those words to her...and she wasn't sure how to act. Part of her wanted to climb into his lap and kiss him senseless, while the other part of her wanted to leap into the air and do a fist pump.

He loves me. The words played around in her head on loop. *He loves me.*

Myles pulled her to his side and kissed the top of her head, then sighed heavily. "What am I going to do with you?" he mumbled against her hair and wrapped both arms around her and held her close.

"Well...I can think of a few things," Geneva said, unable to help herself.

A chuckle rumbled inside of his chest against her ear, and Geneva smiled. She hadn't been kidding when she said they needed each other. No matter how different they were, they completed one another.

She settled into the comforts of his embrace and savored the moment of peace. This was what she'd been missing the last few days—them alone together, enjoying each other's company.

But that wasn't all she'd missed.

She pulled out of his hold and straddled his lap. Leaning her forehead against his, she said, "For the record. I love you, too, and you're stuck with me."

Myles smiled. "Yeah, I'm starting to get that. I guess I'll just have to deal with it."

"Yeah, I guess you will."

When his lips touched hers, Geneva could've sworn she heard angels singing. She molded against him, relishing the sweetness of his kiss. But as their lip-lock grew more intense, Geneva fumbled with his belt buckle. Arguing with him always turned her on, and she had a few ideas on how she wanted them to make up.

Myles pulled his mouth from hers and brushed her hands away from his belt. "Nope, we're not doing that here. I want you on a flat surface and before you suggest it, not here on the sofa or the kitchen counter."

All she could do was laugh and think about him saying something similar the last time they had bathroom sex.

"Hold on." When he stood with her in his arms, she tightened her arms and legs around him as he carried her down the short hallway.

"I'm glad we came to an understanding," she said just as they entered the bedroom.

Now she planned to show him what else he would be missing if he disappeared.

Chapter Twenty-Two

Myles carried Geneva into the bedroom, wondering what he'd done to deserve her. He'd wanted to shield her from his past life, from anything that could hurt her. Instead, he almost pushed away the only person to have worked her way into the deepest crevices of his heart.

Yeah, he might fear that his CIA life could come back and haunt him, but more than anything, he was afraid of losing her. They might've been still getting to know each other, but Myles knew enough. He knew he wanted Geneva in his life for the foreseeable future.

Laying her on the bed, he stared down at the woman who had dared him to walk out of her life. She was the toughest woman he knew and he was a fool ever to think he could've moved on with life without her.

"Stop thinking and make love to me," she said, cutting into his thoughts.

Myles smiled. *Yep, toughest woman I know.*

While he quickly got undressed, she started wiggling out of her clothes. Within seconds, she had stripped down to her red bra and skimpy panties. The smoldering flame in her eyes grew hotter and had his heart beating a little faster.

Especially when she tossed the bra to the floor.

"Damn, girl. That body, though."

"Funny, I was just thinking the same about you."

Her bold and heated gaze traveled down the length of him, making him even harder if that was possible. There was nothing shy about his woman. She was quick to tell him what she wanted or what she didn't want, but there was no mistaking that, at that moment, she wanted him.

He opened the nightstand drawer and set a couple of condoms on top of it before climbing on the bed next to her.

"I'm planning to love on this enticing body of yours until you scream my name."

She pulled his face closer. "And with your persuasive lips and powerful hands, I have a feeling that won't take long."

When their lips touched, Geneva kissed him with an intensity that had Myles's head spinning. The way their tongues tangled and their moans filled the quietness of the room while their bodies were hugged up together, it was like taking a stroll through paradise.

Myles would never get enough of her. How the heck had he thought he could walk away from this fearless woman? For days he had tortured himself with worst-case scenarios. He failed to acknowledge that Geneva wasn't like most women. She knew how to handle herself. She didn't cower when things got scary or tough. Yes, he would always worry about her safety, but together they'd be able to get through anything.

Myles eased his mouth from hers and lifted slightly onto his elbow to admire her beautiful curves. He glided his hand down the center of her toned body, loving the way she squirmed beneath his touch.

His pulse galloped as his hand went lower. Soft, smooth skin beneath his palm was like silk as he slid his hand between her legs. Geneva arched her back and moaned with pleasure. The sound revved his heart as he found the apex between her thighs.

Capturing her mouth again, Myles kissed her passionately as he found the entrance to her core. When he slid a finger into her sweet heat, she was wet and hot, just the way he liked.

"Oh...yes," she whimpered against his lips, digging her nails into his bare back.

She humped his hand with each thrust of his finger and almost leaped off the bed when he added another. She ripped her mouth from his, breathing hard as he increased his speed, going deeper and faster.

Hearing her erotic moans and watching the way her hips lifted up and down had his body tightening with need. She was close. Her interior muscles tightened around his fingers as she moved uncontrollably, bucking against his hand.

"Come for me, baby," he crooned.

"Myles!" she screamed. Her body thrashed against the mattress as she kept calling out his name before shattering around his hand. "Oh, my God," she panted, her chest heaving. "That was...man, amazing."

"And just think. I'm not even done with you yet."

*

Geneva was still trying to catch her breath as Myles peppered tantalizing kisses over her heated body. She was riding high after that intense orgasm, and it was as if she'd been transported to someplace out of this world.

"God, you smell good," he said as he worked his way back up her body, licking, sucking, kissing.

Goosebumps skittered across her skin when his large hands cupped her breasts and squeezed them together. He gently captured a nipple between his teeth and sucked. The man definitely knew how to make her come undone. The way he swirled his tongue around the hardened peak, teasing her mercilessly, had her breaths coming hard and fast.

Geneva squirmed beneath him, squeezing her legs together to tap down the deliciously throbbing pulse between her thighs. But when he paid the same homage to the other breast, electric shock waves touched every nerve in her body. If he kept up the sweet torture, she was going to lose it.

Twisting slightly, she reached between their bodies and slid her hand over his six-pack abs and down to his engorged shaft. The man was huge.

He released her nipple and sucked in a breath. "Babe," he said, shifting onto his side.

Geneva didn't let up. She glided her hands up and down his thick length, caressing him and loving how worked up she was getting him. He moved against her hand as she increased the pressure. Stroking. Squeezing. Picking up speed. A deep groan rumbled inside of his chest when her thumb brushed over the tip of his penis.

Cursing under his breath, Myles covered her hand with his to stop her. "Keep that up and you're going to make me lose control, and I'm not letting that happen. At least not until I'm buried deep inside of you."

He eased out of her grasp and reached over to grab a condom. Geneva watched in pleasure as he quickly sheathed himself. The desire pumping through her body was at an all-time high when he nudged her thighs apart and settled between her legs.

Myles captured her lips again. His demanding kiss matched the erratic beat of her heart as he slid into her core, filling her to the hilt. Geneva's pulse thumped a little faster. He felt so good...and thick...and hard. She would never get enough of him. And the way he pumped his hips, driving into her with smooth, even strokes, had her about ready to lose her mind.

Her eyes slid closed as the enticing pressure building inside of her intensified. With her hands gripping his butt, she held on, matching him stroke for stroke as he thrust in and out of her. The harder he pumped, the deeper he went, and an erotic force swirled inside of her, stirring a passion that was threatening to erupt.

"M—Myles," she whispered as he increased the pace. His thrusts were faster and rougher as he pushed her closer to her release, and she struggled to hang on. Within the next heartbeat, Myles hit that spot, the one that practically had her jackknifing off the bed and hurling her beyond the point of control. Geneva screamed her release as her body shook, and she shattered into a million pieces.

Myles's moves grew more intense. Frantic. Powerful. Out of control. He was rocking her body with such force, the bed was shaking and the headboard banged against the wall.

"Gen..." he ground out, and his body bucked and jerked, then stiffened seconds before he growled his release. He collapsed on top of her, panting loudly against her ear. When he rolled onto his side, he took her with him.

They held onto each other. Hearts pounding. Breaths mingling. It didn't matter how many times they came together, each time got better than the last.

Geneva kept her arm across his waist and placed her leg over his hip, holding him in place. "You still thinking about leaving?"

Myles chuckled, and the hearty sound warmed her spirit. "Nope. Not in this lifetime."

Chapter Twenty-Three

Myles had finally tracked down the apartment number for Cyrus—Cyrus Ferguson, to be exact—but he had a feeling that wasn't the man's real name. Probably because if it were Myles, he would've been using an alias, especially if he was gunning for someone.

"Going in there alone is a bad idea," Laz said. "Even if Angelo and I haven't seen this guy leave or return in the past six hours, it doesn't mean he's not somewhere in the building."

Myles was a little surprised by Laz's concern, considering all the chances his friend usually took. But he appreciated his willingness to be there in the first place. Breaking and entering wasn't something they usually did, but Myles had been prepared to go it alone if he had to.

However, that's not how it worked with Atlanta's Finest. They were a team...family. They stuck together, good or bad, and the team members were always there if they needed each other.

Myles stared out the tinted window of the SUV that they were sitting in. The six-story brick apartment building had three entrances, and they were positioned in the back row of the huge parking lot, where they could easily see two of the doors. Angelo was stationed at the back entrance closest to the apartment unit Myles wanted to enter.

Whether Cyrus was in there or not, Myles was going in. When this all started, he was hell-bent on killing the man who took Whitney's life, but he had since changed his tune. He needed to keep his head on straight. He had a child to raise and a woman to go home to. He couldn't afford to take chances like he did in his former life. He had too much to lose now.

His conversation with Geneva earlier made him think twice about his initial intentions for Cyrus. He hadn't expected his discussion with Geneva to go easy, knowing that she would push back. But her passionate plea for him to stick it out with her had caught him by surprise. She was more of a *'see ya, don't let the door hit you in the ass on your way out'* type of woman.

Today, though, she showed him a different side of herself, a vulnerability Myles didn't know she possessed. Spending the afternoon with her had been just what he needed to get his head back on straight. The woman was a force to be reckoned with, and Myles loved everything about her. He was glad she set him straight.

Otherwise, had he walked away from her, he would've regretted it. Now he just had to stay alive so that he could spend the rest of his life with her.

With that thought in mind, though, Myles was still determined to find Cyrus. He needed to know what their connection was, and if breaking into Cyrus's place got him the information he needed, he had to go for it. Sneaking in and out of places undetected for years was what Myles did...what he was good at.

One more time, he told himself. This would be the last time he broke into someone's home to gather information.

"You sure about this, Myles?" Kenton asked from the passenger seat.

Myles was sure he wanted answers, but he didn't like the idea of making his friends accessories in case he got caught.

But he had never been caught before, so he was hoping his luck held on.

"It's still all clear. Are we gon' do this or what?" Angelo asked into their earpieces. They were all outfitted with tactical earpieces that they often used for jobs where they needed to stay in touch.

"Give me five minutes," Myles said to Angelo and slipped on his gloves. To Laz and Kenton, he said, "I'll let you know if Ashton is needed."

With Ashton being a detective with Atlanta PD, Myles didn't want to do anything that would put his friend in a compromising position. Instead of letting him know in advance that they got a lead, the plan was to give Ashton a heads-up if they found anything that could link Cyrus to Whitney's murder. Myles just wanted to be out of the apartment before any cops showed up.

"I'll be back," he said and climbed out of the vehicle.

Dressed in all black, he faded into the night and darted between parked cars. The dimly lit lot, along with the building not being very secure, was to his advantage. He wasn't expecting any problems getting in, especially after Laz used a thermal energy camera to determine that no one was in the apartment unit.

Myles eased into the building. It was eleven o'clock at night, and there hadn't been too many people entering or exiting for the last couple of hours. The building wasn't in the worst neighborhood, but it was in an area where neighbors tended to mind their own business. No one would think twice if they happened to see him in the hallways.

Instead of the elevator, Myles took the steps two at a time until he arrived on the top floor.

"On your six," Angelo whispered, letting him know he wasn't too far behind him.

Myles heard him loud and clear in his ear, but he had also sensed him nearby. A former DEA agent, Angelo was used to undercover work and slipping in and out of places undetected. Myles was glad he had his back.

Cyrus's apartment was an end unit closest to the back stairwell. Once on the sixth floor, Myles peeked through the stairwell door window, glad to see the hallway empty. He pulled his lock-picking tools from his pocket and approached the apartment.

In a sense, the guy was a psycho for coming after him, but Myles hoped he wasn't one of those paranoid guys who set booby traps.

I'll soon find out, he thought.

Once the door was unlocked, he dropped his tools back into his pocket and pulled out his penlight. Easing the door open, he started with the light pointed down and checked for wires or sensors before stepping into the dark apartment.

Once inside, Myles shut the door, leaving it open just a crack. Accustomed to searching a place in the dark, he didn't bother with a light. Instead, he strategically swept the space with his penlight and moved farther into the unit. He already knew it was only a one-bedroom, which meant he should be able to search the space quickly.

"Eight minutes," Laz's voice came through the earpiece.

The open floor plan was going to make it easier.

Myles crept past the tiny kitchen. So far, there were no traps or cameras. He also noticed how clean the place was. The reason he knew someone lived there was by a few dishes in the dish rack that was in the sink, and there was a pair of men's combat boots near the door.

His boots were quiet on the hardwood floors as he crept toward the small dining table. The only sound in the space was the furnace kicking on, and a television could be heard, but it was in the distance, like next door or from the apartment below.

Myles stopped at the table and looked through the few pieces of mail that were neatly stacked. He moved the envelopes around, taking in the names.

Cyrus Ferguson.

Cyrus Ferguson.

Then he stopped and zoned in on the next envelope with a different name.

Cyrus Furnell.

Well, that answered one question. One of those names was an alias. *Figures.* He'd just have to determine which one.

Now to see what else he could find out about this Cyrus guy.

Myles started down a short hallway but stopped abruptly. Voices filtered in from the main hallway, and he leaned his back against a nearby wall. Then he waited. Pulse pounding loudly in his ear, he stood there for a few seconds, wanting to make sure no one entered the unit.

"Coast is still clear," Angelo said into his ear.

Myles started moving again. He wondered where Angelo had positioned himself. It wasn't like there were potted plants in the hallway to hide behind.

Stay focused, he told himself. He needed to hurry it up and get the heck out of there. Straight ahead was the bedroom, and to his right, a bathroom. Myles went right. He stopped at the bathroom door, making sure it was clear before peeking behind the shower curtain.

Clear.

Swinging his light around the tiny space, he took in a towel hanging on the single rod, a toothbrush sitting on the counter, and then he checked the trash can.

Blood.

Tissue and gauze soaked in blood.

Apparently, I did hit the guy. Good. That was, still assuming they really did have the right guy.

"Five minutes," Laz said in his ear.

Myles already knew if he didn't get out of there soon, Laz would be at the apartment in exactly five minutes. He picked up the pace and stood at the door of the bedroom. Again, he swept the light around the room.

Full-sized neatly made bed. One semi-cluttered nightstand. Dresser on the far side of the room with a small flat-screen television sitting on top.

He moved further into the space, flashed his light on the wall to his left, and froze. His heart slammed against his chest, and shock gripped his body.

"Son of..." The rest of his words caught in his throat.

"What's up?"

"What is it?'

"You all right?"

Angelo, Kenton, and Laz all spoke at once. Laz threatened to come in if he didn't respond immediately.

"Call Ashton," Myles said. His heart practically rocketed out of his chest as he approached the wall. "Shit...this is definitely our guy."

There were at least fifty pictures taped to the wall.

All were of him, Whitney and...

Myles's blood ran cold when he spotted pictures of Collin. Everything from grocery store parking lot shots to photos of him and Whitney in front of her house. But there was one of just him playing in the outdoor sandbox at daycare.

When I get my hands on this guy...

Myles quickly took his phone out and snapped pictures of the collage. Not only did the display contain pictures of them, but it also had the last aliases that he and Whitney had used—Norris and Samantha. Myles had no idea how the man got the classified information, but he planned to find out.

But first, he needed to finish searching the room. He went to the nightstand and rummaged through it before moving to the dresser. He pulled open one drawer after another, digging around in them, searching for anything that would give him a clue to how he and this guy were connected.

When he didn't find anything in the dresser, he went to the closet—a walk-in. No longer caring, he flipped on the light switch and looked around. His gaze swept over the meager amount of clothes and shoes but zoned in on the army uniform and snapped a picture of the jacket. Then he checked the shelves.

On the floor at the back of the closet, he found a box.
Files.

He hurried through the first couple of manila folders and stopped when he ran across printed articles.

Senator Furnell Accused of Treason

FBI Probe into Senator Furnell Oversees Dealings.

Suicide. Senator Furnell Found Dead in Hotel Room.

Myles's pulse pounded in his ears as he read one headline after another.

He remembered. He remembered the assignment.

"Time's up. Get out, or we're coming in," Laz threatened. "Ashton's on the way."

"Coming," Myles said, stuffing one of the articles into his pocket and making sure everything was as he'd found it.

He backtracked to the door and exited the same way he entered.

Anger propelled him down the stairs in half the time it took him to climb them.

Pulse pounding. Head swimming. Chest tightening. He needed air. He couldn't get out of there fast enough.

When he reached the main floor, he pushed open the exterior door with more force than he intended. The moment he stepped outside, he took a breath, then another.

Angelo exited seconds after he did. He went left toward his vehicle. Myles went right and had barely taken three steps when the SUV that Laz was driving screeched to a stop.

Myles climbed in without a word.

He didn't know when, he didn't know how, but Cyrus's days were numbered.

*

Hours later, Myles got word that Ashton had put out an APB—all-points bulletin—on Cyrus Furnell. The killer's real name.

Evidence found at the apartment, including his DNA, matched blood found in the stolen car he had abandoned the night of the shooting. Law enforcement agencies were made aware that not only was Cyrus a person of interest, he should also be considered armed and dangerous.

Cyrus Furnell, the son of senator Theodore Furnell, former United States presidential candidate.

Myles stared at the information on the laptop.

The murky details of a CIA assignment he and Whitney had been on together surfaced in his brain. He still wasn't sure what made his former partner start researching gun trafficking, but he could see a connection with this case. He just wished he would've seen it sooner, then maybe he and Geneva wouldn't have gotten ambushed.

"It started as an off-the-books operation," Myles said to those in the room, including Laz and Kenton.

They, along with Hamilton, Ashton, and one of the detectives from Whitney's murder case, had met at Supreme Security and were in one of the conference rooms.

"We were tasked with gathering intelligence about an organization in South Sudan that was trafficking guns."

"Walk us through it," Ashton said. "Whatever you can remember might help us get inside Cyrus's head and figure out his motive."

"All right, well, what started as an off-the-books operation turned into a disaster…depending how you look at it. Everything that could go wrong on a job did. That included discovering that a US senator was funding a trafficking operation."

Myles told them as much as he could remember about one of the last cases he and Whitney worked on together. While they were collecting information overseas, Senator Theodore Furnell's name popped up. They caught him on tape blasting someone about a problem with a gun shipment that was delayed. Whitney had recognized his voice, but neither of them had actually named him in the report.

As a rule, when agents submitted their findings, they didn't share the actual names of US citizens who might show up during intelligence-gathering. As per protocol, Myles had given the senator a code name when he wrote up his final report.

"When we turned in the document," Myles said, "a US official who reviewed the report had questions about some of the information. Tons of questions.

"Of course, they were concerned that a US citizen was listed in the report, one who was thought to be participating in illegal activity overseas. Unfortunately, that's not all that uncommon," Myles explained. "But when that does happen, those reviewing the reports typically focus on the operation assigned to us. Not necessarily other intelligence that might show up in the process."

"Does that mean the senator's dealings weren't directly connected to the information you were assigned to gather?" Ashton asked.

"Correct. At least as far as we could tell, his gun dealings were a separate situation. But the official requesting additional information from us wanted the American involved to be unmasked. It hadn't mattered to the official that the senator hadn't been a target of the investigation. They still wanted his name because he was funding gunrunners overseas."

"I remember that case from when I was with the FBI," Kenton said, shaking his head. "It was filled with drama. Didn't the senator end up committing suicide?"

Myles nodded. Like everyone else in the room, it was safe to narrow down Cyrus's motive for coming after him and Whitney. Not only had Cyrus's father killed himself, but his mother had died soon after.

"Someone leaked the confidential information to the media shortly after Senator Furnell announced his intention to run for president," Myles added.

The room went silent. Some were probably remembering that moment in history. The media had blasted the information all around the country.

"Why now?" Laz asked. It was the first time he had spoken since the meeting started. "That was years ago. Why come after you now?"

"It probably took Cyrus that long to find Myles and Whitney," Kenton said, "But I think a more important question is who leaked your identity, and why?"

"Yeah, I'm wondering that myself," Myles said.

Their employment was classified information. The only person right now who could answer Kenton's question was in the wind. The cops had no leads and probably could care less that Myles's identity was leaked. They just wanted to catch a killer.

Which was why Myles needed to find Cyrus Furnell before the cops did.

Chapter Twenty-Four

"Do you think it's a good idea for you to be leaving the property?" Parker asked Geneva. He and Angelo were tasked with taking her anywhere she wanted to go. And right now, she didn't care where she went. She mainly needed some air.

"I've been cooped up for days, and if I had stayed inside another minute, I would've exploded. Do you mind taking me to my salon?"

The restoration contractors had been hired, and Geneva wanted to see how far along they'd gotten. Once their part was completed, she'd be able to gauge more accurately what else needed to be done.

"Where's Myles?" Angelo asked from the passenger seat.

He knew just the right question to make her feel guilty. Not about leaving for a little while, but for not letting Myles know she was going. After taking Collin and Coco to Aunt Carolyn, who loved having them around 24/7, Geneva had left Myles a note saying she'd be back.

"He was asleep when I left," she said to Angelo. "I'm sure you know he was out most of the night."

Myles was lucky she trusted him. Otherwise, she would've thought he was out with another woman, especially coming in after two. At least he had called her earlier in the night, filling her in on his findings at Cyrus's place. She could tell he was upset at knowing the guy had been following Whitney and Collin for weeks, if not months. The man also knew one of Myles and Whitney's aliases.

Geneva was glad to learn that she wasn't on Cyrus's radar, but Myles insisted he still wanted her protected. She loved that he was looking out for her, but she was concerned about him. He was more determined than ever to find the killer, and she didn't want him getting killed in the process.

To say the last few weeks had been trying would be an understatement. Between waiting for parts for her Mustang, her shop being under construction, and having to temporarily move from her home, Geneva needed some good news, which was why she hoped the contractor working on the salon was making progress.

"You should call Myles, Gen," Angelo said, cutting into her thoughts. "He'll be worried if you're not there when he wakes up."

He probably would be, but Geneva needed this time to herself, and he needed sleep.

She decided she'd call him after they left the salon.

Geneva noted the crowded parking lot and how busy the strip mall was when they pulled into the lot. As they drove around to her salon, Parker and Angelo were quietly checking out the area. Geneva appreciated their thoroughness and how selfless and attentive Atlanta's Finest had been since the shooting, but she was ready for her life to get back to normal. She especially wanted to get back to work.

When Parker pulled up to the front of the building, Geneva tried to remain optimistic despite the huge front window and glass door that were still boarded up.

Angelo opened her door. "I'll go in with you," he said and ushered her to the front door, all the while glancing around at their surroundings.

She could get used to the service they offered. As one of the country's best personal security firms, they were in high demand, and rightfully so. They were the best at what they did.

"Do you have keys?" Angelo asked.

"I do," she said and unlocked the padlock that Myles had put on the temporary wood door.

Geneva braced herself for whatever she would find as she followed behind Angelo as they entered the building. The smell of smoke was still in the air, and it was dark inside except for a couple of temporary lamps.

"Whoever was working in here must be planning on returning since they left the lights on."

"Maybe," Geneva said, disappointed at the lack of progress. The furniture had been removed, but very little else had been done. "This is ridiculous," she grumbled. The contractor had barely gotten started.

Anger burned inside of her. If she didn't get back to work soon, everything she'd worked for over the years would be gone.

The front door opened, and Angelo was in front of her before she could even see who walked inside.

"What can we do for you?" he asked.

"I'm the restoration contractor," a male's voice boomed. "And you are?"

"Actually, he's with me," Geneva said, stepping around Angelo to approach the man. "I'm Geneva, the owner of the shop."

"I'm Ed. Nice to meet you in person."

"I was told that the shop would be scrubbed and soot removed by now. You guys haven't even started."

"I'm sorry, ma'am. We've been slammed these last few weeks and are a little behind on—"

"Then you shouldn't have taken the job," Geneva snapped. "I could've hired another company, but I was told yours was the best. Clearly, that was a lie."

"We are the best, which is why we're so busy," the guy said, raising his voice to match hers.

"Tone it down, man," Angelo said, looking menacing, which wasn't hard to do with his height and build.

That was something else about Supreme Security. Not only did they hire the best, but their men were drool-worthy gorgeous, and Angelo González was no exception.

"I apologize," Ed said to Geneva. "We should be able to start the day after tomorrow, and I'll have two crews in here working. Once that happens, it should only take a few days for us to have the walls and floors done.

"As I mentioned before, the floors are in bad shape. I'm not sure we'll be able to salvage them. Hopefully, we can, but if not, you might want to start thinking about what type of flooring you want in here."

Geneva listened as he explained all that they planned to do. It was the second time she received the spiel, and all it did was make her more frustrated. She also didn't want excuses for why the job wasn't started. She wanted it done, and that's exactly what she told the contractor.

It was probably time she conceded that Myles was right. She needed to look for a new place. Even if this company got her current salon space cleaned up, would it meet her expectations? Probably not. Now was actually the perfect time to relocate if that's what she wanted to do.

The thought of starting over was scary and exciting rolled into one, but that's how it had been when she first opened. It was hard work, but she had made it a success. She could do it again.

"Ready to head to your place?" Parker asked once she and Angelo were back in the Cadillac Escalade.

"Yeah, that's fine."

"Good, because Myles said he'll meet you there."

Geneva shook her head. "Damn, I guess I don't have to ask how he knew I was heading there next. You guys really stick together, don't you?"

"Yes," Angelo said and gave her a dimpled smile. Geneva rolled her eyes at him, but inside, she was thrilled that Myles was meeting them.

*

Myles tapped his fingers against the back door of the Chevy Suburban, trying to control his frustration. He understood Geneva's need to get out and get some air, but he wished she would've told him. He would've gone with her.

Myles released a long breath. That wasn't true. He probably would've talked her out of it, which was why she hadn't said anything. Actually, he was surprised she had lasted this long. Geneva was social and liked to stay on the move. He shouldn't have expected her to be satisfied being cooped up so that he wouldn't worry about her. That wasn't fair to her.

"I can't wait until this crap is over with," he mumbled.

"Yeah, me too. I'm tired of driving your ass around like you're Ms. Daisy or something," Laz said, and Myles laughed.

"I wasn't talking to you, but for the record, I'm tired of you driving me around, too. I may never sit in the back seat of a vehicle again."

"Well, on the way back, you can sit up here and I'll take your spot," Kenton said on a yawn. "I can use a nap. I'm getting too old for all of these late nights."

Myles nodded. "I feel you, man. When this is all over, drinks on me."

"Drinks?" Laz snorted. "That ain't gon' cut it. We're gonna need some steaks and potatoes to go along with that."

"Well, make sure I stay alive until Cyrus is apprehended or dead, and then dinner is on me."

Cyrus was off the grid. The cops had no leads, and there'd been no sign of him. If Myles were lucky, the guy would turn up dead somewhere, but he doubted if he'd be that lucky.

"Looks like we beat them here," Laz said and parked in front of Geneva's house.

Myles stayed put and glanced around her neighborhood. She lived on a quiet tree-lined street in a cute house that didn't fit her bigger-than-life personality. A better fit for her would be a luxury high-rise or maybe even a loft. His loft, to be more specific. Since their conversation the other day, he'd been thinking about asking her to move in with him and Collin. Their relationship was still relatively new, but Myles knew without a doubt that he didn't want anyone else.

"Here they are now," Kenton said, as Parker pulled up behind them. "Do you want us to stick around, or are you planning to ride back with them?"

"I'll hitch a ride with them. Thanks, fellas, I'll catch you later."

Myles didn't wait for Kenton to open the back door for him. He climbed out before the big guy had a chance. He hadn't seen Geneva all day and couldn't wait a moment longer.

He hated that she'd left the house without telling him, but at least she hadn't ventured out on her own.

"Thanks for bringing her, man," Myles said to Angelo, who opened the truck door for Geneva.

"No problem."

Myles smiled when Geneva climbed out of the vehicle. It didn't matter that he shared her bed and saw her every day. His heart still thumped a little faster whenever she was near.

His grin grew wider when she sashayed to him. Just the sight of her in the short, body-hugging sweater and jeans that accentuated her curves had his body stirring with need.

He couldn't wait to get her back to the guest house and have his way with her. Or better yet, maybe they'd be able to get in a quickie while they were at her place.

"When you look at me like that, you make me want to strip out of my clothes and strut around butt-naked in front of you," she said by way of greeting, that wicked gleam in her eyes shining brightly.

Myles slipped his arm around her waist and kissed her before they strolled up the walkway. "And when you talk dirty like that, you make me want to take you roughly up against the nearest wall."

Geneva burst out laughing. "Ohh, Mr. Carrington, I'm loving this talk-dirty-to-me side of you. You've come a long way, baby."

"Sweetheart, you ain't heard nothing yet. Wait until I tell you about all the ways I'm going to make love to you tonight. But first, let's talk about why you're out running around town. I thought we had an agreement that you would lay low."

"Myles, I tried. A week is my limit. I needed air. You know I can't stay cooped up for long. Don't worry, though; this is my last stop, and I'll make it quick. I just want to grab some more clothes and my cosmetic bag. A girl can only live on just concealer and lip gloss for so long."

"Okay, well, let's make it quick. I told Collin we'll watch a movie with him. We just have to pick up popcorn and gummy bears on the way back."

"Oh, gummy bears, my favorite," Geneva cracked.

She unlocked the front door and they strolled inside.

"I promise. It'll only take me a minute. Angelo is challenging me to grab everything I need and be outside in seven minutes," she said and headed down the hallway toward the bedrooms.

"All right, I'll be right here. I'm just going to grab some water or whatever you have in the frig."

Myles strolled into the kitchen and flipped on the light. He had just opened the refrigerator when he noticed the dishes in the sink, which was odd. Dirty dishes in the sink were one of Geneva's pet peeves. He knew that because she had fussed at him the other morning about that exact thing. Besides, she hadn't been to the house in over a week.

Myles glanced around the kitchen and the adjacent dining room. Something wasn't right. It wasn't anything major that stood out, only small things, like a dirty mug next to the stove and a cereal box on the counter near the pantry.

It might've been nothing, but...

It was also too quiet. Nothing about Geneva was quiet. Even if she were just gathering clothes, she would be singing, laughing, or even talking to herself.

"Hey, babe. How much longer?" he called out, hoping she'd say something so he'd know that she was all right.

Nothing.

Something was definitely wrong.

Myles bent down and removed his pistol from his ankle holster, and slipped it into the back of his waistband. He might've preferred using his knife, but he wasn't sure what to expect, and his gun would be a better choice.

When she still didn't respond, Myles sent a quick text to Angelo, letting him know they had company. He told them to stay put and give him ten minutes before breaching the back door. Now all Myles had to do was lead whoever their unwanted visitor was to the front of the house.

Dropping the phone back into his pocket, he remembered seeing a bat behind Geneva's front door and grabbed it. Maybe the person would think that was his only weapon. But Geneva would know better.

Myles moved slowly down the hallway toward her bedroom. That's when he heard feet shuffling and muffled sounds.

"Geneva, don't forget to grab that red dress of yours that I like. I'm thinking you can wear it tomorrow evening." He had no idea if she had a red dress, but at least she'd know that he knew she had company.

He moved past the guest bathroom, where the door was open, and the room was dark. There was no other sound, and only her bedroom light was on.

When he finally reached her door and glanced into the room, his gut twisted. Ice clogged his veins.

Bile rose to his throat at the sight of a man with his arm around her neck and a pistol against her temple.

Myles assumed this was Cyrus. The man's pale face and dark circles under his eyes made him look as if he was physically ill or hadn't slept in days.

Either way, he was a dangerous man with a gun pointed at Geneva.

Myles moved to the center of the doorway with the bat in his hand. Instead of entering the room, he stayed in the hallway. He wanted the guy out of the bedroom just in case

Angelo and Parker entered before Myles could get Cyrus out in the open.

"Well, well, well, we finally meet," the guy said. "I was wondering when she'd return home. But today must be my lucky day since you came with her. And just think, I thought I would have to have her call you. This makes my job so much easier."

"You okay, baby?" Myles asked, ignoring Cyrus and giving his full attention to Geneva. A tear slipped from her eye, but she looked more angry than scared.

"Yes," she said through gritted teeth.

"Instead of worrying about her, you need to be concerned with what I plan to do to you," the man growled.

"And who are you?"

"Don't play dumb. I know you were in my apartment. I spotted you and your friends leave."

"Okay, so what do you want?" Myles asked, gripping the bat tighter and slowly easing away from the door, hoping Cyrus would follow.

"I want you dead, but first, drop the bat."

Myles took another step back. "Not until you release her."

Cyrus was still holding Geneva close when they appeared in the hallway. "You're in no position to be making demands," Cyrus said. "You either put the bat down, or I put a bullet in her head. Your choice."

"Okay, fine, I'm setting it down."

He lowered it to the floor. Now that they were all in the hallway, that gave Myles and his guys better access to the man.

"Now, let her go. Whatever this is about, it's between you and me, but I'm at a loss here. What did I do to you?"

"You ruined my life! It's because of *you* that my parents are dead."

"Is that why you killed Whitney and shot at me the other night? You think I did something to your family? That's crazy. I don't even know you or your family."

"Don't lie to me!" the man roared and charged forward with Geneva in tow. "It took me four years to hunt you and Samantha down," Cyrus said, using Whitney's alias. His eyes bulged out of his pale face, making him look crazed and on edge. "But I did it. I killed her, and you're next!"

"How did you find me?" Myles asked, trying to stay calm while fuming inside.

"Senator Pickett. I blackmailed him. He was a friend of my dad's, and I knew he'd give me your names. At first, he wouldn't help me, but I convinced him." Cyrus released a sinister laugh, and the sound was like that of fingernails clawing down a blackboard. "He was cheating on his wife with an agent named Ruby Wallace, and he didn't want anyone to know."

A sick feeling settled inside of Myles's gut. He recognized both names.

Ruby was an FBI agent who had worked on Cyrus's father's case. She and Pickett had been found dead a few months ago. Gunshot wounds to the head.

Myles made eye contact with Geneva, who hadn't taken her eyes off him the whole time. It was as if she was asking him: *what should I do?* He needed her to stay calm while he tried to get Cyrus to lower his weapon. Myles didn't want the man to shoot her, intentionally or unintentionally.

"Okay, if you think I had something to do with your parents' death, fine. Be angry at me, but leave her out of this. Let her go, and then it'll be just you and me. Be a man. Come get me."

Cyrus growled under his breath, and his agitation visibly amped up. Myles was getting to him. At some point, the man would make a mistake and give him just the opening he needed. But first, he had to get Geneva out of the way.

"I should've known you were a coward," Myles taunted. "Using a woman as your shield. What kind of man—"

"Shut up!" Cyrus roared and swung his gun to Myles, but he still had a death grip around Geneva's neck. "Just shut up.

You don't know anything about me or what I've been through."

"I don't give a damn about you," Myles continued. "Let. Her. Go!"

"You don't tell me what to do!" Cyrus shoved Geneva to the ground. "I'm the one who—"

The back door burst open just as Myles whipped his gun from around his back and shot Cyrus between the eyes. He dropped to the hardwood floor with a loud thud, and Myles raced to Geneva, who was screaming and scooting away from the body.

Myles's heart hammered loud enough to be heard in the next county as he pulled Geneva up and practically carried her into the living room while Angelo and Parker tended to the body.

Myles blocked her view of the hallway and frantically cupped her face between his hands. "You okay? Did he hurt you?"

"No. No. I'm fine," she panted while swiping at her eyes. "My ears are ringing, but I'm okay. I'm okay," she kept saying before burying her face against his chest.

Myles held her tight. "It's over, baby. It's all over."

"I'm so glad," Geneva said, her voice muffled against his chest. She leaned back and looked at him, tears hanging from her lashes. "I thought he was going to kill me. I didn't know how to warn you that he was in the bedroom. He was hiding in the bathroom, Myles." Her composure shattered, and she dissolved into sobs.

"Baby, I'm so sorry you went through this. I never meant—"

"You saved my life," she sniffled as she pulled herself together. "How did you know he was here?"

"I didn't know at first. I noticed a few things out of place, but what really gave it away was how quiet you were. You're never quiet."

Geneva sputtered a laugh and swiped at a rogue tear. "God, I'm so glad you know me."

"Not as glad as I am." A few more tears leaked from her eyes, and Myles brushed them away with the pad of his thumb. "I love you so much, and I'm going to spend the rest of my life making sure you know that."

"I already know, and I love you, too."

Epilogue

Eight weeks later...

Geneva wasn't used to letting anyone drive her Mustang, especially considering how long it had been in the shop. But Myles wasn't just anyone. He was the man she planned to spend the rest of her life with.

He was also the man who was up to something. She just didn't know what.

He pulled her car into Lenox Mall's parking lot and found a parking spot a long way from the building. He'd been driving around Buckhead, a suburb of Atlanta, stopping at a few stores and picking up items he claimed he needed for their picnic. So far, he hadn't bought any food, but maybe some edible items were in the large basket he had in the backseat.

Geneva turned to him and frowned. "I love the mall as much as the next person, but why are we here?"

His picnic idea sounded crazy since it was the middle of December. Atlanta's weather was unpredictable this time of year. The day before had been thirty-five degrees, while today it was fifty-five. That was still a little too cold to be eating outside, in her opinion. Yet, Geneva agreed to go along with his anniversary plan.

They'd been dating for over two months, and it had been some of the best months of her life. Sure, their relationship might've started out like a nightmare, but after Cyrus's death, their lives eased back into some normalcy.

"Don't worry. This is just a little detour," Myles said, putting the car in park, then turning to her. "You'll get that picnic, but we have one more stop to make first." He reached into the center console and pulled out a red and white bandana. "Here, put this over your eyes."

"What? And mess up my eye makeup? I don't think so."

Myles laughed, something he was doing a lot more frequently. "Just do it. I promise it'll be worth it."

"It better be," she joked.

Geneva wrapped the scarf around her head and made sure her eyes were covered. She secretly loved surprises and was just giving him a hard time, not that it bothered him at all. Myles was a master at dealing with her fickle personality.

When she felt the car moving again, she didn't question it. Instead, her excitement grew. Over the last couple of months, they'd been getting to know each other better. Geneva hadn't known that she could fall more in love with him with each passing day.

A week after Cyrus was killed, she put her house on the market, something she never thought she'd do. She loved her little gingerbread house, but it was impossible to live there after what had happened. She considered herself pretty tough and unflappable, but watching someone get shot and die right in front of her had rocked her. Nightmares, cold sweats, and anxiousness had been a part of her life for a couple of weeks after the shooting.

But through it all, Myles was right there. He had moved her into his loft with him and Collin, and the two of them, along with Coco, were the best cure for dealing with a traumatic experience.

That and therapy.

Her house had sold within a week, even after the buyer, a mystery writer, was told about the killing. He claimed that bit of history might help his muse.

Myles had also sold Whitney's home. Though she hadn't wanted a funeral, Yvette had insisted on having a very small memorial service for her, which was held at the house.

Collin still didn't understand the concept of death, but he was adjusting to his new life. He talked about Whitney from time to time, and occasionally, he'd have crying spells, saying that he wanted her to come back from heaven. The family therapist said it would take time, and already Geneva could see the changes in him.

His friendship with Miracle also helped. Collin had pitched a fit when they moved out of the guest house. He didn't want to leave Miracle. He eventually settled down when Geneva and London came up with the idea of the kids having weekly play dates.

Then there was Coco. The dog had been a godsend to all of them. When Geneva first adopted her from the shelter, she never imagined how much her baby would change her life. Not only hers but also Myles and Collin's. She was such an essential part of their family, and now they were thinking about getting another dog.

Myles was turning out to be full of surprises. It had been his suggestion for them all to start seeing a therapist. He had taken a month off of work to try and make sense of his new life.

He amazed Geneva. Watching how he was with his son, how he also made her feel loved and cherished, all the while taking care of Whitney's estate. He was a real-life superhero. Task-oriented and organized, she was convinced that there was nothing he couldn't do. Myles was the reason the three of them were doing as well as they were. They'd become a family overnight, and Geneva never knew she could be as happy as she was with him and Collin.

"Okay, we're almost there," Myles said, cutting into her thoughts. "I need you to keep your blindfold on until I say you can take it off."

"God, you're bossy but all right."

He chuckled. "You know you like it when I'm bossy."

"I more than like it. I love it. I love you."

Myles grabbed her hand and kissed the back of it. "Not as much as I love you. Okay, are you ready for this?"

"Well, considering I don't know what *this* is, I guess I'm ready."

"Sit tight. I'll grab the picnic basket, then come around and help you out of the car."

Giddiness bubbled inside of Geneva. She loved surprises, and Myles had been full of them over the last couple of months. Not in a million years would she have guessed that he was a romantic. Everything from candlelight dinners to bubble baths for two, he pulled out all the stops when it came to her.

Myles opened the car door and grabbed hold of her hand. "We'll go slow, especially since you decided to wear four-inch heels. Who wears heels to a picnic, anyway?"

"I do. Now quit yapping and tell me what you're up to," Geneva said.

She had a death grip on his hand. Walking blindfolded in high heels over uneven pavement wasn't an easy feat.

"Okay, you're going to take a small step up," Myles instructed.

A few minutes later, they were inside some type of structure because it was a lot warmer than it had been outside a few minutes ago.

Geneva inhaled, expecting to smell food, but instead smelled perfume...the type Journey wore.

"Wait. Is my sister here?"

Myles laughed and guided her a few more feet. Instead of answering her question, he removed the bandana from over her eyes.

Geneva blinked several times, trying to get her eyes to adjust to the brightness of the space.

"Surprise!"

Her heart hitched, and her mouth dropped open at the sight before her. Placing her hand on her chest, Geneva stood speechless.

"What is this?" she asked.

Her gaze bounced around the large, beautifully decorated space, and the smiling faces staring back at her. There had to be at least fifty people there, and it looked as if they had recreated her salon, except on a larger scale. Everything from the pink and black paint job to the hot pink salon chairs she'd had at her old place. Instead of six work stations, there were eight. Where she stood, she could also see a shampoo area and dryers toward the back of the building.

"I can't believe this," she whispered, still taking it all in. "How…" Her words caught in her throat as emotion swirled inside of her.

"It was a team effort," Journey said, walking toward her with two champagne flutes. She handed one to Geneva and the other one to Myles. "But mostly, your man did this."

"Trust me; I had a lot of help. I couldn't have done it without all of you," Myles said to the group and lifted his glass to them.

Geneva looked at him through teary eyes and fell in love with him all over again. "How were you able to keep this a secret?"

Before he could answer, Collin and Coco seemed to come out of nowhere. They ran toward her, and Collin practically knocked her over when he wrapped his arms around her legs. When he looked up at her with eyes that were so similar to his father's, her heart melted.

"Surprise!" he screamed. "Do you like it?"

Geneva laughed through her tears and bent down to kiss his cheek. "Baby, I love it."

For the next thirty minutes, Geneva was overwhelmed by all of the love in the building. All her family and friends, and even the stylists from her old shop, were there. She couldn't remember the last time she'd been hugged and kissed so much, but she loved every minute of it.

"Come with me," Myles whispered near her ear, then grabbed her hand and pulled her toward the back of the building. In his other hand was the picnic basket.

They walked down a small hall, then stopped at the last door on the left. He pushed it open, and Geneva gasped.

"Oh, Myles. You're just full of surprises today."

She strolled into her new office, which wasn't much bigger than the old one, but it didn't matter. In the center of the room was a small table for two covered in a white tablecloth with a candle flickering in the center.

"Here's the picnic I promised," he said and set the basket down before pulling her into his arms. "Happy anniversary, sweetheart."

Geneva wrapped her arms around his neck and couldn't stop grinning. "If this is what you do for a two-month *dating* anniversary, what are you going to do when we've been together for a year?"

"I guess you'll just have to stick around and find out."

He lowered his head and kissed her, and Geneva's heart sang. She didn't know what the future held, but she knew she'd be spending it with her amazing man.

*

Join Sharon's Mailing List

To get sneak peeks of upcoming stories and to hear about giveaways that Sharon is sponsoring, go to https://sharoncooper.net/newsletter to join her mailing list.

ABOUT THE AUTHOR

Award-winning and bestselling author, Sharon C. Cooper, is a romance-a-holic - loving anything that involves romance with a happily-ever-after, whether in books, movies, or real life. Sharon writes contemporary romance, as well as romantic suspense and enjoys rainy days, carpet picnics, and peanut butter and jelly sandwiches. She's been nominated for numerous awards and is the recipient of Emma Awards (RSJ) for Author of the Year 2019, Favorite Hero 2019 (INDEBTED), Romantic Suspense of the Year 2015 (TRUTH OR CONSEQUENCES), Interracial Romance of the Year 2015 (ALL YOU'LL EVER NEED), and BRAB (book club) Award -Breakout Author of the Year 2014. When Sharon isn't writing, she's hanging out with her amazing husband, doing volunteer work or reading a good book (a romance of course). To read more about Sharon and her novels, visit www.sharoncooper.net

Website: https://sharoncooper.net

Join Sharon's mailing list: https://bit.ly/31Xsm36

Facebook fan page:
http://www.facebook.com/AuthorSharonCCooper21?ref=hl

Twitter: https://twitter.com/#!/Sharon_Cooper1

Subscribe to her blog:
http://sharonccooper.wordpress.com/

Goodreads:
http://www.goodreads.com/author/show/5823574.Sharon_C_Cooper

Pinterest: https://www.pinterest.com/sharonccooper/

Instagram:
https://www.instagram.com/authorsharonccooper/

Other Titles

Sharon C. Cooper

When Love Calls (Novella)

More Than Love (Novella)

Reunited Series (Romantic Suspense)

Blue Roses (book 1)

Secret Rendezvous (Prequel to Rendezvous with Danger)

Rendezvous with Danger (book 2)

Truth or Consequences (book 3)

Operation Midnight (book 4)

Stand Alones

Something New ("Edgy" Sweet Romance)

Legal Seduction (Harlequin Kimani – Contemporary Romance)

Sin City Temptation (Harlequin Kimani – Contemporary Romance)

A Dose of Passion (Harlequin Kimani – Contemporary Romance)

Model Attraction (Harlequin Kimani – Contemporary Romance)

Soul's Desire (Contemporary Romance)

Show Me (Contemporary Romance)

Made in United States
Orlando, FL
15 April 2024

45835948R00150